The Vampire and the Case of the Cursed Canine

Heather G. Harris & Jilleen Dolbeare

Published by Hellhound Press Limited

Copyright © 2024 by Heather G. Harris and Jilleen Dolbeare.

All rights reserved.

No portion of this book may be reproduced in any form without written permission from the publisher or authors, except as permitted by U.S. copyright law.

Published by Hellhound Press Limited.

Cover Design by Christian Bentulan.

Artificial Intelligence (AI): No part of this manuscript, including text/graphics and/or cover design, was produced or assisted by AI technologies.

AI Restrictions: The authors expressly prohibits any entity from using any part of this publication, including text and/or graphics, for the purpose of training AI technologies to generate text or graphics, including without limitation to technologies that are capable of generating works in the same style or genre as this publication. The author reserves all rights to license uses of this work for generative AI training and development of machine learning language models.

Heather's Dedication

For my awesome supporters on Patreon, with special mention to Amanda Peterman and Melissa. I will never stop being amazed by your support.
To all the people who help us behind the scenes: our cover designer Christian, our editor Karen, and our proofreader Sara – thank you all. Special thanks to Alyse Gibbs whose astounding talents really brings our books to life!

Jill's Dedication

I dedicate this book to all the creatures that have come in and out of my life. The dogs, the cats, the horses, the chickens, and even the possum. You were all fiercely loved. Also, to my current two little beasties, thanks for being loving and understanding when you want my attention and I'm busy writing! Also, as always, to my husband and family for supporting my writing habit. I know it's tough sometimes! Last but not least, a big shout out to my wonderful and fabulous Alpha, Beta, and ARC readers you rock!

Foreword

If you'd like to hear the latest gossip, bargains and new releases from us, then please join our newsletters!

If you'd like FREE BOOKS then join Heather's newsletter on her website and you can get a couple of free stories, as well as pictures of her dog and other helpful things.

Jill will also give you FREE BOOKS, but she will send you cat images instead! Sign up to Jill's Newsletter on her website.

Chapter 1

I don't think I breathed all the way to the North Harbour. Naturally, Edgy had landed his plane – and my mum – on the bloody North Harbour. Where else would she be, but *death* harbour? In a way, it seemed oddly appropriate.

Mum isn't that bad, I told myself firmly. *She's particular but not murderous – unless you ate her last pickled egg, then admittedly you'd take your life in your hands.*

As we approached the harbour of death, I could already see the one-armed pilot. Next to him was another man. It wasn't my father pulling a surprise trip – as if! – but nevertheless I recognised him and my tummy roiled. It was John, the vampire who'd been instrumental in my escape to Alaska. I owed him everything but as I looked at him, his shoulders bowed, I felt a measure of trepidation. John had helped me but first he'd betrayed me. Which John was I getting today?

Don't judge a man by his first action but by his final one, I told myself, and stiffened my spine. John *had* betrayed me but he'd saved me in the end, to his own detriment. He was controlled – owned – by my father's business partner, Octavius the Vampire King of Europe. Octavius had something over John that was so strong he couldn't do anything *but* work for that arsehole.

The vampire king was adept at all sorts of dark arts, including blackmail. No matter what John had done for me, he still marched to the king's tune. I would greet him warmly and keep one eye on him at all times.

He and Edgy were unloading a truly monstrous amount of luggage off the pint-sized plane. I turned to Connor, eyes wide; we'd have to make at least three trips in his sports car to get that lot to my house. Connor had reached the same conclusion and he pulled out his phone. 'Get a Suburban to the North Harbour, stat.' He hung up.

I looked around nervously for my mother. I doubted she'd be in a good mood after a ride on a small, worn-out plane. I couldn't see past Edgy, John and the tower of luggage ... but then I heard her voice over the crash of the surf, her tone both imperious and saccharine sweet. Hearing her overly dulcet tones made me wince.

I looked around, weighing up how mad she'd be if I ran away. Or maybe I could push her into the harbour and hope the water dragon ate her. Everything in me screamed to get her far away from here. Portlock was my new home and I loved it. She was going to criticise everything, look down her sharp, pointed nose at all the rough edges of the life I'd built there.

'Easy,' Connor murmured, his hand rubbing slow circles on my back. I took a deep breath and let it out slowly. 'You've got this,' he continued, letting his hand fall away.

No, I hadn't; I was so far from having this.

'Mr Pilot, you've forgotten to retrieve my darling! Now that you've seen to your ... plane ... you must fetch my Arabella! Go along now.' Her tone when she said 'plane' made it very clear that she thought the small aircraft barely qualified for the moniker. Edgy rolled his eyes but did as she bade him and hurried back to retrieve the dog.

I finally saw my mother. She was wearing a silk dress, kitten heels, a full face of makeup and carrying a garish handbag over her arm. She was standing with pinched lips glaring into the plane.

I could already hear her little beast yapping. I'd met many a lovely Pomeranian but Arabella was not one of them. Where others in her breed were soft, fluffy and cute, she was the spawn of the devil. She sensed that I was her rival for Mum's affection and she loved to piss all over me. Literally.

Maybe I could convince Fluffy to eat her. I smiled: that'd work. Heck, Arabella was so small that Shadow could probably eat her. Cats were less picky; Shadow could definitely get the job done.

'What *is* that look on your face for? Whatever it is, I like it.' Connor laced his fingers through mine and my anxiety levels dropped instantly; something about him was so reassuring. I smiled up at him and answered honestly, 'I'm plotting her dog's death.'

He laughed. 'I didn't expect that answer. You're a dog person.'

'I am, but Arabella isn't a dog. She's the spawn of Satan.'

'Ah, that explains it.' He smiled indulgently. Connor MacKenzie was the only thing in my life that Mum would approve of. He was handsome, accomplished and kind, not to mention the son of a vampire king. That thought soured my mood. Mum *would* approve of Connor. Ugh. It made me want to dump him on the spot.

Luckily, he chose that moment to give me my favourite smile and the madness faded. I'd walked out on Connor once before and I wasn't making the same mistake again even if Mum did like him. Connor and I were a team.

I rolled the tension out of my shoulders. Edgy had let Arabella out. The little beast piddled on the dock – better than on me – and Mum praised her lavishly. Yeah, yeah, praise her for breathing, but praise me?

Never. I tried not to let the bitterness show on my face and pushed it deep down into the little box where it lived.

Mum picked up the fluffball, tucked it under her arm and headed towards me. I blew out a breath. *Here we go.*

She minced down the dock to where we were waiting by her gargantuan pile of luggage. 'Oh darling! I've *missed* you!' She air-kissed me on both cheeks using Arabella as an excuse not to get close enough to touch me. I looked at the dog; Mum had painted its nails a horrific shade of fuchsia.

She took a step back and looked me up and down. 'Elizabeth, darling!' Her lips twisted in a moue of distaste. 'What on earth are you wearing?'

Fuck my life.

'Hi, Mum,' I mumbled. I was wearing my best XtraTuf black boots folded down to show their blue, white and red seascape lining. I'd left my uglier brown work boots at home. I had on a cheery bright-blue rain jacket over my best jeans, and a nice top even she'd approve of – if she could see it. I was wearing what I was comfortable in, and she could take a long walk off a short pier. I tightened my hold on Connor's hand.

Right. Connor. Introductions. I had to remember my manners. I chuckled wickedly to myself and turned to him. 'Connor, I'd like you to meet my mother, Victoria Barrington. Mum, I'd like to introduce you to Connor MacKenzie.'

My mother's smile had become fixed. In polite society you always introduced the highest-ranking person to the lowest ranking person, but I had introduced Connor to my mother not the other way around. Her pursed lips told me she understood the slur. Heh, heh, heh.

'Connor is the local vampire leader and my...' I thought about it. In reality we were mates, *fated* mates, but even though Mum knew about the existence of magic she was as ped as they come. 'Boyfriend,' I finished lamely.

Connor didn't bat an eyelid. 'Pleased to meet you, Mrs Barrington,' he said graciously and held out his hand.

Mum tapped a finger on her cheek and snubbed his offer to shake, probably because I'd pissed her off with my introduction thing. Whoops. She frowned. 'MacKenzie? That name sounds awfully familiar. Do you have relatives in England?' She smiled too politely.

Connor dropped his hand. 'Scotland,' he replied. He didn't bring up his father, so neither did I. 'I'll help with the luggage,' he offered. He picked up several bags and started to haul them along the dock.

Edgy looked relieved to have some help. John helped too and between them they made short work of the pile. I watched John: was he planning to stay with me as well? I only had two bedrooms and offering him the sofa didn't seem fair.

'Umm, Mum, is John staying with us?' I asked. 'I don't have a very large place.'

'Don't be silly, darling. The vampires have arranged a place for him.' She waved her hand in the air like it was sorted.

I frowned. Connor hadn't mentioned anything; I'd have to ask him about it. 'Connor will give us a ride home, and then I guess he or his men will come back for the rest of your luggage.'

No doubt Lee Margrave would show up with that big SUV that Connor had summoned and collect the remaining bags. Anyone would think my mother was moving in, not coming for a month: she must have packed the kitchen sink. She was going to be very disappointed with the limited space she'd have at mine.

Maybe I should give the house to Mum and John and stay with Connor? The idea made me brighten, then I looked at my mother and sighed. She'd make my life miserable if I did that. More than miserable.

Mum's small, practical heels weren't practical enough for the climb. The tide was out and the incline, which wasn't much when the tide was high, was pretty damn steep. I offered her my arm but naturally she refused it; she was too proud to admit that my ugly boots were the better choice. To add insult to injury, the heavens burst and it started pouring with rain. I flipped my hood over my head but I didn't have an umbrella to offer her. Mother powered on to the car through the deluge, and I felt her disapproval of everything around her like a flame burning next to me.

Well, so what? She could take her disapproval and shove it where the sun didn't shine.

Chapter 2

John placed the last bag that would fit in the boot of Connor's car then turned. Our eyes met and for some reason mine filled with tears. 'I never got the chance to thank you,' I choked out. I threw my arms around him and hugged him.

He stayed still for a beat before returning the embrace. 'I'm so glad you made it here safely,' he murmured. 'And under Connor MacKenzie's protection, no less. I'm impressed.'

I gave him one last squeeze and let him go. 'And now you're here with me!' I drew back and smiled. 'Are you going to stay in Alaska?'

His smile faded and the darkness returned. 'I can't.'

Whatever he was being blackmailed with, it hadn't changed in the few months I'd been gone. Poor man. 'I'm sorry, John.' I touched his arm lightly.

'Oh, you've met the help,' Mum remarked, an edge to her voice. What a bitch.

I gritted my teeth. 'John helped me escape from London.' I managed not to add 'unlike you', but it was a struggle.

I climbed in the back seat with John so Mum could have the front seat. She hastily repaired her make up; she was wet and bedraggled after the heavy downpour but that didn't stop her putting her best foot forward.

Thankfully the painfully silent drive wasn't too long. I sensed Mum's disappointment when we pulled up to my council-supplied bungalow; where I saw quaint charm, she saw a small home that was far beneath her social station.

'Better than your old flat, I suppose,' she muttered under her breath. As we were all vampires, we heard her bitchy comment as clearly as if she'd shouted it. Both men politely pretended not to hear while I ground my teeth.

Mum waited in the car for someone to open her door for her. Ever the gentleman, Connor quickly offered a hand to help her out. She smiled brightly, and this time she took it.

I climbed out of the cramped back seat and rushed to the front door, opening it as quickly as I could so that Mum could get in the house without getting any wetter. I winced as I stepped inside; I hadn't had time to clean since I'd come in the day before with a muddy Connor and a very muddy dog. I'd cleaned the bathroom, but the floors in the rest of the house needed a serious mopping. Seeing it with my mum's eyes made me cringe.

Luckily Fluffy arrived to distract me. He barrelled forward, wagged his tail and greeted me with enthusiasm and happiness as if I'd been gone for several days rather than half an hour. I rubbed his head and told him he was a good boy.

Mum came in with Arabella in her arms, not even trying to hide her disapproval as she looked around. Fluffy took one look at the pair of them and let out a low rumbling growl. He didn't like her expression any more than I did. 'Oh shush,' I ordered him half-heartedly.

My mother reached out, swiped a finger along a windowsill and inspected her finger. Her frown deepened when she saw the dust that now coated it.

'I haven't had much time to clean,' I said stiffly. I didn't owe her an explanation.

Then I gritted my teeth; I was going to have to be the bigger person. Mum and I would be living together; if I didn't make some sort of effort, the next few weeks would be hellacious. I relented enough to apologise for Fluffy's growl. 'Sorry about my dog,' I managed. 'He's usually quite friendly.'

She glanced at Fluffy, then did a double take. Her mouth dropped open for a second before she closed it and blinked rapidly. 'My goodness,' she said faintly, clutching a hand to her chest like I had a pet werewolf. 'Where on earth did you get such a large dog? I expected a small one like my precious Arabella.'

'I brought him with me from London. Some monster had locked him in the commercial bin outside my flat. I rescued him.'

Mum stared at me, judging me, until I grew uncomfortable. Not only was my dog inappropriately large, he wasn't papered and pampered. Arabella had pink nails, for Pete's sake. 'Hmmm,' she said finally.

'Your room is this way,' I said hastily to distract her from making more complaints about Fluffy.

The spare bedroom had a bed, a dresser and a walk-in wardrobe; it was rather plain but luckily it was clean and prepared with fresh bedding. 'Oh my,' Mum said faintly. 'It *is* rather basic.'

Did she expect the Ritz? I bit my cheek and cleared my throat. 'It's not much but it's mine.' And her comment in the car had been right: it was *much* better than my miniscule studio flat back in London.

There was a ruckus from the kitchen – high-pitched barking and a kitten screaming. I ran out to save Shadow, but I should have known better because my lynx kitten Shadow wasn't in any danger – he was *creating* it. All puffed up, with his stubby little tail looking like a pom-pom, he had Arabella trapped in a corner. His claws were extended and his attitude was sassy. Whoops: Shadow could definitely eat Arabella if he wanted to.

I hastily scooped him up before Mum could see him threatening her darling. No doubt Arabella had done something to provoke the fight because Shadow was a chilled-out lynx – unless you were the beast beyond the barrier and then he was a warrior of epic proportions.

I deposited him with Fluffy. 'Keep an eye on him and don't let him go Rambo on Arabella,' I murmured to my dog. He barked and sat to attention.

I went out to help John and Connor bring in the remaining bags from the sports car then lugged them to Mum's room, stacking them in a row like a mini-Wall of China. And to think there were still twice as many bags at the docks ... I shook my head in disbelief at her sheer excess.

I left my mother to potter with her bags and went to complete the next British ritual in welcoming a guest: making them a cup of tea. For her and me, it was our favourite form of familial pretence.

By the time I'd prepared the tea the way Mum required, Lee had arrived with the rest of the bags. A quick glance outside showed the monstrous size of the vehicle that had been necessary. I caught Connor's eye and mouthed a quick thank you. He smiled warmly, melting me with his icy blue eyes.

After we'd unloaded, I snagged him and tugged him into my bedroom. As I kissed him, the reassuring zing shot through me; where once it had been a torment, now it was a comfort.

I drew back. 'I'm not sure I can cope with this. With her.'

He tucked some stray hair behind my ear. 'Bunny, you're the law around here. You're strong, fiercely independent, totally contrary, incredibly clever and kind to boot. I am grateful to your mother for birthing you – but say the word and I'll run her out of town quicker than you can say "Fuck awf!" in your cute British accent.'

I grinned. 'I can say it pretty fast.'

'I know.'

I blew out a breath; it felt like that was all I'd done since Mum had arrived – deep breathing and sighing.

He was right; she was getting under my skin and making me forget all I'd done, all I'd become. I was a *new* Bunny, and she didn't know this one; she wasn't going to stomp all over me, like she'd done my whole life. I was going to be polite, respectful – and firm.

I kissed Connor again. 'You're the best. Do you know whether Mum has found a place for John to stay?'

He shook his head. 'Not with me, but we have facilities. I'll run him out to Kamluck and set him up in the barracks before dawn. I didn't see a daylight charm on him.'

'Thanks. You're the best boyfriend ever.'

He looked amused. 'I'm not sure the boyfriend label fits me. You'll eventually have to tell her that we're more than that.'

'I know, but she's ped. It'll take a bit of explaining.'

'Plenty of peds believe in soulmates,' he pointed out.

'True.' Although I agreed, I was pretty certain that Mum wasn't one of them. I couldn't recall seeing my parents ever kiss – heck, they barely touched – but everyone's relationships were different; what you saw on the surface might be very different from what went on behind closed doors. I found myself hoping that Mum and Dad *were* affectionate to each other when they were alone because if they weren't...? I shook my head. To go through life with such coldness was no way to live.

'I'll grab John after a cup of tea,' Connor offered.

I kissed him more firmly and mentioned out loud what I'd thought earlier. 'How about we leave John and Mum here, and Fluffy, Shadow and I come and live with you?'

His eyes heated up. 'Don't tease me,' he growled. 'I'd love that, but we both know you can't.'

I sighed. 'I know, but it was worth a shot.'

'We should go back out there.' Connor was still looking at me like I was lunch. 'But first, a quick lesson in not teasing me...' His lips touched mine and this time the zing was so hard I gasped. Could he control its force? My head swam and the kiss left me heated and panting.

He drew back and assessed the state of me with a satisfied smirk. 'Tea time.'

For the first time in my life, I didn't want tea at all.

Chapter 3

After a brew, Connor took John to Kamluck. I felt my lover's absence like the loss of a limb.

I was alone with my mother now and her judgement was heavy in the air. The silence drew out, and the longer it went on the tenser it felt. We sat at my kitchen table politely sipping our tea. Try as I might, I couldn't think of a single thing to say to her.

When she finally spoke, I was relieved that one of us had broken the uncomfortable silence. 'Love, I have something to discuss with you.' She stirred some sugar into her cup and my eyebrows rose: she believed that having sugar in tea was uncouth. She only did it when she was stressed, which was rare because she was a lady who lunched; she had chefs, cleaners and drivers so what did she have to be stressed about – except for how successful her charity luncheons were?

Something to discuss with me? My stomach clenched. Here it was: she was about to tell me how disappointed she was about my small house, chaotic job and apparently overly large dog.

I felt Fluffy's weight against my legs, comforting and protective. He'd sensed something was off and was putting himself between us. Shadow had retreated to my bedroom, away from Arabella who was sitting primly on Mum's lap.

I raised my eyebrows in invitation. *Go on then, hit me – tell me how wrong my life is.* I squared my shoulders; I wasn't going to bite my tongue in response, not this time.

'It's like this, darling.' She looked down at her tea and took a sip almost as if she were gathering her courage. She took a deep breath. 'I've wanted to talk to you about this since you became a vampire, but I didn't find the time before you left.' She frowned at me, 'Of course you didn't clue us into your plans to leave, so that's hardly my fault.'

I clenched my teeth and didn't point out that I *had* asked for their help to leave and they'd said no. 'Mum, get to the point. What are you talking about?' How did me becoming a vampire change anything besides my diet and my vulnerability to the sun?

'Well, Elizabeth, it's like this. Supernats aren't supposed to reveal themselves to the pedestrian world.'

I blinked. Something in the way she'd phrased it made my stomach clench. Suddenly I was sure that she wasn't lecturing me because I'd once blurted out to her that I was a vampire. *Pedestrian world*: she'd phrased it like *she* wasn't pedestrian.

'Mum...'

She raised a hand to stop me. 'Listen. This is difficult enough as it is.'

I closed my mouth and clenched my jaw, my slow heart hammering as I waited.

She drew herself up stiffly into her normal imperious posture. 'You see, Elizabeth ... I'm a witch, darling.'

I stared at her. All this time she'd been a supernat? My mouth hung open and for once I had nothing to say.

Mum trilled an awkward laugh. 'An elemental fire witch.' As if to prove it, she summoned a small flame to her fingertip. 'I always have been. Unlike you, I manifested my powers at a *proper* age – I was three when I summoned my first flame by accident.'

Gods: even while she was telling me something so important, she couldn't help getting in a dig. My mum might be a witch but she was definitely a total bitch.

'Nope.' The word flew from my lips and I shook my head like I had when I was a child, hair flying, eyes wide in disbelief.

I'd seen and accepted plenty of things since I'd arrived in Portlock: dead banshee spirits – fine; red-eyed werewolves – I got it; smoky murderous beasts – sure. But my mother a witch? Nope. No. All the no's, because if she *was*, that could mean my nana was one, too. The thought of her keeping that from me was crippling. Mum always let me down – that was her modus operandi – but Nana?

My mother nodded primly. 'Deny it all you like, Elizabeth, but I assure you I am a fire witch. See?' She waved her flaming finger at me.

'That's a tiny flame,' I said inanely. I could throw huge fireballs; maybe I was even more powerful than my mother. Fire came to me easily, and now I realised that I'd inherited that ability from *her*.

My mum was a fire witch. No matter how many times I repeated it, my brain couldn't accept it. I was in shock.

'It is tiny, isn't it?' she said smugly. At my less-than-impressed look, she elaborated. 'Any old idiot can throw a huge fireball but it takes years of study to perfect the control required to produce such a small flame.'

Right: I was any old idiot.

'That's why there aren't that many fire witches,' she continued sagely. 'Too many accidentally kill themselves before they learn control.'

Yikes. I added 'learn control' to my to-do list.

She doused the flame and took another sip of her sweetened tea. I stared at her as my brain started whirring again. The shock faded and gave way to anger. My mum was a witch, and John had told me a witch had arranged for me to be turned; had an enemy of my mother's arranged for me to be killed? Was my vampirism nothing more than a 'fuck you' to my mum?

I pushed the thought aside for later. I needed to focus on the issue at hand, namely that Mum was a freaking fire witch and she'd never, ever told me about it.

Fluffy must have sensed my distress because he stiffened and growled again, a quiet rumble that I felt against my legs than a sound Mum would hear.

She was taking calm, leisurely sips of tea whilst she shattered the foundations of my entire being. Anger and hurt warred inside me, both wrestling to be the dominant emotion in my broken heart. They writhed like poisonous snakes, slithering through my shocked body. How had she kept something like that from me for my entire life?

Instead of jumping up and slapping her, or running to Connor to cry, I asked, 'Does Dad know?'

Mum gave a very unladylike snort before she hastily held a tissue to her nose as if that could suppress her uncouth noise. 'Excuse me,' she murmured, dabbing her nose. She cleared her throat. 'Of course he knows, Elizabeth. He's a fire witch as well. That's how we met.'

That was too much. Both of them had kept this from me, a joint effort to keep their poor ped daughter ignorant. No wonder I'd always been forbidden to enter my dad's office – no doubt it was full of grimoires and crystals and other witchy things.

I tried to hold it together but the shock forced tears to spill. 'I bet you loved making a fool of me, didn't you?' I spat then burst into uncontrollable sobs that were not even slightly pretty.

Mum looked shocked for a second then grimaced. 'Oh dear,' she murmured. 'This hasn't gone well.' She looked flustered as she put down her tea and popped Arabella on the floor. She came over and rubbed my back awkwardly. 'We weren't being malicious, darling – we didn't keep it from you to *mock* you. We couldn't tell you because you weren't supernatural and it's the *law*.'

'To you I was your awful ped daughter, a constant source of disappointment,' I sobbed bitterly. 'At least now I understand *why* I disappointed you so damned much.'

'That's not true, Elizabeth! We've always been proud of your various – achievements.' Even as she said it, her tone was dubious as if she couldn't quite remember what they were.

My heart was aching and I felt so raw that every instinct told me to flee from the person who had caused me so much pain. I scrubbed the tears from my face.

'Elizabeth—' my mother started.

'Don't,' I snapped, holding up a hand. I wasn't sure what I was going to say next but before I could work it out, the phone rang.

Saved by the bell.

Chapter 4

It was Gunnar. I dug deep to find Portlock Bunny. Work Bunny. Professional Bunny. I wiped my eyes again and cleared my throat. 'I have to take this, it's work,' I said firmly. My mother waved her hand, giving me permission that I didn't damn well need to answer my own bloody phone.

She picked up Arabella and settled back at the kitchen table, sipping her tea again like she hadn't ripped my world in two.

'Gunnar,' I answered a shade hoarsely. 'What's up?'

'Sorry, Bunny. I know your mom arrived and it's your day off, but I could use your help on a case.' His voice dropped an octave. 'Plus, Connor kind of suggested you'd be more than happy to be summoned.'

Despite everything, that made me smile. Even though he wasn't by my side, Connor was still trying to ride to my rescue. In this case the monster I was being rescued from was my own mother, but he'd been right: I was more than happy to be rescued.

It said something about my psyche that a part of me was hoping Gunnar had a juicy murder case that would keep me out of my house for days on end. 'I'll be in ASAP,' I promised. 'Give me a few.' We hung up.

I turned to face She-That-Had-Birthed-Me. 'I have to go in to work,' I said bluntly.

'But I just arrived,' she protested. 'I wanted to talk.'

'I think you've said enough, don't you?' My voice was brittle; I hoped my broken heart wasn't on my sleeve for everyone to see. I gritted my teeth and cast around for something to say that was a little more polite than the 'fuck off' that wanted to leap out. 'Why don't you get cleaned up and grab some rest?' I offered lamely.

My mother looked subdued and her eyes were downcast. I felt a stab of guilt; she'd come all of this way to see me, flown thousands of miles to be with her daughter, and come clean about a huge secret that must have weighed on her for years. Was I being unfair?

I tried to think about it objectively but I was in it too deep to see anything clearly. Later, when I had some time alone, I'd drown in my childhood memories and see everything in a new light, but for now I tried to set it aside. I had work to do.

Mum gave me a tremulous smile. 'All right, darling, I am a bit tired. Rest sounds good.'

I managed my own tight smile. 'Maybe we can grab some food together later.' I offered the olive branch stiffly. Before she could reply, I grabbed Fluffy's lead, stuffed Shadow in his pram and stalked out.

I had a five-minute walk to clear my head. To be honest, even a five-mile hike wouldn't have cleared the detritus in my mind, but I had to try. The fresh air would help. Yeah, and pigs would fly.

I stalked to work, trying to quell my tumultuous emotions, push the feelings down, lock them in a box and focus on work. What a relief work was. God I hoped someone was dead.

I opened the door of the Nomo's office to find April Arctos seated at my desk. I'd forgotten that she was due to start today, and seeing someone usurping my seat gave me another wobble I didn't need. Suddenly I felt utterly replaceable, though I had enough self-awareness to know that was nothing to do with April Arctos.

I pasted on my best smile again and stepped forward; at least Mum's social soirées had been good for something. 'Hello, April, I'm so happy to see you! Welcome!' I *was* thrilled to see her, just not at my desk. We badly needed help in the office and April was a force to be reckoned with.

'Thank you, Bunny.' She gave me a genuine smile that faltered a little as she looked at me. 'Is everything okay?'

April was an observant woman so no doubt she'd spotted the red eyes and splotchy skin that signalled a crying jag. I pinched the bridge of my nose. 'My mum is visiting,' I admitted.

'And you don't get on?'

'Like dragons and knights,' I said flatly.

'Ah. Well, maybe this is an opportunity for you to mend fences.'

'I think our fences are destroyed,' I huffed.

April winked. 'Good thing you're dating the local lumberjack then!'

Her humour surprised a laugh out of me. 'Yeah, that's true.' I felt a little lighter and realised that had been her intention. I touched her shoulder. 'Thanks, April. I really am glad to have you here.' Fuck it, she could have my desk.

I let Shadow out of his carrier to join Fluffy on their matching beds. 'He in?' I asked, thumbing towards Gunnar's office.

She gave an exasperated sigh. 'Is he ever out?' I grinned. She already had her finger on the pulse; she'd fit in fine.

I went to Gunnar's office and tapped at the door. 'What's up boss?'

Gunnar looked up. 'The mayor called to say we have a developing situation down at the North Harbour.'

I'd been there less than an hour ago – what could possibly have cropped up in that amount of time? 'What kind of problem?'

'The kind where tempers are fraying. Mafu's keeping his distance. He said it looks like it's about to get ugly. Ready to rock and roll?'

'You bet. But why is it always the North Harbour?' I complained.

'It's cursed,' Gunnar agreed. He heaved himself out of his chair and we made hasty tracks to the borrowed ancient Suburban on loan from the borough. The Nomo SUV had met it's end at the hands of a possessed wind witch only a day and a half ago.

As we raced to the North Harbour, the place that seemed to be the bane of my existence, I asked, 'What did Mafu say was happening?'

'He said fists were about to fly and we'd better hurry before fur and fangs got involved. I nearly went without you,' he admitted, 'but I knew you wouldn't be long.'

'I appreciate you waiting.' I *needed* this; I needed a sharp reminder that I wasn't a downtrodden waitress anymore.

We parked and hurried down the walk-down ramp; the tide was coming back in so it was much less steep. People had gathered on the dock next to Edgy's plane and a fishing boat that was moored nearby. The crowd was rumbling and the tang of blood danced on the air.

As I stepped onto the boards, my stomach gave a low rumble of hunger. Dammit, I hadn't had any blood before I'd come out. It was a rookie error. I got hangry: someone was bleeding from a stray punch and suddenly I was feeling a whole lot of rage. I cursed myself for not remembering that I'd needed blood, no matter how distasteful I found it.

The mayor was trying to control the small crowd from a distance with a loud hailer, but he was obviously fighting a losing battle. I watched as one man shoved another with significant force. Despite the strength of the shove, the other barely moved – shifter strength. He gave a taunting smile and his aggressor stepped back and crouched low. I'd seen that stance before: he was going to shift. Mafu wasn't wrong about the fur and fangs. Luckily, I was the one with the fangs.

I pulled a set of magic-cancelling cuffs out of my belt and, using vampiric speed, sprinted towards the crouched man. His shift stopped abruptly as I closed his new jewellery around his wrists and his eyes cleared. 'What?' he asked in confusion, still kneeling. He looked around. 'Gary?' he said to the taunting man. 'What's going on?'

Gary pulled his hand back to shove his fist into the kneeling man's face, but before he could make contact Gunnar had wrestled him to the ground. The minute the cuffs were on him, Gary looking around in confusion. 'Carl?' he said to his friend. 'What the fuck?'

'I don't know, man. You were fixing for a fight.'

'So were you,' I interrupted. 'And you're not alone.' Around us another seven people were vying for a heavyweight title. Fists were flying; even worse, I could feel my own anger rising. The heat in me was scorching and I wanted to give into it to burn away the feelings of inadequacy my mother's confession had raised in me.

Gunnar bellowed. 'Everyone stop!' No one paid him any mind.

'Cuffs!' I barked. 'Cuff them all quickly!' I briefly considered putting a cuff on myself before I lost control but dismissed the idea. The last thing I wanted right now was to be in a hostile situation without my magic. I could keep a lid on my rage. Probably.

We made quick work of the irate crowd because they were focused on each other, barely aware of their surroundings. Soon all nine men were cuffed, confused and subdued.

I was standing near the edge of the harbour. A familiar glint of gold in the water made me step closer: the water dragon. It looked at me pointedly, and I moved closer to meet its ancient eyes. The problem was that I didn't speak Water Dragon and I was still wrestling with my rage issues, which were becoming almost unbearable.

'You got some rage growing?' Gunnar grunted.

'Oh yeah. Like a forest fire,' I warned him pointedly.

He shot me a look. 'Hold it steady,' he commanded. He wasn't talking about my temper but about my flames.

I nodded tightly and stepped closer to the water; if I lost control, at least I could direct the flames into the bay. The sea was hellish cold – it could cope with being a degree or two warmer.

'The anger – it's a curse,' Gunnar rumbled. 'We need to find and disrupt the rune work. It'll be here somewhere.'

'Disrupt it how?'

'We need to scrub it out.' Gunnar's huge fists were opening and closing rhythmically. He was fighting the urge to start kicking ass, too.

Scrub out rune work: that seemed simple enough. I was about to go back to the crowd when the water dragon flicked water over me with its tail. 'Hey!' I objected. I hadn't taken care with my appearance but at least I'd been clean; now I was swampy. Son of a bitch.

My watery friend was trying to tell me something, but what? There had been a time not long ago that the thought of being near an ancient water dragon would have been enough to make me piss my pants, so in a way it was a nice reminder that I *had* changed and grown. I was stronger now, and I wasn't going to let my mum unmake my progress.

I moved closer to the water dragon. It rolled on its side then one golden eye blinked at me and pointedly looked up. I followed its gaze.

The dock was anchored with six tall metal poles so it could slide up and down with the tide. Although it was dark, the smell of blood and the dragon's eye led me to glimpse what could definitely be the cursed rune work on the metal's surface.

I wiped my hands down my pants. The poles were smooth so this would take my full vampiric strength – and luck. I jumped, grabbed hold with my hands and knees then used my feet to propel me and started shimmying up the pole.

The smell of blood became stronger; no wonder my tummy had rumbled. I hadn't smelled a nosebleed, it had been this: runes drawn in blood. I could see them clearly now, painted on the metal surface.

I anchored myself as best I could with one arm and both legs, got out my phone, used the flash and snapped some pictures. Once I'd secured the evidence, I used my jacket sleeve to swipe through the runes. Ewww. I tried not to think about the blood that was now covering my jacket.

Once I was certain I'd destroyed the dangerous runes, I slid down the post. Hopefully I'd destroyed them before Gunnar's rage accidentally started him wiping the floor with the cuffed men below me.

Chapter 5

Once I was back at the dock, Gunnar shot me a relieved look. 'You found the curse.' With his own rage settling, it wasn't even a question.

'I found it.'

With the curse neutralised, there was no reason to keep the crowd cuffed; they were victims, in the wrong place at the wrong time. We released them after we'd taken some brief statements. They were shift workers at the fish plant who'd come down to the dock for a few beers. There was nothing illegal in that, for all we were a damp town.

The statements were pretty much the same: they all confirmed that they'd had an indescribable feeling of rage then found themselves down here fighting with their friends. They were confused and their memories were fuzzy, so no one could remember what had caused their anger. I shuddered. I often felt that my sharp memory was the sole weapon in my arsenal so losing it... It didn't bear thinking about.

Gunnar told the crowd that they'd walked into a curse; if they had tiredness or weakness that they couldn't explain, they should go to the hospital immediately. Tense and nervous, the group dispersed.

All their statements confirmed that going to the docks had been spontaneous and wasn't a regular occurrence, so nobody could have known in advance that they would have been there at that time. That told me it was more than likely that they hadn't been the targets of the curse.

They were lucky that Mafu had walked by, seen the beginnings of a scuffle and knew enough to stay out of it. That begged the question: who was the curse really designed for? One of the fishermen? Edgy? Or was it an ill-conceived prank just to trap *someone*? I bit my lip. I didn't think so: this didn't feel like a kids' screw-up.

We spoke briefly to Mafu. He'd seen someone watching the drama unfold from the bushes but they'd scuttled away before he could speak to them. We checked the area carefully but all we found were some small footprints in the mud. If the Peeping Tom had been the perpetrator, they'd had small feet. We took some photographs and Gunnar made a mould of the shoe print in case it *was* the curser watching the action unfold.

After all that, we went back to the Suburban. There wasn't much of a scene to save or analyse, since I'd scrubbed the shit out of it. The thought made me glance towards the water again but I didn't see so much as a hint of gold. The water dragon was long gone; it had done its thing – protected the town – and now it was back to whatever water dragons did in their spare time. Water polo, maybe.

'How's your mom?' Gunnar asked.

Now that was a loaded question. I shrugged. 'She's fine, I guess,' I said tightly, trying to keep a lid on my emotions whilst I was working.

He threw me a sidelong look. 'I'm sorry I'm keeping you from her,' he said mildly.

'I'm not!' Something about Gunnar often reminded me of a priest: his warm demeanour invited confession, and who was I to refuse? With a sigh I told him, 'Apparently she's a witch, a fire elemental like me. She never told me. Ever.'

His eyes were sympathetic. 'I'm sorry, Bunny. That's hard.'

'Yeah, well... It was a double whammy because it turns out my dad's a witch, too. I feel like they were sniggering up their sleeves at me my whole life.'

'Hey,' he objected softly. 'Come on now. I bet it was hard for them. We're supposed to keep the supernat world hidden from ped folk.'

'You're supposed to be on *my* side,' I said, annoyed.

He grinned. 'Oh, I am. Always. They're absolute fuckers. Scum of the earth.' He paused. 'Is that better?'

I laughed. 'Yes, actually it is.' I sobered. 'I do get that. I was ped, now I'm not. The rules – the *laws* – have changed. So okay, she kept it from me for most of my life, but she could have told me after I was turned.' I bit my thumb as I thought. 'Maybe me getting turned into a vampire was nothing to do with *me* – maybe it was one of *their* enemies.' I sighed. 'Why did she wait so long to tell me the truth?'

He was silent for a beat. 'I can't answer that – but you know who can.'

I puffed out a sharp breath. 'My mum?'

'You got it.'

I looked out of the window. I hated that he was right when I wanted him to be wrong.

We were pulling into the Nomo car park. 'How about you bring your mama over for supper with me and Sig tomorrow? You know how Sig feels about you. She'd love to meet your mom.'

My knee-jerk reaction was to refuse because my mother would judge everything about their gorgeous home. I liked Gunnar and Sig too much to subject them to any ridicule from her, but at the same time they could definitely handle it – handle *her*. And if both sides of my life had to meet, far better to control the situation. 'Sure.'

Gunnar beamed. 'Great. Sig will be thrilled.'

She won't be once she's met my mum, I thought darkly, but I kept the thought to myself. Fluffy had no such compunction: he growled then barked a worried sound.

'You're invited too,' Gunnar said, winking at my dog, Fluffy's head lowered; he wasn't happy. He didn't like my mum, and he was a good judge of character.

We went into the office and I checked in with April. The night had been slow. 'Go on,' Gunnar said. 'Get yourself home. Your shift will come soon enough.' He wasn't wrong: Portlock didn't believe in being dull and there was rarely a quiet moment. I needed to seize this one.

I collected my animal friends and set off home. Since I doubted I'd have any privacy once I got there, I called Connor as I was walking.

'Hey, doe. How's it going with your mom?' he asked.

'Great,' I said, faux brightly. 'She's been lying to me my entire life. She's a fire witch.'

There was silence. When he spoke, I heard concern and thinly veiled anger in his tone, anger on my behalf. He really was the best. 'Do you want me to come over?' he asked tightly. 'I'll hold your bag while you kick her ass.' Now *that* was the reaction I'd wanted from Gunnar!

I grinned and my heart lifted a little. 'I can't tell you how much I appreciate that offer. And I do want you here, more than anything ... but I'd better have it out with her. And I kind of promised to take her to the Garden of Eat'n.' I was regretting that olive branch now; the curse had whipped a lot of rage through me and it still hadn't quite settled.

Time for a change of subject. 'How's John? Did you get him settled okay?'

'No problem. He's got a private room. I keep a bunkhouse and a few duplexes on the property for strays, new vamps, or vampires and their families that are between housing. Not everyone is lucky enough to have a daylight charm.'

I couldn't imagine not having one anymore, being restricted to the shadows... My hand clasped the charm at my throat. I remembered all too well the cloying darkness of London. 'Thank you for helping him,' I said. 'John is a good man. He helped me escape London even though it was to his detriment.'

'I'd never leave a vampire in need, especially not one that helped you.'

'I know, but I'm annoyed it was dumped on you because someone – Octavius or whoever sent John – didn't think about him.'

'Perhaps someone else was supposed to have set it up. In big organisations, it's not hard to drop the ball. Someone must have arranged appropriate travel measures or he'd have burnt to death.'

'You're right. Thanks for sorting it, though. I do appreciate it.'

'I'd do anything for you, Bunny.' His voice was husky. 'I miss you. You know I'm here if you need me. You're not alone in this, okay?'

I nodded even though he couldn't see me. It scared me a little how essential Connor was becoming to my life, but I thanked every deity I could think of that I had him by my side so we could face the coming storm together.

I was confident it was going to be a raging one.

Chapter 6

I walked into a wall of silence. My home was never that quiet when I was here; usually Shadow was snoring or Fluffy was chasing cats in his sleep. I guessed Mum was asleep and maybe Arabella was too. I felt bad at the surge of hope that we could maybe forget going out for dinner.

I slunk into the kitchen to feed us. I fed Shadow and Fluffy first because I'm a good fur-mother, and while they were eating I boiled the kettle and microwaved a cup of blood. My stomach was rumbling and I suddenly realised that I could hear my mum's heart beating – worse, it was close. I whirled around just as there was a spate of obnoxious yapping.

'Is that you, darling?' Mum called from the living room.

I bit back the snarky response *'Who else were you expecting?'* and managed a civil, 'Yes, Mum,' instead.

I downed my warm blood, for once savouring its taste. I had needed it too much; I needed to be more careful. My awareness of Mum's heartbeats settled to a steady thrum, background noise that I could disregard. These days, I could easily pick out Shadow's racing heart and the constant comforting beat of Fluffy's; they sounded like home to me.

Since Mum was awake, I prepared a pot of tea – she preferred it to come in a pot. She walked in, her hair wrapped in a silk scarf and wearing her dressing gown and bright-pink, fluffy-heeled slippers. Who wore heels to relax? A psychopath, that's who. She was carrying Arabella.

'I'm sorry if we woke you,' I offered. 'We were trying to be quiet.'

She waved a hand dismissively. 'It was Arabella rather than you. She thinks she's the size of your dog, Fuzzy.' Fuzzy was a ridiculous name for a dog: Fuzzy was a name for a muppet.

'Fluffy,' I corrected flatly. 'Arabella would be a single-bite snack for him.' I looked at Mum's pooch in warning in case she was half as smart as my canine and could understand.

My four-legged companions had disappeared and I assumed they were in my bedroom; they both seemed a little allergic to the Pomeranian. Who could blame them?

After the tea had brewed, I put some milk in Mum's and searched the cabinet for some biscuits. They were gone, eaten by me on a lonely day. I groaned inwardly; I hadn't been to the market for a while.

I passed her the tea and we sipped in awkward silence. Well, this wouldn't do. We wouldn't get anything resolved if we didn't speak. 'We didn't get a chance to finish our conversation, Mum,' I started.

She sipped her tea carefully, avoiding my eyes. I was breaking the rules; we'd always used tea to *avoid* conversation. 'I know that was upsetting for you,' she said carefully, setting down her cup. She laid her hands primly in her lap.

Upsetting? She'd uprooted my whole existence and she thought I was *upset?* I wasn't upset, I was fucking furious. I wanted to scream at her but I held it together and forced myself to take another drink before I spoke. 'I'm not upset; I'm hurt and angry. Imagine how you'd feel if your parents had *lied* to you your entire life. It's a lot to take in. To accept.' *To forgive.*

She sighed. 'We didn't have a choice, Elizabeth. You should have been a strong and powerful witch but your powers never manifested. We couldn't tell you the truth because you weren't a supernat. It wouldn't have been so bad if we weren't so closely aligned with Octavius, but we were. *Are.* We have to follow the letter of the law – we couldn't tell you and risk him finding out that you knew. It was bad enough when you discovered vampires existed. Gods, that was a headache and a half.'

It was time to confront what had been haunting me; I needed to know the truth. 'Nana. She was a witch too?'

She must have been. I touched my triskele charm, remembered some odd things she'd said and done. I realised now that she'd been trying to let me know about the supernat world. She knew about my exceptional memory, and she'd hoped that if she dropped enough crumbs I'd put them together on my own.

She'd told me many times about the power of crystals but I'd dismissed it as 'new-age nonsense'. More fool me: I'd remained clueless. My vaunted powers of memory and observation had failed me because I hadn't wanted to see.

Mum nodded and her chest puffed out with pride. 'Yes, dear, she was. You come from a long line of powerful fire elemental witches.'

For fuck's sake. A long line – and for the longest time I'd been the dud who was ignorant of her fiery heritage. Well, I wasn't ignorant now.

I knew what I could do with the flames within me, but for some reason I didn't tell mum. Maybe I'd tell her after we'd had time to bond. A child-like part of me wanted her approval *without* my magic. Let her think I was an ordinary vampire – that would do for now.

'Fire?' I asked casually, as if I didn't know full well what she was talking about.

'Yes, fire. Of course, I can do many other things with magic but fire comes naturally, like breathing. The other magics require gestures and incantations, rituals and potions.' She paused. 'Do you know any witches here?'

I thought of Elsa Wintersteen, Shirley Thompson and Vitus Vogler. Without exception, they'd all been a tad deadly. 'Um, yes,' I said blandly. 'I've met a few.' I tried to think of a *good* witch that I'd met and Sigrid popped into my mind right away. I'd almost forgotten about Gunnar's invite for dinner. 'Actually, talking of witches, we're invited to my boss's house for supper tomorrow. His wife is a witch.'

Mum brightened and clapped her hands. 'Oh, how delightful. Do you know what manner of witch she is?'

'She's a hearth witch – at least that's what Gunnar calls her. I've never asked her directly.' I waited for my mother's face to screw into a moue of distaste at something so lowly, but her smile broadened.

'Wonderful. I love a good hearth witch – they have such beautiful homes and cook such delicious food.' She hesitated then added, 'Hilda is a hearth witch.'

I blinked. 'Hilda? Our cook?'

'Yes, dear.'

I stored that piece of information in my memory then groaned as I recalled telling Hilda on more than one occasion that her cooking was magic. She'd always grimaced and I'd thought that she had a problem accepting compliments like many women do; it was far easier to cling to our societally imposed low self-esteem. But no, Hilda was grimacing for a whole different reason.

'I try and hire witches when I can,' Mum said primly.

'Because they're better than anyone else?' I asked cynically, prepared for her to wax lyrical about how much better witches were than peds or werewolves or vampires.

'No, because it is so hard to earn an honest living these days. Centuries of persecution mean that witches instinctively stay hidden. We can't play to our strengths, not unless we come to one of the supernat havens, like Portlock.'

'Are there other places like this? In the UK, I mean?'

'Of course! I'd love to take you to a few of them.' Her eager smile faded. That wouldn't be possible because Octavius would seize me for my one hundred years of conclave service if I set foot on UK soil. Officially I might be part of Connor's group but I had no doubt that Octavius would do anything to get me under his control again.

And after the one hundred years were up? By then my mum would be six feet under. There would be no mummy and daughter daytrips to British supernat havens in our future and we both knew it. 'We'll have to enjoy Portlock,' I said finally.

She nodded. 'Yes, I've heard so much about this town. I'm excited to meet its covens.'

'Do you belong to a coven?' I asked curiously.

She gave a brisk nod. 'I do. Actually, I lead all the covens in the United Kingdom.'

I sputtered. You didn't get to lead all the witches in the UK without stepping on some toes, so no doubt she'd made some powerful enemies. It was making more and more sense that my being turned was not about me but about her.

I desperately wanted to ask her about it but I couldn't figure out a way that didn't sound accusatory, and I didn't want to make her feel like I thought it was *her* fault. I put that aside – for now – but, man, the blows kept coming.

'How did you keep *that* a secret?' I demanded.

'You thought I did a lot of charity work and I do, but it's all related to my duties as High Priestix.'

That made sense. I'd been hurt by how often she'd been away; for a stay-at-home mum, she was never home. But if she were heading all the UK covens, she'd have to travel a lot. It didn't alleviate my sense of being unwanted and unloved, but at least it explained some of it. And maybe that was what all her social climbing had been about: a way of covering up her real activities? Maybe she'd really been encouraging me to mix with supernat children?

Before I could ask, my phone rang. I glanced down, expecting it to be Gunnar with another issue, but it was Liv. Why was she calling *me*? I swiped it open. 'Liv. How are you?'

'Peachy,' she said abruptly. 'Did your mother make it into town?'

I frowned. 'Yes, I didn't know you knew she was coming.'

'Of course I did. I invited her,' she said stridently. 'I didn't know she was *your* mom at the time, I only realised when she told me she wouldn't be staying at the Portlock Hotel with the others. Why did you never mention you had a witch mother? Ashamed?'

It felt like the walls were closing in on me. *Liv* had invited my mum here. Mum wasn't here to see me and confess her deepest, darkest secret face to face; she was here to see Liv. I felt such an idiot. Even with my mother's confessions, I'd somehow hoped that she was here for *me,* for us to build something. Instead the heat in my gut told me that I was a consolation prize, like always.

'No,' I snarled, taking out some of my anger on Liv. 'I would never have been ashamed of having a witch as mother.' *If I'd known*. I looked at my mother and met her eyes. 'You invited her to Portlock?' I repeated, letting my hurt show on my face.

Mum flinched.

'Yes,' Liv said impatiently. 'I told you I'd called the four most powerful elemental witches in the world to come help with the barrier gems.'

'Yes, you did. Here she is.' I handed over my phone.

'Elizabeth...' Mum said, her tone pleading.

I turned and left the room. I was fresh out of fucks to give.

Chapter 7

I stroked Fluffy whilst he whined softly in concern. His warmth and visible love helped soothe the dull ache in my heart. Shadow darted in, jumped into my lap and purred loudly as if my pain called to him, as if his acceptance of me could somehow eradicate it. Maybe it could.

I stroked his fur, burying my hands in the softest blanket known to man. I wanted to fall apart; indeed, I was poised to do so and it took everything in me not to. That's what Mum would expect of me. *Bunny the mess. Bunny the fuck up.*

I wiped away my tears and took a minute to centre myself. I wouldn't let her keep hurting me. I was an adult; I had a life of my own. I had my pets, my friends, my job and … I had Connor. I'd keep my focus on those positives. I had so much to be grateful for here.

I went to the bathroom to make sure it didn't look like I'd been crying and grimaced at my reflection. I was splotchy and red. I washed my face and brushed and plaited my hair. I'd promised Mum supper at the diner and I would follow through. Because she'd been a terrible mother didn't mean I had to be a terrible daughter. We were at rock bottom – things could only improve, right? I took another deep breath and went out to face her.

She was sitting at my kitchen table with Arabella on her knee. She looked up as I walked in. 'I've finished with your phone, darling,' she said, still looking reserved. 'Thank you,' she tacked on hastily.

'No problem. Do you still want to go out for supper?' I wasn't ready to tackle the hand grenade of Liv's call yet.

'Absolutely. Let me get myself suitably attired.'

I didn't ask what Liv had wanted and Mum didn't volunteer the information. We were back to our safe zone: polite, empty small talk.

I took Fluffy out while I waited for her to get ready, refilled the animals' water bowls and then, full of nervous energy, I did some much-needed cleaning. After a while, I checked the time: I'd been waiting thirty minutes already.

Mum swanned in. 'I'm ready, dear!' she declared.

I stared at her in disbelief. She was wearing a different silk dress, this one in lavender, with heels. Her hair was in a perfect chignon and she was wearing earrings and pearls. She had a full face of makeup. She would stand out at the diner like a unicorn at a rock concert.

'Aren't you going to change for dinner?' she asked, frowning.

I looked down at myself. I was wearing smart jeans and a nice T-shirt. 'Trust me. I'm overdressed,' I mumbled. 'It's a seven-block walk, Mum. Do you want to change your shoes?'

'I walk everywhere in these, I'll be fine. They have a charm in them to make them feel like flats,' she explained conspiratorially. Now *that* would have come in handy during my teen years.

Mum shut Arabella in her bedroom so there wasn't a ruckus between the animals whilst we were out. I turned on the TV for Fluffy and flipped it to one of his new favourite shows; a cooking program with the Hairy Bikers. For all I knew, he enjoyed salivating over the food.

We walked slowly to The Garden of Eat'n. Yes, Mum could walk forever in her heels – I'd seen her do it before and now I knew how. The little sneak. 'Oh,' she said, eyes wide, when we stopped in front of the diner. 'Is this it?'

I thought it was quaint, quintessentially American, but no doubt she only saw the flaking paint and the tired-looking waitress. The Garden of Eat'n had no airs and graces and no one needed a reservation. We went in, found an empty booth and sat.

'I see why you dressed like you did.' Mum manoeuvred awkwardly into her seat.

'I know it doesn't look much but the food is really good.' Not Michelin-star good, but good enough. I winced; it wouldn't be good enough for Mum. What had I been thinking bringing her here?

With pinched lips, she picked up the menu and frowned at the laminated two pages of small print.

When she put it down, she rummaged through her designer handbag for a wipe to clean her hands.

'Is that the only bag you brought?' I asked, looking at the flowered monstrosity.

'Of course, darling. I wouldn't take a Hermès on an aeroplane!' Her expression was horrified. 'What do you recommend?' she asked, still sounding dubious that anything here would be edible.

'The halibut fish and chips, or the chicken fried steak. Unless you want a full breakfast.'

'What's a chicken fried steak?' she asked.

'Beefsteak beaten until it's flat and tender, breaded and deep fried. They serve it with mashed potatoes and cover the whole thing in gravy.'

Mum stared at me aghast. 'Why on earth would you call beefsteak chicken?'

I shrugged. 'Beats me.'

'And that counts as *cuisine*?'

'It's very tasty.'

'Even so,' she said faintly, 'I believe I'll have the fish and chips.'

To be perverse, I ordered the chicken fried steak. When the waitress left, I braced myself and broached the subject of Liv. 'So what did Liv have to say?'

'She was talking about the general game plan.' It was hilarious to hear my posh mother say something like 'game plan'. She continued. 'I'm the first witch to arrive and she said she'd let me know when the others get here so we can work on the barrier gem issue.'

I seized the bull by the horns. 'That's why you really came? To help Liv? It wasn't to see me – it was just a happy coincidence that I live in the same town.'

To her credit, she looked like I'd slapped her. 'Of course not, darling! I came to see you! To be honest, I would have palmed the job off on one of the other fire witches – I'm not a fan of air travel, as you know. But seeing you gave me the impetus to conquer my fears!' She looked like she was expecting me to give her a standing ovation. 'I couldn't believe that I was being asked to come to the same town in America where you lived. It was like providence herself was smiling upon me.' She beamed at me.

I wanted desperately to believe her and I found myself nodding. 'And Dad?'

She hesitated. 'Well, he wanted to come – of course he did! – but work obligations got in the way. Next time, I'm sure.' She was lying, but what was new? Dad had no plans to visit me, now or ever. That made my eyes prickle, so I hastily looked away and took a long drink of Coke until I could pretend that the ache in my throat was from the bubbles.

For all Mum's faults, she was good at reading a room. She reached out and patted my hand awkwardly. 'Tell me about your young man, Connor. He's a feast for the eyes, that's for sure.'

'Mum!' I gasped, scandalised.

She chuckled. 'I'm allowed to window shop, darling.' She frowned. 'A vampire called Mackenzie... Why is that name so familiar?'

I sighed; I might as well tell her because she'd find out one way or another. 'Connor is the son of the Vampire King of America.' I braced myself; that would get her going.

Her eyes widened. 'Why didn't you tell me so when you introduced us? Good Lord, I had him carrying my luggage like a common bellhop!' Her hand fluttered to her forehead. 'I feel faint.'

'No you don't,' I snorted. 'And Connor isn't like that. This is Alaska – he chops down trees for a living. Besides, he and his father aren't on the best of terms.'

'That doesn't matter! Oh my gosh, he must think I'm *awful*!' She was literally clutching at her pearl necklace. I needed her to calm down before people started looking at us.

'I wouldn't worry. He probably wanted to make a good impression on *you*,' I soothed.

That made perfect sense to her because in her world *everyone* wanted to make a good impression on her. Her expression cleared. 'Even so, I'll have to make it up to him. There has to be a better eating establishment in town. Let's invite him to dinner – my treat.' It was gratifying that she knew me well enough not to suggest that I cook.

'There's the Pizza Kodiak Kitchen, but to be honest it's much the same as this place. You might want to consider coming back here – Connor does love a good chicken fried steak.'

She looked horrified and I smiled inwardly. Rural Alaska was going to be a rude awakening for her and I was looking forward to it.

The waitress arrived with our food. 'Thank you so much,' Mum said calmly. She waited until we were alone again then hissed, 'Why is there so much of it?' She was used to the miniscule portions of posh London cuisine.

'Everything is big in America. Wait until you see the trucks around here.'

'And your young man, I bet,' she muttered salaciously under her breath.

I wished I could unhear that. Sometimes vampire hearing was the worst.

Chapter 8

Thankfully Mum liked the halibut. She was still dubious about the establishment as a whole – she set out the list of failures as we walked home – but I flagged the evening under the 'not a total disaster' column and moved on.

When we got in she excused herself and went to bed, exhausted from her trip. The sun was only an hour away from rising so I took Fluffy out for a toilet break and then crawled into bed too. As I was snuggling in, Shadow curled up on my chest. He had grown again. He purred loudly and moments later his brilliant golden eyes slid closed. Mine soon followed.

I woke to a loud, panicked yip, flung off the covers and ran out of my room. In the lounge, Shadow had Arabella pinned to the floor with one large paw. Arabella's eyes were wide, and she was panting with fear. Whoops. I'd left the bedroom door ajar so Shadow could get to his litter box in the night. My bad.

I picked up Shadow, who yowled in protest at being deprived of his naughty little game. 'Bad Shadow,' I murmured. 'Be nice to the annoying dog.' If I had to be, then so did he.

I carried him into my bedroom and closed the door firmly this time, then went to the kitchen. This called for a brew. Cohabiting was exhausting at the best of times; add in territorial pets and it was a recipe for disaster.

'That is *not* a normal cat!' Mum glowered as she joined me. She picked up Arabella and fussed over her.

'No, he's a lynx kitten.'

'A lynx? As in an actual wild animal?' Eyes wide, she clutched at her throat where her pearls usually rested.

He might be a wild animal, but he fitted in fine with me and Fluffy. What did that say about us? That we were feral? I was strangely okay with that. 'He's pretty gentle most of the time,' I said reassuringly. 'He's a baby and he's still finding his way. The vet thinks he's only a few months old.'

'He's bigger than Arabella!'

'Arabella weighs 1.5 kilos. Most normal house cats are larger than her,' I pointed out.

'That *menace* is going to kill my darling!' Mum squawked.

'He's playing. It'll be fine.' She wasn't buying it. 'I'll take him and Fluffy with me to work, give them time to cool off. Don't forget we're invited to dinner at my boss's tonight. We usually go at midnight, which is around my lunchtime. I'll pick you up.'

'All right,' she said tightly, still unhappy about Shadow. 'It'll take me a while to get used to a night regime. I keep largely to daylight hours in London

– except when I'm dealing with other supernats, of course.'

'Of course,' I said flatly. I knew nothing of her secret meetings with other supernats and that chafed.

The atmosphere was still a little frosty, and I'd never been happier to go in early to work. Sidnee looked up at me in surprise when I arrived, then at the clock then back at me. Yep, I was two hours early. 'Did something happen?' she asked.

'Yes, my mother happened. She's been here one full day and I'm ready to move out.'

'It's your house,' she pointed out.

'Desperate times and all that.'

I pushed Shadow's pram into its spot and lifted him out. He gave his kitten squeak and marched over to rub against Sidnee's legs. I'd never had a cat before and I wasn't sure if he was behaving like a normal one. Kitten or not, he was some kind of cool superhero creature that could drive back the beast beyond the barrier. I pictured him with a cape – then laughed. He'd probably tear it to shreds to play with.

I made some tea and coffee and took them to Sidnee's desk. 'Guess what?' I started.

'What?' she replied dutifully.

'My mum didn't come all this way to see me.'

Sidnee frowned. 'Why did she come then?'

'Well, that's the real kicker. She's a witch.'

'*What*?'

'A fire witch,' I continued, satisfied with the way I'd shocked her. 'She's a High Priestix, a powerful fire elemental, and Liv invited her here to help with the barrier issues. Mum dropped that bomb on me right after she arrived. Can you believe it?'

Sidnee stared at me for a long minute with her mouth open until she realised and closed it with a clack. 'Oh my gosh. I'm so sorry, Bunny. That's a lot to take in, and I know from what you've said before that she was never an award-winning mum.'

'She wasn't an anything mum,' I admitted. 'I had a host of nannies and she was never there. Now I know why – she was working her way up the coven ladder. She rules all the covens in the UK.'

'Wow.'

'Yeah. A part of me thinks I should be proud of all that she's achieved, but I laid in bed looking through a tonne of my childhood memories and there are so many times she wasn't there. She chose her career over me – her secret, supernatural career. That she's successful doesn't make it any less shitty for me.'

'No, I guess not. I think we're told now that as women we can have it all, and I'm sure plenty can, but it's an awful lot to juggle.'

I sighed. 'Yeah, and she dropped some balls. Anyway, she's a fire witch and she's here to save the barrier. My dad is a witch, too. They've been lying to me my whole life.'

'Fuck.' Sidnee reached out to squeeze my hand. It was rare for her to swear so I really appreciated her use of foul language on my behalf.

I paused for a moment and decided to change the subject back to work. 'Okay, I can't wallow more. Any calls?' I really meant cases: I needed something big to take my mind off my mother and our whole raft of issues.

'I picked up a kid for shoplifting a candy bar and a box of condoms at the grocery store,' Sidnee said proudly.

'Nice one. How old was the kid?'

'Fifteen. I brought him back to the station for processing and to call his parents, but Gunnar decided to have words with him. He won't be stealing again after the Nomo got through with him. The kiddo said he was too nervous to buy the condoms, and Gunnar said if he was too embarrassed to buy penis coats then he definitely shouldn't be using them.'

I bust out laughing. 'Penis coats? He said that?'

'Well, no. I'm paraphrasing,' Sidnee admitted, making me laugh even harder.

'So, beside the penis-jacket thief, anything else happen?' I asked when I'd gotten the snickers under control.

It had been a slow few days since we'd caught Elsa Wintersteen, the wind witch who'd been influenced by the cursed gems. She was safely in an institute being rehabilitated. I'd been relieved when the council hadn't simply sent her to jail; yes, she'd done horrific things but they hadn't really been her fault any more than being briefly possessed by the fire gem had been my fault.

'Oh! You made the paper, again.' Sidnee pulled out a copy of *The Supernat Sentinel*. Sure enough, there was a grainy photograph of me cuffing one of the cursed lads from the docks. The headline said: *Fierce Fanged Flopsy Foments Fear.*

I let out a groan. I regretted ever speaking to Lisa, the sole reporter at the *Sentinel*. The article was actually pretty accurate and informative because she'd spoken to some of the cursed lads after Gunnar and I had let them go. It cautioned everyone about the power of curses and ended with a warning to the perpetrator that the Fanged Flopsy was on the case.

'Bloody marvellous,' I groused. I guessed that explained who our peeping Tom had been: Lisa was five foot nothing and the shoe prints would undoubtedly match her delicate feet. Dammit, that meant we were back to square one with the curser. I made a mental note to call Lisa and shout at her for running off like that. No doubt she'd been concerned – rightly – that we would confiscate her photos.

Sidnee grinned. 'Apart from that, it's been a really boring shift.'

'Anything from the hotline?' I wondered if Chris, Sidnee's drug-dealing ex-boyfriend had tried to contact her again.

'Nah. The only call was from Gertrude – another complaint about Remmy. I visited him and told him to quit taunting her.'

'And he agreed?'

Sidnee shrugged. 'For this week, at least.'

'He's going to get himself killed,' I predicted darkly.

She laughed. 'I doubt it. I think Gertrude has a thing for him.'

My jaw dropped. 'No way!'

'Way.'

'She needs flirting lessons,' I said drily. 'You think Remmy fancies her back?'

She waggled her eyebrows. 'There's a reason he's always on her land!'

I shook my head and chugged my tea. 'This chat has blown my mind.'

'Sometimes you have to look at things from a different perspective,' she advised quietly. From her suddenly serious tone she was thinking about Chris, but it was also good advice. I could apply it to the shit with my mum: maybe I should try looking at things from her point of view?

Then again, maybe not.

Chapter 9

Gunnar bellowed for me shortly after Sidnee left for the night. 'You rang, boss?' I said drolly as I strolled into his office.

'Funny,' he said flatly. 'We've got a call to go to the "*black market*".' He said the last two words in a deep spooky voice, wiggling his fingers at me, but he was grinning and he looked excited.

'We have a black market?' That sounded intriguing. I wondered what you could buy there. Then I remembered that our poison-wielding, fireball-throwing witch, Shirley Thompson, had been selling her wares on the dark web. It was probably things like that.

'It's the worst kept secret around,' Gunnar admitted. 'But I've never been able to find it, let alone had an invitation! It moves around the supernat towns, never staying anywhere long enough to bother the local law enforcement, but they sell things that MIB would definitely take issue with. Obviously they don't advertise their presence, but word gets out. I usually find out about their arrival right about the time they're moving on. This time, we've got them early! And they've actually invited us there!' He sounded very enthusiastic.

'Are we arresting them?' I asked, confused.

'They've asked for us to come, so I'm betting there's been some foul play. We'll get the lay of the land and then play it by ear. Take plenty of magic-cancelling cuffs.'

I patted my hip where a number of them were resting on my belt; I always had them on me when I was on duty. In a magical town, they were one of the best weapons in our arsenal.

We left the animals at the office; I could still remember the covetous gleam in Liv's eyes after she'd learned Shadow could fight the beast beyond the barrier, so I wasn't about to tote him into an illegal market which sold who knows what.

'What's the deal with the market?' I asked as we drove. 'It sells illegal stuff?'

'Undoubtedly so, but mostly it's about avoiding paying tax and leaving no trace. Everything in cash. No transactions to chase down.'

It was hard to get excited about tax evasion; tax was essential for our civilisation's infrastructure, but give me a juicy murder over a dull white-collar crime any day.

I was surprised when we pulled up to the Chatham Bay Funeral Home and I looked questioningly at Gunnar. He shrugged. 'Apparently it's here, in the basement.' He hesitated a moment. 'Liv owns it,' he said unhappily.

Of course she did. She was a necromancer; owning a funeral home made a sick sort of sense. 'Who would let her have their dead?' I asked incredulously.

'A lot of people. She gives you a steep discount if you let her use the death to her magical advantage.'

'But ... what does she do to the bodies?'

'She holds a funeral, everyone says goodbye. A closed casket is buried but no one is quite sure what's inside – if anything at all.'

My jaw dropped. 'So she might have an army of undead servants we know nothing about?'

He grinned. 'I think we'd notice some zombies shuffling around town. You've seen the poppets she uses?'

'The creepy doll things?'

'Yeah. She uses nails, skin and hair to imbue them with the life force of the deceased and she uses those to power her spells. I've never seen a zombie rattling about. I'm ninety percent sure she buries the dead after she's done with them.'

The remaining ten percent was a worry. 'You think she knows she has an illegal market in her basement?' I asked.

Gunnar's jaw was working. 'Yes, I do.'

'But she's a councillor!'

'That she is,' he said darkly. 'We'll be having words after this.'

I suddenly wondered if Liv's flirtation with Gunnar was nothing more than a smokescreen, a way of making him so uncomfortable that he wouldn't look at her business too closely. Liv was scary smart so I wouldn't put it past her. I wouldn't have put anything past her.

I looked at the building as we loitered in the car – I hadn't previously paid much attention to it. The facade was basic, inoffensively bland. Parking was around the back out of sight of the road. It was easy to stop there without drawing attention – and that suddenly didn't seem accidental.

The car park was heaving. We stopped next to an ambulance that had parked at the curb. Uh-oh: its presence seemed ominous. Maybe it was precautionary but, given our presence, probably not. I had to admit to being excited. Getting to see a real illegal market was indescribably cool – but I retracted my wish for a juicy murder.

The double doors were wide to allow for coffins and funeral parties to leave easily. We went into a broad corridor and turned right towards some stairs leading downwards. There was nothing to indicate that anything dodgy was going on, no big sign saying: *Black market this way!* I was quite disappointed.

We went down a flight of stairs and faced another double metal door. Gunnar twisted the knob and *voilà* – we were in the black market.

A low roar greeted us. There must have been a silencing spell to keep the place secret because it was packed with people and noisy. There were five rows of ten tables, fifty stalls laden with books and with weapons, from knives and swords to maces and bow and arrows. There were also tables with crystals, tables with herbs, and some with what I assumed were potion ingredients. Then there were tables with the potions themselves.

The room was lit by dozens of fairy lights. I looked up and saw fluorescent tubes on the ceiling, so clearly the dim lighting was a deliberate choice to create ambience. All the people hawking their wares were wearing cloaks with the hoods up, casting long shadows over their faces. Maybe they wanted to be anonymous, but it also added to the atmosphere. Part of the allure of the black market was its mystique.

I felt a fizz of excitement: this was *so* cool. I wondered if there were tomes about fire elementals. I had some cash on me; on a scale of one to ten, how pissed off would Gunnar be if I went shopping?

The room fell silent as every eye turned to us, then the whispering began. A figure walked hastily toward us, a woman I'd never seen before. Although I didn't know everyone in town, I didn't think she was from Portlock. She wasn't dressed in a robe or the town uniform of jeans, sweatshirt and brown XtraTufs; instead she was wearing a flowing, multi-coloured maxi dress and large hoop earrings. Her dark brown hair was a mass of wild curls.

'Are you the Nomo?' she asked impatiently.

'That's me – Gunnar Johansen. This is my colleague, Bunny Barrington. You're the one who called me? Laura?'

'Yeah. Come with me.' She turned and we followed, weaving through the crowds and the stalls. She took us to a booth in the back corner that had been roped off. I looked at its display of books; I'd have bet my month's salary I was looking at magical grimoires, though the stall also had some more commercial items like stickers and mugs. A mug that said *I Survived the Black Market* made me grin. It was like a booth at a fair, only with paranormal accoutrements.

'Jeff collapsed,' Laura said briskly. 'We called the paramedics but they won't approach him because apparently he's been cursed.'

The two paramedics were standing impatiently to one side. 'It's still active,' one of them confirmed. 'If we approach, chances are we'll fall foul of it too.'

We walked around the U-shaped table arrangement. Sure enough, a man was lying behind it, his back arched, his eyes staring unseeing at the ceiling. His mouth was open in a silent scream. A chill ran down my spine.

'It's a living nightmare curse, but we haven't been able to find the source,' the other paramedic said.

Gunnar grimaced. 'Bunny, we'd best check over the booth. Slow and steady. If you feel odd, step back and call me.'

'The last curse, the one on the dock, was done with blood. Let me see if I can smell anything.'

Gunnar brightened. 'Great idea.'

There was a riot of smells in the basement, including old blood, formaldehyde and a tonne of incense and floral ingredients. I closed my eyes and put my hands over my ears to block my other senses so I could focus on smelling blood. It helped that I was a little hungry.

I sank into my baser nature, embracing it. Suddenly the heartbeats around me were thunderous. Too many. Far too many. I opened my eyes. 'Can we clear this place out? The heartbeats are distracting me.' I wished we'd brought Fluffy with us; I bet he'd find the bloody curse in a minute. Well, fetching him could be Plan B.

Laura grimaced at my request but moved off to do as I asked. I heard her use the words 'temporary closure' a lot but then I blocked her out too. As the room emptied, I was able to ignore the few heartbeats that remained like Gunnar's and the paramedics.

I walked slowly around the booth. As I got closer to Jeff, the scent of blood pulled at my nose. Deer blood. It wasn't as tantalising as human blood but it was there.

Cautiously, I moved closer. 'Bunny,' Gunnar said warningly.

'I'm being careful,' I promised. Now that I had the scent, I opened my eyes. The blood smell was coming from Jeff, but it couldn't be from an injury – the curse was *on* him. Somehow someone had lifted up his T-shirt, held him still and painted a curse on him with deer blood. No way could that have been done without someone seeing something.

Jeff's back was arched, so I moved closer to look under his T-shirt. Sure enough, rune work. 'Don't touch him!' Gunnar barked.

I rolled my eyes. As if. 'I'm not the one with the history of touching dodgy substances, am I?' I shot back. 'The curse is on his back. Get me something to wipe it off with.' One of the paramedics opened their bag and passed me a sterile wipe.

'Gloves first,' Gunnar ordered, chucking me a pair nitrile gloves. I caught them, but before I donned them I used my phone to document the runes and Jeff in situ. Then I snapped on the gloves and started wiping.

As soon as I disrupted the curse Jeff's body went limp, his eyes rolled back into his head and he passed out. The paramedics rushed forward and started to do their thing. As they worked, they assured us that he would live; however, the curse he'd been under was horrendously strong, and they weren't sure he'd recover mentally from it.

Things weren't looking good for Jeff.

Chapter 10

The illegal market was entirely too good and too quick at closing up shop. By the time the paramedics had stabilised Jeff and taken him to hospital, every last person had cleared out of the funeral home – including Laura – and the fifty tables were bare. Only Jeff's table remained laden.

I had a look through the pile of books, and sure enough there was a grimoire for fire elementals. Mum had said that without control I'd set myself on fire, so it seemed like a good investment. I turned to Gunnar, the heavy book in my hands.

He looked at me for a moment. 'I didn't see anything,' he said finally.

I grinned and put all the cash I had on the table. It was meagre payment but I had kind of saved Jeff's life so I figured we were square.

Gunnar and I turned back to assess the empty basement. 'This blows,' I muttered. 'I really wanted to have a snoop around. Some of the wares looked cool.' Gunnar slid me a glance. 'And interview all the vendors as suspects!' I added hastily.

His lips twitched. 'Uh-huh. We'd better box this stuff up and take it into custody.'

We turned back to Jeff's table – but now it was completely bare. All that remained was that one mug that said *I Survived the Black Market*. Someone was a total wiseass. 'How the fuck did they do that?' I demanded.

Gunnar sighed and wiggled his fingers. 'Magic.'

'Son of a bitch,' I grumped. At least I had the book – and apparently a new mug. Gunnar pulled on some gloves, picked it up and bagged it. 'Hey! I wanted that,' I protested.

He grinned. 'You can have it back after I've had Sig check it for hexes or curses.'

'Oh! Good idea.'

He tapped his forehead. 'I do have them sometimes,' he said drily. 'Let's go. This place is a bust.'

We drove back to the office in silence. Fluffy was overjoyed to see us, giving us his finest barks and turning around in circles. Shadow lifted his head, looked at us, then closed his eyes and settled down again. It was a hard life being a cat.

Once we'd made a hot drink, we retreated to Gunnar's office to plot our next moves. 'Can I see the pictures you took?' he asked. I unlocked my phone and passed it to him. He scrolled through the photos, looked at the runes on Jeff's back then flicked to the runes on the docks. 'Same style,' he grunted.

'What do you mean? Runes are runes, right?'

'Yes, but in the same way letters are letters and we all have different handwriting. I'd bet good money these two curses were done by the same person.'

'So the incident at the dock wasn't a prank gone wrong?'

'Not by half. At a guess, I'd say the curse on the docks was a practice run. Maybe they decided runing rage onto Jeff wasn't punishment enough because the runes on him were stronger. Darker.'

'We've got a stray evil witch? *Again?*'

He smiled wryly. 'The witch population takes up a good portion of Portlock. There are plenty of *good* witches– and it's not just witches that use runes. Necromancers and shamans use them, too.'

'Wonderful.' I sighed and crossed my arms. 'So our suspect pool is large.'

'Huge,' he agreed. 'But, like handwriting, someone might be able to recognise the rune style.'

'Liv,' I suggested.

'Liv,' he agreed with a heavy sigh. He took a deep breath to brace himself then he pressed speed-dial seven on the phone. As it rang, he hit the speakerphone button so I could listen in.

The phone rang several times before Liv picked up. 'Gunnar, to what do I owe the pleasure?' she purred. 'I hope it's not about the barrier because only one of my elementals has arrived so far, though I'm pleased to report the new programme is working out. For now, I've got all the gems secured. Moving forward, after the barrier is restored no one will be a gem caretaker for longer than a year, and I'm also working on a permanent solution. There's a small fly in the ointment, though.'

'Of course there is,' Gunnar responded. 'Hit me.'

'Well, the other witches will be here in the next couple of days. Once we've all gathered, I'll have to take the gems offline for a time to … um … recalibrate them.'

'Offline?'

The chills that raced down my spine made my knees weak. What did that mean? Offline sounded *bad.*

Gunnar swallowed as he shared a nervous glance with me. 'Does that mean the barrier will be down?'

'We don't know for sure but possibly. I'm working on a temporary fix, but you need to put a plan in place just in case.'

Gunnar and I both had identical expressions of horror. He shook his head. 'Liv, there *is* no plan. If that barrier goes down, we're screwed.'

'If we don't deal with the gems, the barrier will fail anyway,' she pointed out.

'Goddammit, Liv! What about a temporary barrier? Anything your magic users can do?'

'We'll see. I'm working on things at my end but I need you to have a backup.' She was being weirdly insistent.

'All right, I'll look into an emergency procedure. To be honest, we should have one in place regardless. Anyway, that's not why I called.'

'No?' her voice turned sultry. 'Did you ring to whisper sweet nothings in my ear?'

'No. I rang to talk about curses and runes and about the black market in the basement of *your* funeral home.'

'Ah,' she said delicately. 'That.' She paused and I could well imagine her biting her lip whilst she tried to think of a way to blag her way out of that one. 'We both know that the black market is a necessary evil, Gunnar. By hosting it myself, I can control what the market brings into our community. It's in our best interests to have it hosted by someone we trust.'

Gunnar ground his teeth. He didn't like her answer but he needed her for the rune thing, so evidently he decided to let it go. For now. 'You're walking a fine line, council member,' he growled, pointedly using her title.

'Perhaps, but by now there's no evidence the market was ever there.'

I could believe it. By now, no doubt the tables themselves had disappeared too.

'That's what they do,' Liv continued. 'The vendors don't run this market over several paranormal towns without being able to set up and take down quickly.'

'If I get so much as whiff that they're still in town, I'll shut them down,' he threatened.

Liv gave a tinkling laugh. 'But Gunnar ... you'd have to find them first.' She hung up.

Gunnar glared at the phone, his face red with anger.

'Well, shit. And we didn't get a chance to ask her about the runes,' I pointed out.

'I'm well aware of that. We need to ask her in person so we can watch her face and see if she's lying to us. Come on, let's track her down.'

'You think she'd lie to us?'

He snorted. 'Do elves love archery?'

I paused. 'I don't know. Do they?'

'They're obsessed,' Gunnar confirmed. 'Let's go to the funeral home first, and then her home. This time we take Fluffy.'

'Agreed.'

Shadow was still snoozing, so we left him curled up. We were soon pulling back into the car park of the funeral home; this time it was empty. 'I guess they all left,' I said drily. 'And no sign of Liv's car.'

'Nope.' Gunnar parked up. 'Well, let's go make sure, do our due diligence.'

We climbed out, taking Fluffy with us. The rear door was locked, but after testing it Gunnar did his thing and it opened. We went down the hall and then the stairs. When he opened the double steel door, nothing but darkness and silence greeted us.

He found the lights and the fluorescent tubes flicked on, pouring a harsh light down onto the space. The whole place was empty and surprisingly clean; it had been swept, and the smell of bleach and disinfectant was heavy in the air. If any evidence of Jeff's curse *had* remained, it was long gone.

I turned to Fluffy, 'Can you find anything they missed in the clean up?' I wasn't optimistic.

He trotted around obligingly, sniffing at certain spots before returning and sitting silently in front of me. No barking, no wagging. He agreed: no one and nothing was left. Dammit. I ruffled the top of his head. 'Good boy.' He gave a single bark that I interpreted as, 'Well, I did what I could.'

'Let's go,' Gunnar said. 'They've obviously got a second site and it's probably already running.'

'Any other place in a town this big?' I asked.

'There are tonnes of places they could use. There's a bunch of warehouses on the waterfront, three large churches, several large houses, the fish plant, the cannery, Kamluck Logging, tents in the woods...'

'Got it. Could be anywhere.'

'Yup.'

I sighed. 'So, without Liv telling us, or without an invite, we won't find it again?'

'It's not likely.' Then Gunnar's phone rang and he looked down. 'It's the hospital.'

I leaned against the car and waited as he swiped to open it. He didn't put it on speaker, so I waited until he was done. It wasn't a long conversation but it was long enough for me to grow concerned.

Finally he hung up and looked at his mobile for a minute. 'It was about Jeff,' he said finally. 'Apparently removing the runes didn't end the curse like it did at the docks, though it stopped it ensnaring more people, so we did the right thing.' He looked serious. 'This is dark magic.'

'A curse isn't inherently dark?' I asked incredulously.

'Like anything, it's a matter of degrees. The doctors have put Jeff in stasis so they can try and find a cure without the curse progressing. Unfortunately, they can't keep him like that for too long. He's in real danger - if the curse remains on him, his mind will fail and his body will follow. And then we'll be investigating a murder.'

Chapter 11

We were both grim as we drew up to Liv's house. It wasn't too far from Connor's but was set back, gated, and didn't look so modern; the stone build had been deliberately designed to look old.

Gunnar didn't press the intercom to alert Liv; instead he held the little keypad for a moment and the gate swung open. 'Nice,' I commented. A small smile curved his lips.

We parked on the gravel drive, but before we could climb out of the car Liv opened the front door. 'Come to waterboard me in person?' she asked archly. 'I'm always willing to get wet for you, Gunnar.' She licked her full lips.

She was wearing a see-through baby-doll nightdress and nothing else. Her hair was in a loose Afro and she looked untameable and wild; I could well imagine she'd be amazing in the sack. As I felt my cheeks grow warm, I looked away. Then it occurred to me that was probably her purpose in opening the door dressed like that: she loved to shock.

I forced my eyes back to her face and she met my gaze. Looking amused, she gave me a wink and my skin warmed further. Being a vampire, you'd think that I wouldn't be able to blush but I really could. Damned heartbeat. Hopefully the darkness hid quite how red my face was.

I cleared my throat then briskly pulled up the photos on my phone and passed them to Gunnar. He could get closer to Liv: I was keeping my distance. When I stepped back a few feet, she smirked even more.

'We've had two incidents with curses,' Gunnar said.

'And you're here to accuse little old *moi*?' She fluttered her eyelashes in fake distress.

'Not at all. We're here to see if you recognise the writing. They're done by the same caster.'

Liv sobered, took the phone and flicked through the curses. 'The first one is pretty mild, but the second one is nasty. You'll need a shaman to break that.'

'Do you recognise it?' Gunnar asked.

She shook her head slowly. 'Sorry, no. You have to understand, curses are kept private and so is ordinary rune work. Everyone has their own style, and their own family runes that others don't know or use, and they're closely guarded. I've seen some curses and rune work in Portlock but mostly when they've gone wrong, so I've seen a lot of junior work. This isn't junior, this is expert. It was done by someone experienced.'

'Could you name them?' Gunnar pressed.

Liv tapped a finger on her lips. 'I'll investigate and report back. Now, are we done here or are you coming inside?' She opened the door a little wider. 'You're *both* more than welcome,' she said throatily. She drew her gaze over us, letting it heat up.

As I all-but ran to the car, her laughter followed me. Gunnar slammed the car door shut at about the same time I did. 'Let's not mention this to Sig,' he suggested.

I grinned. 'Deal.'

Back at the office, Sidnee was at her desk. 'You're not supposed to be in,' Gunnar said, looking at her with concern.

She shrugged. 'I had some bad dreams. I fancied company.'

His eyes softened. 'And we weren't here. I'm sorry, Sidnee.'

'It's okay, I had Shadow. Give me the rundown. Anything juicy?'

We told her everything. When we were done, she hauled out her phone, typed a message and hit send. 'Okay,' she said brightly. 'You need a shaman and I happen to know one. Do you remember Anissa Popov?'

I remembered her well: she'd been on our list to investigate when we were searching for Eric the werewolf's killer. We'd taken her off that list pretty quickly when we discovered she'd been in Anchorage having a baby at the time of the murder. 'Yes, of course.'

'She was one of the nurses when I was in the hospital, and she was super lovely. We keep talking about meeting for a coffee. I've asked her to visit Jeff and let me know if she can do anything.'

'That's great.' Gunnar clapped her shoulder. 'Thanks, Sidnee.'

'How about I run around looking for a suspicious number of parked cars?' I suggested.

Gunnar nodded. 'You do that. I'm going to check through our records of magic users, shamans and necromancers and see if any of them are worth a closer look.'

'Isn't Liv doing that?' I asked.

'Do you trust her?' he shot back.

'Kind of.'

His shoulders slumped. 'So did I, but she's running an illegal market so...'

'She did have a point – it comes to the supernat towns regardless.'

'Maybe,' Gunnar admitted begrudgingly.

'Anyway, I'll do a recce and look for lots of cars.'

'Take Fluffy with you,' Gunnar ordered as he handed me the keys to the Suburban.

'You got it, boss.' I flipped him a cheeky salute.

'I used to be respected,' he muttered as he went into his office.

Sidnee and I exchanged grins. 'Email me the photos from your phone,' she said, 'and I'll start a draft of the paperwork.'

'You're the best!' I sent the photos then I studied her; she looked tired. 'You sure you're okay?'

'I'll be fine. Thanks.' She gave me a quick hug. 'Go on, now. Let me steal your cat while you fight crime.'

'I have to find it first,' I groused.

Fluffy and I left together, determined to find the highly illegal, carefully hidden black market – before someone else got cursed.

Chapter 12

Portlock wasn't that large, so I decided to go down by the docks and look for extra cars around the warehouse district. I went to the South Harbour, my favourite of the harbours, and headed for the fish plant. There were plenty of cars parked out front, but probably no more than usual. Even so, I decided to check inside; if Liv would host a black market, there was every chance that Calliope would as well.

I let myself in and walked around briskly, powering through the overwhelming stench of fish. I'd already covered most of the place before Soapy found me. 'Hey,' I gave him a jaunty wave.

His dark expression didn't waver. 'She wants to see you. She doesn't take kindly to trespassers.'

No need to ask who he was referring to. I followed him dutifully to the office knowing I was about to get a verbal spanking for snooping around uninvited.

As usual, Calliope Galanis was sitting at her desk exuding the aura of a general. Today her blue hair was piled on her head in a series of intricate braids. Her light blue eyes met mine, and they were calm like the waters she lived in. I reminded myself that still waters ran deep and Calliope ate people who pissed her off.

'Lovely to see you,' I started.

'Indeed. How nice of you to drop by so ... *unexpectedly*.' Her glacial tone made it clear she didn't think it was nice of me at all.

I'd already checked her fish plant and there was no black market there, so I saw little reason in keeping the truth from her. 'The black market is in town,' I explained. 'I'm looking for it.'

Her lips curled. 'And you think *I'm* hosting it?'

'Liv was,' I shrugged.

Her smile widened, showing her sharp teeth. 'Yes, it's her turn. I did it last year.'

I blinked. 'You take it in *turns*?'

'Along with other concerned citizens. Sometimes we need more items than the proper channels allow.' She studied me. 'Are you going to report me?'

I sighed. Portlock was fifty shades of grey; I'd talk it over with Gunnar but no, I wouldn't be writing up a citation. 'I doubt it.'

'I've so enjoyed having you join us here in Portlock. I do love some fresh blood. And I understand Connor enjoys your company...'

I grimaced: our dating was bound to come out but I'd hoped we could keep the whole 'fated mates' thing to ourselves until we were a little more established as a couple. Everything between us was fresh, wonderful and *private*. I wanted to keep it that way.

'I'm delightful,' I said flatly. 'Everyone enjoys my company. Whilst I'm here, have you made any progress in finding out more about Chris and the general's organisation?'

Soapy spoke up. 'We've sent three men in undercover to join the remaining splinter military group. Contact has to be sporadic or we risk them.'

I sat up straighter. 'Any sightings of Chris Jubatus?'

Soapy nodded. 'He's still hip deep in the organisation, but he's cautious about our men so far. It will take time to earn his trust.'

'But we'll do it,' Calliope snarled. 'And when he trusts them, we'll bite off the head of the beast that dared to attack us.' She paused. 'Figuratively speaking, of course.'

'Of course,' I said faintly. We both knew she wasn't speaking figuratively at all. I stood. 'Well, if you don't wish to divulge the current location of the black market...'

'It has not been confirmed yet.'

'And when it is?'

She smiled. 'Of course I'll let you know, Officer Barrington.' She was lying.

'Thank you for your time,' I said politely.

'I'll show you out,' Soapy said. It wasn't an offer. I let him herd me out of the building. 'Next time make an appointment, Barrington.' He slammed the door shut behind me.

After the fish plant, I moseyed around the warehouse district. I passed one empty warehouse but it had no cars outside. The AML warehouse, where Chris Jubatus and his black-ops crew had held my friends hostage, was also a no-go; it was busy, but the workers were offloading a barge.

I was about to continue my search when my phone vibrated with a text from Sidnee: *Anissa thinks she can break the curse with the right ingredients for a potion.*

Did she say what she needed? Maybe we can order them?

She has to consult her elders. She said she'd get back to me. That was promising.

I continued to drive around. The next warehouse I came to had quite a few cars outside and was large enough to house the market easily. Fluffy and I got out for some more snooping but it was another dead end. It looked like someone was renovating it and the cars belonged to the construction personnel. I was getting discouraged.

My phone buzzed. *Bunny, get back here. Anissa came through!* Sidnee's text read.

On my way, I replied. I looked down at Fluffy. 'Let's go boy, we might have a cure for poor old Jeff.'

Fluffy wagged his tail and we hurried to the vehicle. I drove back as fast as I dared, excitement buzzing; if we could cure Jeff, he could tell us who'd cursed him. He must have seen who'd painted runes on his skin.

This was going to be easy! We'd have this case cracked in no time at all.

Chapter 13

When Fluffy and I strolled into the office, John was sitting on the hard plastic chairs on the civilian side of the counter and Sidnee was talking to Anissa. Anissa looked slightly more rested than the last time I'd met her, but not much. She was dressed in pink scrubs, her dark hair braided down her back.

'Hey, Anissa,' I greeted her. 'How are you?'

'I'm okay, thanks, Officer Barrington.'

'Please, call me Bunny.'

She smiled. 'Thank you, Bunny.'

'How's your daughter?'

Anissa beamed and it warmed her stern looks. 'She's wonderful.'

I smiled back. 'That's lovely to hear. I know those early months can be tricky. Can you excuse me a moment?' I turned to John. 'Hi, John, how are you doing? Is everything all right at Kamluck?'

'Yes, everything is fine. Connor has been so welcoming.'

'How can I help you?'

'I need to talk to you about something.'

I looked back at Anissa. 'Is it urgent?'

He weighed up the question before slowly shaking his head. 'No, it's important but it's not time sensitive. It can wait. I see you're busy right now.'

'I'll come out and talk to you tomorrow, or we can do dinner when you're in town,' I offered.

'Either works. I'll be in touch.' He walked out and my gut curdled with anxiety. What could he possibly have to say to me that was important? Nothing good, that was for sure.

I turned back to Anissa. 'I'm sorry about the interruption. Thanks for coming in. Can you tell us a little about what we can do about the curse?'

'I consulted the elders and they think that the curse can be broken with an ancient ritual that requires the afflicted to consume a potion made from a bunch of native ingredients. The problem is that one of them is hard to get here, and we don't know if we have time to send someone to collect it from the nearest supernat town.'

I frowned. 'What's the ingredient?'

'It's a plant that's generally found in the sub-Arctic called alpine azalea, or *Loiseleuria procumbens*. It's an evergreen shrub with tiny pink flowers.'

I made a mental note to look it up. 'You said *hard* to get. *Can* we find it here?'

Her face grim. 'Yes, it also grows up there.' She pointed at the mountains. 'At the top.'

Well, fuck. We could only get it from there if we went beyond the barrier.

'The elders have contacted tribal members in the subarctic, but it'll be a few days, maybe a week before they can send some. Realistically, if we're going to save Jeff someone has to get the plant from the mountain.' Her look at me felt pointed.

I wanted to look behind me for someone else who could get it, but I knew no one was there. Besides, the only people who had successfully returned from beyond the barrier lately were me, Fluffy, Gunnar and Thomas.

'Anything else?' I asked, my voice amazingly steady even if my knees were weak.

'We need some devil's club, too. That grows everywhere, although if someone is going up there it would be better if it were naturally grown with no plant food or pesticides. The potion will be a little more potent.'

Great: devil's club was covered in thorns and prickles. And, of course, we'd have to survive long enough to bring it and the alpine azalea back. 'Thanks, Anissa,' I made myself say even though I wanted to run away screaming.

She looked at Fluffy and paused. 'How long have you had your dog?' she asked curiously.

'I got him right before I moved here.'

She frowned. 'There's something off about him.' She stared at him and hummed a low tune in her throat. Fluffy's tongue lolled out, then he looked at me and whined. I felt the little hairs on my arms lifting like they were full of static. Was she using magic?

She stopped humming and shot me a worried glance. 'I don't know if you know this, but your dog is cursed.'

'What do you mean cursed?' I said. 'Is he going to be okay?' Panic filled me. How could that have happened? Fluffy hadn't been with me at the docks or the funeral home so he couldn't have stumbled across either curse accidentally.

'Not like Jeff's curse,' Anissa clarified. 'This is something else. It's a few weeks old at least – it's worn a bit. I can't see what kind it is, not without some proper study. But yeah, definitely cursed. It's lying around him like an orange haze.'

'Can we get it off of him?' I begged. 'Now?'

She grimaced. 'I'm sorry; it's not going to be simple to remove. I'm not saying it's impossible but I need to look into it.'

My heart hurt. 'Is he in pain?'

'No,' she assured me hastily. 'He'd be whining if he was.'

'I can't leave him like this! Will the potion work on him, too?'

'The one we have in mind is specifically for the nightmare curse, but alpine azalea is in the base of a lot of curse-breaking potions. Get me enough of it and I'll do what I can for your dog.'

'Thank you so much. Obviously I'll pay for your time. How soon can you work out what's going on with him?'

'I'll need to prioritise Jeff,' she admitted. 'He's in jeopardy right now whereas whatever is on your dog isn't life-threatening. If it were, the haze would be red. But after we've sorted Jeff, I'll get right on it. It might be a week or so – I'll have to fit it in around childcare and shifts.'

'I really appreciate your help. The sooner you can get to him, the better.' I was freaking out at the idea that Fluffy was cursed when I didn't know when, why, or even how it was affecting him. I dropped to my knees and cuddled him. 'We'll fix you,' I promised fiercely. He gave me a lick.

I looked up Anissa. 'If ever you need a favour, let me know.'

She gave a shy smile. 'No worries. Helping you is the right thing to do. I'll start prepping things, but I can't do much without the last few ingredients.'

I nodded. 'I'm on it.' And I was. Sure I wanted to help Jeff – but would I hurry beyond the barrier for him? No. For my dog, though, I'd tear the world apart.

As Anissa hugged Sidnee goodbye, I felt a weird twinge of jealousy. 'I didn't realise you knew Anissa well,' I said after the door shut behind her.

'Yeah, she was my nurse after the ... *incident*.' The incident she was referring to was when we'd rescued her from black-ops drug dealers, her ex and a terrifying kushtaka.

'Oh yeah, you mentioned that, but I didn't know you'd stayed in touch.'

'We hit it off. She's really cool, and she doesn't have a lot of friends. Like me.'

The door opened and April Arctos walked in. She frowned when she saw Sidnee. 'Have I got my shifts wrong?'

'I'm not supposed to be here,' Sidnee said cheerfully.

'You're all workaholics,' April muttered. 'You're young, you should be out having fun, not loitering here.'

'We like loitering here,' Sidnee objected. 'There's free coffee.'

'Good point.' April nodded and sat at my desk. 'I'll check on things.' She logged into the system. 'Ooh – curses! They're always exciting. I remember once when my brother paid a witch to transform my other brother into a fish.' She laughed. 'Mum was furious. My youngest sister kept trying to eat him whenever she was in bear form. It cost a pretty penny to uncurse him, which my brother had to pay back in full. He had to pull double shifts at Kodiak Kitchen for years.'

'What did the fish brother do to get himself cursed?' Sidnee asked.

'Oh, he kissed my cursing brother's girlfriend. They're married now.'

'The cursing brother or the fish one?'

'The fish one. It was true love. Cursing brother is over it – turns out he was gay and was very much in denial about it. He's happily married, too. Grant is perfect for him.'

Sidnee was grinning. 'Your family sounds fun.'

April beamed. 'Thank you. They sure are something.'

'Talking of curses,' Sidnee said, 'Fluffy is cursed too!'

'Oh no!' April bustled round to Fluffy to check him over.

'Apparently he's not in pain,' I assured her.

'What's the curse doing to him?'

'We have no idea.' I admitted, but my head wasn't really in the conversation; it was on Fluffy and going beyond the barrier. I was determined to go but I was already pooping my pants at the prospect.

Sidnee shook her head. 'Fluffy is the absolute bestest boy. I can't imagine how he was cursed!'

'Me neither,' I said. 'Maybe someone on a case did it and we never noticed. But I'm worried. I don't want anything to happen to him.' Thinking about losing him was making me sick to my stomach. I wanted to run home and shove him into a cocoon of blankets. I needed a distraction – fast. 'I'm going to update Gunnar before we clock off,' I said. Besides, we were due at Sig's for dinner shortly.

I went into his office with Fluffy on my heels. Gunnar was leaning back in his chair, his feet up on the desk, scrolling through his phone. 'Busy?' I asked a shade sarcastically.

He looked up. 'Nope.'

'We have a lead on a way to help Jeff.'

His eyebrows shot up; he put his feet down and leaned forward. 'But?'

'Anissa Popov, the shaman, said her elders have a cure but it requires a hard-to-get ingredient.'

'How hard?'

'Beyond-the-barrier hard.'

Gunnar gulped. The last time we'd been beyond the barrier, we'd barely escaped the beast and Gunnar had ended up with both shoulders dislocated. It wasn't an experience either of us was in a hurry to repeat.

'Is there a way we could helicopter in or something?' I asked optimistically. 'I know they're expensive and we don't have much of a budget, but it would be the easiest way by far.'

He grimaced. 'Unfortunately there isn't a chopper in town, nor does anyone have a licence to fly one. Edgy couldn't fly one without it being properly modified. Jim used to be able to fly one.'

But I'd burnt Jim to a crisp.

'The truth is,' Gunnar went on, 'the mountain is so rocky and uneven I don't think a chopper could land there anyway even if we sourced one and could afford it...'

I squared my shoulders. 'So we're on foot. That's fine. I'll go,' I volunteered.

'Not alone. I'll call Patkotak.'

'Yeah,' I brightened. 'That would be good.'

Gunnar fixed me with a firm look. 'I'm going, too. You don't have to go if you don't want to.'

I blew out a breath and explained about the alpine azalea and Fluffy's curse.

'I'm sorry to hear about Fluffy being cursed. Whatever it is, we'll fix him.' Gunnar reached over and touched my arm. 'If he's not been harmed by it so far, I'm sure he'll be okay a little while longer. Either way, Patkotak and I can go alone.'

I wanted to take him up on that, but what kind of officer would I be if I had others do my job? 'Thanks, Gunnar, but I'll go.' Last time my fire had saved us; in fact it had saved us more than once.

'Are you sure?'

'Definitely.' I was no shirker.

He pressed the number five on his phone and hit the speaker button. Thomas Patkotak picked up after three rings. 'Gunnar, what can I do for the Nomo?' he asked, his tone friendly.

'It's a pretty big favour,' Gunnar said heavily. 'We have an out of towner in the hospital because of a curse. We have a limited amount of time to save him, and we need to go fetch some weed from beyond the barrier. And Fluffy is cursed too. We were hoping for your assistance.'

The phone was quiet; even Thomas Patkotak, the scariest human I knew, wasn't thrilled with the task. 'I'll help – for Bunny. Small problem, though – I'm in Homer. I'm not due back until tomorrow.'

'We have a little time,' Gunnar confirmed. 'But not much. We'll wait for you, but it would be great if you'd get back as quickly as you can.'

'You got it.' Thomas hung up; he wasn't great with hellos or goodbyes.

'Well, Bunny Rabbit, we have a day's reprieve.'

I sighed. 'Frankly, I'd rather get it over and done with.'

'This way we can plan better, make sure we have what we need to fight the beast,' Gunnar said.

Fight? Survive, more like.

Sidnee wandered in carrying Shadow draped around the back of her neck. Gunnar looked at her sharply. 'Maybe this time we should take your cat,' he suggested.

I considered it but shook my head. 'He's too small – he's only a baby. Plus, he isn't Fluffy and he's not trained to walk on a lead. I'd be devastated if something happened to him.' I couldn't cope if I saved one pet only to lose another.

'True, I wouldn't want anything to happen to the little fella. Still, I saw what he did to the beast when it was trying to get through the rift.'

'And that bit of action wiped him out for over a day,' I argued. 'And that was a little smoke from the beast, not the whole creature itself!' I wanted my dog and my cat safely at home. We didn't need Fluffy to find a body this time, it was a *plant* we were after and he wouldn't know its scent any more than I did. The animals could stay home safe whilst we blundered head first into danger.

'Calm down, Bunny. I agree – but maybe when Shadow is full-grown we should think about training him. He could be the first-ever police cat.' Gunnar grinned. He was trying to ease my fears. Shadow was safe, Fluffy would be fine for now and Anissa would fix him. I clung to that. First, I had to go beyond the barrier.

I coughed out a small laugh, more from nerves than humour. I had twenty-four hours before I set off and I was already terrified.

Chapter 14

The dinner at Sig's had grown from the four of us to include Stan and Sidnee. 'Why don't you see if Connor wants to come?' Gunnar asked indulgently. 'You know Sigrid will have made enough food for a small army.'

I weighed it up. Stan and Connor could be a bit fractious and I didn't want them bickering in front of my mum, but even more I wanted to see Connor. *Needed* to see Connor. 'If you're sure it's okay.'

'Go ahead!' Gunnar grinned.

I excused myself to call Connor and he answered straight away. 'Hey, Bunny, how's it going?'

I blew out a breath. 'I've had better days. I've been rolling around the black market and stepped on Soapy's toes a little. And I found out Fluffy is cursed.'

'Fluffy is *cursed*? With what?'

'We're not sure. It's not a simple rune curse because he's been washed plenty of times. Anissa is working on it – but I have to go beyond the barrier for an ingredient.'

'I'll come with you,' he said firmly.

'I appreciate the offer but we're going to keep it small. In and out. The fewer people there are, the less chance we have of being spotted by the creature.'

'You'll wear your vest?'

I wanted to say it wasn't going to protect me from having my head ripped off but he probably knew that. 'Sure I'll wear it. Anyway, I'm going to Sigrid's for dinner to introduce Mum to Gunnar, Sigrid, Stan and Sidnee. You want to come?'

'Of course. I need to see you anyway.'

'Why? What's up?' I asked, worried.

'Nothing. I just need to see you.'

'Aww.' I melted. 'You're so cute.'

'Cute?' Outrage crackled in his voice. 'I am not *cute*. I am sexy and debonair.'

I giggled. 'Yup, those things, too. See you in half an hour at Sig's?'

'Wild horses wouldn't drag me away.'

We rang off and I felt lighter. I loved that he'd offered to come with me beyond the barrier, and I also loved that he trusted me enough to let me go without him.

'Connor's in,' I called to Gunnar.

'Great. Why don't you head home and I'll swing by to pick you up in thirty minutes? That way you can warn your mom.'

I smiled. 'Yeah, I should warn her it's not quite the cosy dinner she's expecting. Thanks.' I collected Shadow and Fluffy and we headed out. This was either going to be an epic disaster or a mild disaster – but *definitely* a disaster.

I walked into my house and found my mother sitting on the sofa watching TV. I didn't think I'd ever seen her watch TV – that had been something I'd done with my nana. It was oddly humanising – not that I thought she wasn't human now I knew that she was a witch. She was still my mum, my cold and aloof mum.

She clicked the TV off hurriedly before I could see what she was watching. It had sounded suspiciously like a soap opera. 'How was your evening, darling?' she asked.

'It was fine,' I said, brushing over the curses and the market. 'Gunnar invited a couple of my friends to dinner with us. He's going to pick us up in about thirty minutes. Are you ready?' I asked to be polite because she was sitting there fully made-up and dressed for dinner.

'Yes, dear, I'm ready. What do you do with your animals? Do you take them? I don't know the customs here.'

'Gunnar loves animals – he has a husky. I usually take Fluffy so he and Loki can play. I'll let you decide about Arabella.'

'Well, I can't leave her alone with that *cat*.' She glared at my innocent looking lynx kitten.

'If you want to leave Arabella behind, I'll lock Shadow in my bedroom before we leave,' I offered, keeping my eye roll to myself. I couldn't imagine

Arabella would get on with Loki any more than she got on with my pets.

'Fine, I'll leave her here. She'd feel overwhelmed with two large dogs, poor darling.' She stroked her pooch, which was reclining on her lap. Uh-huh.

I prepared a cup of blood so I could enjoy my meal later. When the timer on the microwave dinged, I plugged my nose and downed the stuff that kept me alive. As I walked back into the lounge, Mum stopped talking. Fluffy was a few feet away from her, his gaze locked on Arabella. 'Who were you talking to?' I asked, looking around.

'Oh, you know me. I was blathering to Arabella.'

Fluffy gave a low growl: he had evidently decided that Mum was a threat, probably because she kept making me cry. He positioned himself between her and me. Arabella yapped at us and he growled again. 'Stop it, you bully,' Mum snapped.

My temper flared and I felt the heat rise in my chest. He was cursed, he could be dying and he *wasn't* a bully. Before anything could happen that I'd regret, I took Fluffy with me to the bedroom to change my clothes. I figured I'd dress up for my mother's sake, although I'd have to change back after supper to finish the remainder of my shift.

Fluffy whined at me. 'What's up boy, why are you so upset? Is it about the curse?'

He couldn't answer me, but his expressive eyes were trying to tell me *something*. I sighed again. 'Sorry, boy. I don't understand.'

He huffed and lay down with his head on his paws. Shadow came out from under the bed and jumped up on it, then gave one of his kitten squeaks. I scratched behind his ears. His fur was dense and soft, and his presence calmed me. I smushed his face and kissed him. 'Okay, I'm sorry to say it but you're staying home, little one, so be good. No taunting Arabella!' His little golden eyes promised nothing.

I went into the bathroom to brush my hair. I usually wore it in a long braid for work, but now I undid it and twisted it into a knot at the back of my head. I still didn't have much in the way of jewellery since the fire, but I'd bought a pair of silver stud earrings to dress up my look. I applied the barest amount of makeup and then, when I was ready, I shut the bedroom door behind me leaving Shadow inside. He was quiet, so I hoped he'd curl up and have a nap.

Gunnar knocked on the door as I was pulling on my shoes. Perfect timing. I opened it with a warm smile and, when he walked in, I introduced him to my mum. This time I did it properly and addressed her first. 'Mum, this is Gunnar Johansen, my boss. Gunnar, this is my mother, Victoria Barrington.'

'Pleased to meet you, ma'am,' Gunnar said, his big voice rumbling out and filling the house. Mum blushed a little, smiled and took his hand. What was it with women and Gunnar? Even my mother was blushing over the brawny Viking-esque man.

We followed him out to the Suburban; his truck wasn't the best vehicle for climbing into while wearing a dress so it was much more date-friendly.

We made polite conversation until we pulled up outside his home. As always, I admired the red-painted house with the little painted flowers and beautiful front garden, but I wondered if Mum thought it was kitsch rather than whimsical and homey.

Gunnar led us into the house, usually Loki barrelled into us full of exuberance, but today he remained stretched out on his bed. Fluffy went to go and see him, and Loki gave a wide yawn. Gunnar frowned. 'Odd,' he murmured.

'That's not like Loki,' I said.

'No,' his frown deepened. 'It's not. We'll keep an eye on him. Maybe he's just feeling lazy, but if it carries on a day or two, we'll take him to the vet.'

Fluffy laid down next to Loki and Loki yawned and licked him. Loki's tail gave a happy tap tap, but he still didn't move to get up to play.

The smell of Sig's cooking wafted through the house making my stomach rumble; her food wasn't super fancy but it was always divine and somehow comforting. Mum gave an appreciative smile.

I could hear Sidnee and Stan in the kitchen laughing about something, so we walked through the living room and joined them. They looked up at us as we entered.

'Hey, everyone, I'd like you to meet my mum. Mum, this is my best friend Sidnee. Stan is a friend and one of the councilmen and the shifter leader.' I knew that even though I called him my friend, she would care more about his leader status.

'So nice to meet you, Mrs Barrington.' Stan held out his hand.

Mum looked up at him. 'Gosh they grow everything big in America,' she said, eyes wide.

He grinned, his ego happily massaged. 'Well, thank you, ma'am. I'm even bigger in my other form.' He winked. Was he flirting with my mum?

I narrowed my eyes at him. 'Behave,' I mouthed.

He gave me an innocent look. 'What?' he mouthed back.

Mum turned to Sidnee. 'I'm so glad that you are here for my daughter,' she said, a genuine note of gratitude in her voice. My heart warmed; she *did* care about me, even if she was terrible at showing it most of the time.

Sidnee virtually bounced up and down in her seat as she beamed at my mother. 'I am so glad she came to live here! She's so wonderful – and I'm super-happy to meet you!' Her exuberance coaxed an answering smile from Mum, and once again I was so grateful for my friend.

Finally I introduced Mum to Sigrid. 'This is Gunnar's wife, Sigrid.'

'Pleased to meet you,' Mum said. 'The food smells delightful. Elizabeth said you were a hearth witch, but I could tell that right away from your lovely home and garden. It's perfect.'

It was Sigrid's turn to blush. 'Thank you.'

Mum was making friends everywhere and I was impressed. I'd underestimated her, and I didn't know why: if there was one thing my mum could do, it was socialise.

Chapter 15

The doorbell rang. 'Mine!' I yelled as I ran to open it. 'I'll get it.'

'"Connor and Bunny, sitting in a tree,"' Sidnee sang. I ignored her, but she wasn't wrong: I would happily kiss that man anywhere. Even if the bark was scratchy, I'd still give it a go.

I flung open the door and there he stood. He'd made an effort. For once, he'd foregone his usual flannel shirt – and I missed it – in favour of a pale-blue one that matched his eyes. His black curls were perfect and he was clean-shaven.

I leapt into his arms and he caught me, a crooked smile curling those gorgeous lips. 'Hey,' he breathed, and then he kissed me.

I melted into him and everything in me *breathed*. Tension drained out of my shoulders as the delicious scent of him surrounded me. This, right here, pressed up against this divine man, was my happy place.

Eventually I pulled away, but it took a supreme force of will. 'You wanna have a quickie in a tree?' I asked when I had breath.

He threw back his head and laughed. When his guffaws had settled to chuckles he nodded. 'Sure, I'm game. But maybe not now. I'm supposed to be meeting your mother properly, remember?'

I huffed. 'I'm the one that needs you.'

His eyes softened. 'Glad to hear it, doe, I need you too.' He pulled me in for a hug and I nestled happily in his arms.

'Shall we run away?' I said into his neck.

His chest rumbled with suppressed laughter. 'One day – but for now I can smell Sigrid's cooking and I'm starving. Come on, we'll face them together.'

I sighed. 'Okay. Did I tell you Stan's here? Can you be on your best behaviour?'

Amusement danced in his eyes. 'I'll play nice if he plays nice.' That was probably the best I could hope for.

I drew back from him to shut the door and spotted Lee Margrave camped out front in Connor's car. 'Does Lee want to come in?'

'Probably,' Connor said lightly. 'But he's on bodyguard duty.'

'Shouldn't he, you know, guard your body?'

'I figured you'd do close detail and he could do the distance thing.'

'Oh, I can definitely do close detail.' I gave him another soft brush of my lips.

'Promises, promises,' he murmured. He laced our fingers and we walked into the dining room where everyone had gathered. Mum was chatting with Gunnar and Stan, and Sidnee shot me a knowing grin.

'Oh good,' Sigrid smiled. 'Connor's here! I'll grab the food. Everyone, seat yourselves.' She went out to the kitchen; moments later she returned with a platter holding a huge fish, a large bowl of rice and some mixed vegetables from her garden. Good basic food, but my mouth was already watering.

'This is chinook, also known as king salmon,' she said as she laid it down.

'I love how you cook fish.' Stan's eyes were already glued to it, waiting to dig in.

'You have some drool here.' I pointed to the corner of his mouth.

'Ha-ha.'

Sigrid served my mother first as she was the honoured guest, then it was a free for all. Mum kept shooting Connor covert glances that she thought I didn't see, but she was as obvious as a brick in the face. Now she knew he was royalty, she wanted a chance to apologise for thinking he was her bellboy.

Stan told good-natured Bunny jokes and I only had to kick him once under the table. Conversation flowed easily and we soon made short work of the food. Finally Sigrid brought in a tray of hot drinks and plied us with tea and coffee. She handed my *I Survived the Black Market* mug to Stan, who took it with a chuckle. I guess she'd checked and determined it was curse free.

'That was truly wonderful,' Mum enthused. 'An absolute delight. Thank you so much, Sigrid.'

'You're very welcome, Mrs Barrington.'

'Please, do call me Victoria.'

Stan took a big sip of his coffee and had a small coughing fit, which progressed to a bigger coughing fit. 'Okay?' I asked.

'Went down the wrong pipe.' He smiled and took another sip – but then his eyes widened and he stared into the corner of the room. 'Good gods!' he exclaimed suddenly, leaping up so quickly that his chair toppled over.

I followed his gaze but saw nothing. 'Stan? What's wrong?' I asked.

He was sweating and panting. He raised a hand and pointed again to the corner. 'The beast!' he shouted, then gave a horrific scream before he fell to the floor, his back arched and his mouth opened in a soundless scream.

'He's been cursed!' Mum barked. 'Everyone away from him while we determine the source.' And that was when Sigrid let out a blood-curdling scream, too. Her eyes were wide and her back was arched uncomfortably in her chair.

'Sigrid!' Gunnar roared,

As he reached out to her, I slapped his hand down. 'No touching!' He glared at me. 'She's been cursed. The last thing we need is you being affected too. If you need to do something helpful, call the ambulance.'

I turned to Sidnee. 'Can you contact Anissa?' She was trembling as she looked at Sigrid and Stan, but she pulled out her phone and started dialling her friend.

My eyes zeroed in on the mug from the black market. 'Nobody touch the mug!' It was the only thing that Stan and Sigrid had both handled.

'Sigrid said it was clear,' Gunnar said faintly.

'Evidently not. Maybe the curse was hidden. Let's box it up – we can take it with us to the hospital. Anissa can verify if it's the cause.'

Mum's hands were out doing God-knows-what. 'This curse is a strong one and it's incredibly malevolent.'

I nodded. 'If we can get them to the hospital they can be put into stasis. We know what we have to do to break it, but we can't do anything without that damned plant.'

'I can help,' Mum said firmly.

I looked at her. 'Please.'

She stood over Sigrid, hands outstretched, and chanted low and rhythmically in Latin. It had been a while since I'd done high-school Latin but luckily my memory never let me down. She was chanting something like 'Give my energy to them, keep them safe'.

As she put a protective, energising ward around Sigrid, my skin started to itch. She went to Stan and did the same. When she was done, she looked wrung out and ready to collapse. Connor carried a chair over to her and she sank gratefully into it. 'I gave them some extra energy to help them fight the curse a little longer.' She sat back in the chair. 'I'm not a curse breaker or maker, but it's something.'

'Thanks, Mum,' I said, meaning it with all my heart.

'While they're warded, they're safe to touch,' Mum promised.

Gunnar ran to Sigrid, picked her up and cradled her in his arms. 'I'm here, baby.' He kissed her forehead.

Sidnee knelt beside Stan and wrapped an arm around his waist. 'You'll be okay,' she whispered. 'Come on, big bro, fight this shit.'

Outside, the screaming wail from the sirens told me the ambulances were here. Just in the nick of time.

We followed the ambulances to the hospital. Anissa was waiting when we arrived and she hurried over. She looked at both victims, her eyes glassy as her magic thrummed around us, then she nodded solemnly. 'It is the same curse.'

Gunnar swore loudly. 'The nightmare curse? They're both stuck in their nightmares?'

Anissa nodded. 'I'm sorry. Yes.'

'There's no runes painted on them.'

She grimaced. 'Then the curse is even more potent. Hurry. Let's get them settled and in proper stasis.' She touched my mother's arm. 'I don't know you but I can see your magic around them. You've really helped. Thank you.'

Mum smiled tightly. 'You're quite welcome, I'm sure.'

'I'm going to find the ingredients tomorrow,' I said firmly to Gunnar. 'You stay here with Sig and Stan.'

'I don't know what to do.' Gunnar's eyes were locked on Sigrid as she was hooked up to all manner of tubes.

'Trust me to get it done.'

He turned to me. 'I do.'

'Then be with Sig. As soon as Thomas is here, we'll head out.'

Gunnar bundled me into his arms, gave me a quick kiss on the forehead then released me and hustled after his wife.

Anissa spoke up. 'The elders are ready to use the ingredients as soon as you can get them. The sooner, the better.'

'I'll get them ASAP. Thanks for doing this and for taking care of them.'

She smiled warmly then went after Sigrid and Stan.

'Are you staying, Sidnee?' I asked.

She squared her shoulders. 'No, I'm going with you.'

'Okay, I'll drop you home.'

'I mean to get the potion ingredients.'

'It's outside the barrier,' I said incredulously. Sidnee had only recently decided she liked real police work and she'd been a bit timid about doing anything too wild; nothing was wilder than going beyond the barrier.

'I know, but it's Sigrid and Stan. They're my only family, Bunny. I have to go.'

I understood exactly how she felt. 'Okay. Let's go home and get some rest, because tomorrow we're going to go find the plants and save them all,' I vowed.

Connor had asked Lee to follow us to the hospital so we all climbed into his car. Lee dropped Sidnee home then drove us back to my house. I wasn't surprised when Connor followed me out of the car while Lee stayed outside. 'Has he got a charm?' I asked.

'Yeah, he has Juan's.' A small flash of grief passed across Connor's eyes.

'I'll be heading to bed.' Mum was still swaying a little. 'I need some rest.'

Connor offered her his elbow and walked her to her room; it was a mark of how tired she was that she simply patted his hand in thanks and didn't try to curtsey and call him 'Your Majesty' or something embarrassing like that.

I rang April and updated her; she promised to hold the fort in our absence and I trusted her to do exactly that.

I had a hot shower to wash away the nightmare events of the evening – and then I started to cry at the thought of Stan and Sigrid trapped in *their* nightmares. Connor pulled back the shower curtain and pulled the sobbing mess that was me into his arms. 'Your shirt!' I hiccupped between sobs. 'You're getting it wet.'

'I couldn't give less of a fuck,' he said pleasantly. 'Come here.' He held me whilst I wept, and after I was done I felt better. Calmer. He helped dry me, then he undressed and slid into bed naked.

'What if there's a fire and you need to run out?' I asked. 'We can't have my mum seeing the goods!'

He grinned. 'I'm happy to have them so named, but I promise she's already seen similar goods.' I glowered. He relented. 'If there's a fire, I promise I'll grab some boxers.'

'Okay, good.' I settled down against him.

He kissed my shoulder. 'So,' he cleared his throat. 'Now that Gunnar can't go, I'd like to come with you through the barrier.'

I hesitated; I didn't want him in danger's way but I also knew that he'd be an asset, not a liability. And this wasn't about me; it was about Sigrid, Stan and Fluffy. And yeah, Jeff. 'Okay,' I agreed. 'Thanks. Now can you do me a favour?'

'Anything.'

'Distract me.'

'Your wish is my command,' he promised.

Chapter 16

I slept fitfully with bad dreams full of the beast and the kushtaka. When my phone alarm finally sounded, I was relieved to get up; I needed to actually *do* something to save my nearest and dearest.

Connor and I got up and dressed. When I checked my phone, I saw I'd missed a call and a text from John so I hurriedly texted that I'd call him when I got back from a case. I felt bad for foisting him off but I really needed to focus. I also had a message from Thomas Patkotak who said he'd meet us in an hour at the spot where we'd exited the barrier last time, up past the Grimes' brother's house.

Mum questioned me as Connor and I packed bags for the trip with all the essentials: blood, snacks, water and a first aid kit. I really hoped we wouldn't need the last one. 'Are you sure someone else can't do this?' she asked anxiously, almost wringing her hands, though I noticed that she didn't volunteer.

I shook my head. 'Gunnar won't leave Sig's side and I'm the law when he's down – me and Sidnee.'

'Elizabeth, you should look for a job that better fits your station,' she started, but I shut that down fast. I was tired, cranky and cross, definitely not in the mood to be lectured to. I'd rolled out of bed Portlock Bunny; it was time for Mum to meet her and hear some hard truths.

I faced her. 'I'm here because you wouldn't help me escape from London. You were quite willing to have me press-ganged into servitude. I love this job, I'm good at it and I'm going to help my friends. I have no *station* – what I have are friends, a lover and some happiness. This is the happiest I've ever been, even if it's far from you and Dad. I will never give up this job. You can bury me in the uniform. End of discussion.'

She sat down heavily and her eyes filled with tears. 'Where did I go so wrong with you?'

I didn't pull my punches. 'You didn't want a ped daughter and chose to foist me off on other people.

Just think how lucky you are. Problem sorted. That's what this is.'

Tears fell and she ran to her bedroom; in her defence, she didn't slam the door. I sighed. My conscience was already pricking, I'd have to apologise later. I didn't regret what I'd said but I could have said it in a better way.

I looked around for paper and pencil to leave her a note. If I didn't come back, I wanted her to know I was sorry.

Sorry, Mum. I'm anxious and worried. I didn't mean to take it out on you.

I love you, Bunny.

P.S. Please look after my pets.

I fed the animals, then Connor and I went to pick up Sidnee. 'You think I was too harsh?' I asked.

He squeezed my hand. 'Honestly? No, not harsh enough.'

April had taken over the Nomo's office – she promised she'd even sleep there if she needed to. She was a real team player, a smart hire on our part, but hopefully no one would need *real* police help since the entire force was occupied and three council members were also out of action. If someone did need something, they'd have to brave Liv or Calliope or try to find the mayor – who was usually out fishing.

I longed for Fluffy's company, but with him being cursed he was better off at home.

Sidnee looked pale but determined and I knew how she felt. I smiled tightly but had no words; what we were about to do was incredibly dangerous. I reached out to Connor and touching him steadied me. Nothing was going quite how I'd envisaged, but with him by my side, I was steady. My feet felt like they were more connected to the ground and my stomach settled. I took a deep breath and drew my determination around me like a cloak.

We parked next to Thomas's truck. 'Hey,' I greeted him as I hopped out.

'Morning, all,' he replied. He was right: it was morning. The sun was high in the sky and it was just shy of midday. Last time I'd been scampering around the barrier at night; maybe the beast was nocturnal and would hide, I thought hopefully, though I didn't say it out loud in case one of the others disabused me of my happy notion.

We shouldered our packs. Mine felt surprisingly heavy: why I'd felt the need to pack *that* many biscuits was anyone's guess. Never pack a bag when you're hungry.

'Hi, Sidnee.' Thomas smiled. 'I didn't know you were coming.'

'Sig's been cursed. I'm here in Gunnar's place.'

Thomas's admiration was plain to see. 'I'm sorry to hear about Sigrid. You really are a brave woman.'

Sidnee squared her shoulders. 'I'm trying, but I'm actually scared shitless.'

'That's all that bravery is – you're scared shitless but you still do the right thing.' His tone was gentle and I suppressed a smile. This was the man who'd said he could kill me ten different ways before my fangs dropped. He had it *baaaad*.

Sidnee nervously checked her gun one more time. I didn't tell her that last time bullets had barely registered with the beast.

Connor tugged me behind the car for a moment alone. 'Before we go,' he murmured and pulled me in for a scorching kiss. The zing rocketed through me in the very best way. I wanted to stay frozen in the moment with him forever but we had a job to do. Lives were at stake, possibly ours but certainly Sigrid's, Stan's and Jeff's. Not to mention Fluffy's. Failure was not an option.

Sidnee was talking quietly to Thomas; they were giving us a moment and – unless I was mistaken – having a little one of their own. Thomas wasn't at all forward but he was definitely interested. Yes, he was older than her but he was steady and dependable, and he wasn't hard on the eyes, either. I could see that Sidnee had noticed that too when she gave him a warm smile.

Connor's hand rested comfortably on the small of my back as we joined them. I looked at the barrier; the last time, I'd sensed dissonance and discovered it had a tear, but this time I felt nothing but the usual hum in my back teeth. The barrier was healthy – for now – but with the gems acting wonky, you never knew. Hopefully Mum and the other three witches who were coming would heal it for good.

This time I knew the spell to re-enter, which I hadn't the previous time. Thomas looked me over, judging my emotional state. He was far too observant for a human, far too good at everything. 'Are you ready?' he asked.

I wasn't, but I had no choice. At least this time I knew what my fire magic could do to the beast and I was better prepared. 'I'm good.'

He stared at me a moment longer then gave an approving nod. 'What are we going up there for? Gunnar said some weed but I doubt he has much use for the devil's lettuce.'

I snorted a laugh. 'We need to come back with alpine azalea and devil's club. Do you know what alpine azalea looks like?' I'd printed some pictures to show them.

Thomas frowned. 'I do – but I don't recall seeing it up there.'

My stomach sank. If we couldn't find that bloody plant, there was no guarantee that we'd get the stuff from the subarctic in time. We could lose Sigrid and Stan. Thomas saw the panic on my face and hurriedly reassured me. 'I haven't been up there in years and I wasn't looking for plants. Don't freak out. We aren't going to stop until we find it.'

I took a few deep breaths, as did Sidnee. 'We're going to find it. It's there.' I'd manifest it, dammit.

Thomas turned and we followed him through the barrier.

Chapter 17

The first time I'd gone through the barrier I'd been scared, but not as much as I was now. I'd been ignorant then and ignorance was bliss. Sadly, I was no longer ignorant.

From the moment we stepped through, I was on high alert. Since no one drove out here anymore, the road was overgrown and it soon became no more than a trail. We were all tense; our heads were constantly swivelling to look around. Last time we'd had GPS coordinates as a starting place, but now we were heading up the mountain looking for plants. It would have been a nice day out but for the dangers around us. And the beast wasn't the only worry: the nantinaq hadn't been too pleased with us last time, either.

Sidnee grasped my hand and I felt her tremble. Her eyes were mer black; if she'd been anywhere near a body of water, she would have shifted. I squeezed her hand reassuringly.

Thomas veered off the path at a place that seemed sensible to him; since I was still a newbie at bushcraft, I was happy to follow. Connor's footfalls were as silent as Thomas's. I still didn't know how they did that. I had vampire reflexes but I couldn't do it – at least, not yet.

The sunlight was coming through the conifers and I could see where to step. It was much easier than stumbling around at night, but I still crashed about. At least Sidnee was just as noisy. I'd have been reassured by that except that we were trying to be quiet and not attract the beast. I prayed it was sleeping somewhere far, far away. It had to sleep, right?

Thomas was moving ridiculously quickly; if I'd still been human, I'd have been hard pressed to keep up. I took a shuddering breath when we came across the remnants of the Savik brothers' firepit, and I couldn't help wondering if we'd be next. Nope! No negativity allowed on this trip. We were going to find the plants and be in and out before anything scary found us. Easy-peasy.

Thomas found animal trails for us to walk along when he could, but the terrain was rough. Even though people like the Saviks had been coming out here to hunt, there hadn't been enough of them to wear footpaths into the forest. Soon he and Connor were deploying machetes.

Thomas paused every now and again to make sure we were all together and to determine where we were going. He pointed out trees and other landmarks so that if we got separated, we'd have an idea how to get back. The very thought of being alone out here was terrifying. Sidnee stayed by him as the trail narrowed and I brought up the rear with Connor.

When I heard a branch crack behind me I whirled around so fast I nearly fell on my arse. It was a deer, as surprised as I was. It was small and brown, with a darker patch on its forehead and a white strip around its nose. Its dark eyes looked at me for a moment and one ear flicked at me, listening.

Connor must have heard me stop because he came back and put his arm around me. He whispered in my ear, 'It's a Sitka blacktail. Watch when it turns.' Sure enough, the deer flipped around on its back feet and bounded off. Its short dark tail flicked and it was gone.

I released my breath. That had been almost magical: for one moment I'd enjoyed nature and not worried about the beast. 'It's beautiful,' I murmured. And not tasty in the slightest. Deer blood was gross.

'Yes,' he agreed and kissed my forehead.

From Portlock at sea level the mountain was only around a thousand feet high, but it was covered in brush and tough going; we were all panting with effort before we reached the top. As we neared the summit, we started searching for a life-saving evergreen shrub with tiny pink blossoms. Luckily, we were there at a time when it bloomed, so in theory it shouldn't be hard to spot, but Thomas's earlier comment had fear curling in my gut. What if it wasn't there?

Thomas stopped abruptly and the rest of us nearly barrelled into him. 'If it's anywhere, it'll be here. Keep your eyes sharp.'

I looked around hopefully. No pink blossoms anywhere.

Thomas reached the same conclusion. 'We'll have to spread out and cover the whole of the mountain top. It's not going to jump up and announce itself. We can collect the devil's club on the way down. I've seen a tonne of that already.' I had too: we'd had to avoid the prickly plant all the way up. It made sense to collect it on the way down so it would be as fresh as possible.

Sweat was dripping down my back, and it wasn't entirely due to the climb. This was the most dangerous part, where we split up and our attention would be divided between watching for signs of the beast and looking for the plant.

I caught Connor's eye and knew he felt the same: he didn't want to leave me. I tore my gaze away from him and checked on Sidnee. She looked small and lost; if we weren't being driven by such an urgent need, I'd have insisted she stick with one of us. But we had a mission and our loved ones' lives depended on it.

We agreed to meet in one hour and each took a different direction. I deliberately thought about my mum and all she'd put me through, using my anger to build the fire in my gut so it was ready. I felt alone, afraid – and utterly determined.

I walked in a zigzag across my section, checking every plant I saw – which was a lot. After a while I looked at my phone to check how long I'd been looking and was horrified to see it had only been fifteen minutes. It had seemed like forever: it turns out that time crawls when you're petrified for your life.

The next time I checked it had been forty-five minutes and I'd run out of fresh ground. That was when I heard it: an eerie howl. My floppy heart gave two quick beats and a chill ran down my spine. I knew that sound because it haunted my dreams.

Our time was up. The beast was awake, abroad and we were about to be hunted.

I rushed back to our starting point. The others must have heard the howl too, because they all returned within moments of me. 'It knows we're here,' Thomas said grimly.

Fear threatened to overwhelm me but I pushed it down. We were here for the plant and we weren't leaving without it, no matter how much the beast yodelled at us. 'Anyone find it?' I asked, even though I could see from their empty hands that they hadn't.

Another eerie howl came and it sounded closer. It was coming our way – and fast. 'Time's up,' Thomas said. 'We have to go.'

I didn't know what to do. We had to find that plant but we also had to survive long enough to take it back. Sidnee grasped my hand again. 'We can't leave,' she pleaded with Thomas. 'This is their only chance. I can't lose them. I *won't*.'

She was right. 'You go, I'll stay and look,' I said. 'I have my fire.'

'Fuck that,' Connor growled. 'I'm not leaving you.'

In the end, it didn't matter because the beast decided for us.

Chapter 18

Sidnee's eyes were fixed on something behind me, wide with fear. I turned to see what had made her turn sheet white, though I already knew. Black smoke was writhing through the trees behind us. 'God save us,' she whimpered.

Thomas grabbed her arm. 'Run!'

We took off over the top of the mountain and down the other side. It was foolish to run so fast – there were plenty of cliff edges and lots of scree to slip on – but we had little choice. Death by plummeting or death by beast. I felt a shade hysterical. I didn't want death at all! I'd already done the death thing once and it hadn't agreed with me.

Thomas took the lead, dragging Sidnee with him. Connor and I stuck together a few steps behind them.

Thomas stopped at the edge of a steep precipice and indicated that we should veer to the left.

As I teetered on the edge, I saw something on a ledge about twenty feet down. Alpine azalea. The little flowers were dying and dropping off, but the pink caught my eye. 'Oh my God! It's there!' I cried. That caught everyone's attention and I suddenly realised that they probably thought I meant the beast. 'The plant,' I clarified. 'It's down there.'

'We've got to go!' Thomas reminded us. 'It's right behind us. Move!'

I ignored him; I was already climbing down and Connor was right with me.

'Come on, the beast can't fit down here,' I said confidently, even though I had no idea what its capabilities were. The ledge was barely fifteen inches wide and it would be hard for any of us to stand on it for long, let alone a giant marauding beast. I hoped my friends were good rock climbers because we'd either have to go up and brave the beast or go down about fifty more feet to a less steep part of the mountain.

I had no climbing experience but I trusted my athletic body and my vampire strength. I could absolutely do this. Probably. I clung to small protruding rocks and brush and slowly made it down to the ledge.

Connor was behind me so I slid as far to the side as I could on the narrow ledge. He looked as if he knew what he was doing because the second I was out of the way he descended at twice the rate of my trembling progress.

I looked up to see Sidnee start down, miss a handhold and slide down about five feet. My breath caught and my heart beat an extra thud in my chest. She grabbed a branch and steadied herself. Connor was standing below her in case she fell, hands outstretched ready to catch her, and he only stepped away when she joined us on the ledge. Thomas, of course, was smarter and came down on a rope. Dammit, I didn't know we had a rope!

The beast howled its rage from the summit, its smoke and red eyes peering over the edge at us, then it started down head first like Dracula. I shut my eyes and opened them again; it was over the cliff edge and heading for us. 'Cut the plant,' I yelled. 'We have to get off this ledge! It's coming!'

Thomas whacked half of the plant with his machete. I grabbed it, opened my bag to put it inside – and gasped. Two golden eyes winked out at me. No wonder my bag had felt so heavy – I had a stowaway. The weight wasn't biscuits; it was motherfucking Shadow!

The kitten spotted the smoky beast over my shoulder, leapt out of my rucksack and bounded towards it. His own shadow magic lifted from him and his tendrils of smoke went to confront the beast's. 'Shadow!' I yelled. 'You get back here right this instant!'

'He's saving us,' Connor barked. 'Don't waste his efforts. He knows the way to the barrier. Move!' He shoved the azalea into my rucksack, closed it and shouldered it.

My heart rate was almost at human speed. My panic was at a level I'd never experienced but that increased my adrenaline. I couldn't leave my cat in order to save my dog! My heart was breaking. My gorgeous, brave – stupid – Shadow!

As Thomas reached for his rope, it brushed against the beast, broke on contact with the black smoke and tumbled down to us.

Thomas didn't miss a beat and immediately looked around for somewhere else to tie it off. There was nothing but the remnants of the alpine azalea bush. No way was that strong enough to hold any of us.

The black smoke was battling with Shadow. My kitten's yowls and hisses filled the air but I couldn't see where he or the beast began. If I sent in a fireball, I'd risk hurting my baby!

Finally Thomas tied the rope around Sidnee, and he and Connor lowered her down the cliff face using their body weight to keep her steady.

The reality was that Connor and I could take our chances. If we fell, we might suffer broken limbs but we'd heal with some blood. More urgently, we needed the beast off of our asses and away from my Shadow.

'Shadow!' I shouted. 'Get away! Flame time!' I didn't know whether he was smart enough to understand me – he was not Fluffy. Then, with relief, I saw a small patch of Shadow disentangle and head back towards me. That was all I needed.

My fire was raging in my centre; fear for my fur baby amping it up to whole new levels. I had to make the hit count. If I couldn't kill the beast, at least I could discourage it from following us long enough for us to get to the barrier. But I needed to be closer. I skirted along the ledge until I was as near to the beast as I could get. Connor and Thomas were still working double time to get Sidnee to safety.

Shadow barrelled towards me and leapt up next to me. 'Good boy,' I praised him. 'Clever, clever boy.' Whatever he'd done, it had definitely injured the beast; its progress towards us was far slower than it had been before.

The fire within me was so hot it felt like I was scorching from the inside out. With a cry, I held out my hands to direct the flames, channelling them through me – and then I let go. A huge, scorching fireball launched from my hands. The blast was of such strength that for a split second I could see the huge wild cat at the centre of the inky shadows.

It looked a lot like Shadow. Oh fuck: Shadow and the beast were the same species!

Chapter 19

My fire struck true and the beast yowled. The sound was so intense that we all froze. The men couldn't cover their ears or they'd risk dropping Sidnee, but I had no such problem. I clamped my hands over my ears, but even so my eardrums burst.

Blood dripped out through my fingers and everything went quiet. Discombobulated, I picked up Shadow. A few seconds passed and then, with a tiny snick, I could hear once again. I guessed the injury wasn't severe enough to need blood to kick-start the healing process.

Thomas's ears were still trickling blood, but I assumed Connor was also good as new.

The yowling quietened as the beast scrambled back up the cliff face as easily as it had come down. It was retreating; I had no idea how badly we'd hurt it but hopefully it was enough for us to escape.

Sidnee had reached the bottom. Connor made Thomas wrap the rope around himself and we lowered him down next. Once he was safe, Connor pulled up the rope. 'You go next. I'll lower you down.'

I shook my head. 'I can go down on my own. I'll lower you.'

'Don't be ridiculous. I'm a full vampire and we don't know what you are. If I fall, I'll heal. If you fall, you could die.'

'I'll be fine after I drink some blood.'

'Are you going to drink from Thomas or Sidnee?'

I blinked. 'I brought some with me.'

'And you brought at least two bags? Because when you were shot, you drank more than one.'

That stopped me. He knew I didn't have two, and no way could I drink from my friends. 'Fine, dammit.' I took the rope and grudgingly tied it around my waist. My rucksack was full of the plant so I couldn't tuck Shadow in there; however, he jumped out of my arms and started down the cliff face like he was a mountain goat.

I grasped the rope and walked backwards off the cliff, trying to help Connor bear the weight of me by finding hand and footholds. It felt like it took forever to get to the bottom.

Thomas was holding Sidnee, who was visibly pale and shaking. She was scared, and who could blame her, but I was weirdly all out of fear. I guess there comes a time when fear isn't of use so your body gets rid of it.

It was unbelievable: I'd seen the beast, and it was the hugest big cat I'd ever seen. Its malevolent red eyes were unlike Shadow's golden ones but I knew there was some sort of connection between them. My kitten was curling around Sidnee's ankles, purring loudly and trying to reassure her; he was as far from evil as you could get.

I could only spare a cursory glance for my companions because my heart was in my throat as I watched Connor descend. He coiled the rope over his shoulder and free climbed down. Even though I'd seen every inch of the rock surface on my way down, I had no idea what he was clinging on to. When he was about ten feet from the ground, he leapt free and landed gracefully.

An explosive breath burst out of me and I fell into his arms. 'That was terrifying. Never do that again. Thank God you're safe.'

He chuckled into my neck. 'That was fun. I'd forgotten how much I enjoy climbing.'

'Let's move,' Thomas said, still with one arm around Sidnee. He was right: we weren't out of the woods yet, literally or figuratively.

Thomas consulted his phone's map. I had no idea which way to go and that was disconcerting. With my eidetic memory I'd never had much opportunity to be lost before, but after running blindly and going over a cliff I honestly didn't know where I was.

Thomas chose a direction and we followed. Sidnee stayed close to him and he kept a careful eye on her, though he relinquished his hold so he could navigate. He set a bruising pace, wanting to get off the mountain and back within the safety of the barrier as much as I did. He only paused once to hack some devil's club to add to our plant collection.

Soon we were on our way down the trail and onto the road. Thank all that was holy; there was no sign of the beast or the nantinaq.

I crouched down to speak to Shadow. 'Is it your mum or dad? Because if you want to stay with it...?' Shadow climbed onto my lap. Okay, then.

Last time I'd gone through the barrier it had been damaged and it had refused us entry, so I was a little nervous. Holding my kitten, I muttered the spell, and this time it worked like a charm. Once I made it to the safe side, I almost collapsed in relief.

I smirked a little when I noticed that Thomas was holding Sidnee's hand as they came through. Connor and I turned away so they wouldn't see we'd noticed. If this was the beginning of something between them, I didn't want to interfere. Dangerous as Thomas was, he was steady and true – unlike Sidnee's last boyfriend. Thomas was at least fifteen years older than Sidnee – but who was I to talk? I had no idea how old

Connor was, but he was definitely *much* older than me. I was currently queen of the age-gap romance.

Now that we were safe, Sidnee gave me a radiant smile. 'I'll ride with Thomas,' she said. 'Give you two some space.'

I stifled a smile. 'That's kind of you. Why don't you take the plants to Anissa? I'll go back to the office to relieve April.'

Sidnee nodded, 'Sure thing.' She got out her phone. 'I'll text Anissa to let her know we're coming now. You hold the fort and I'll get the rest of our troops up and running again.' Now that hope had returned, Sidnee was bouncing again, all trace of her earlier pique gone.

I passed her my bag with the plant in and turned to Connor. 'Can you drive?' I asked, chucking him the Nomo SUV's keys. 'I want to ring Gunnar.'

'Sure.'

We climbed in and headed down the rough country road. Once we were in phone range again, I called Gunnar. 'Tell me good news,' he answered, his voice tight.

'We got both plants and we're all safe.'

'Thank God.' The words exploded out of him.

'We're going to the office to relieve April; Sidnee is taking the plants to Anissa as we speak. Sigrid's going to be okay, Gunnar.'

He blew out a shaky breath. 'I owe you, Bunny Rabbit. You know that, right?'

'You don't owe me a thing. See you soon, boss.' I rang off before I could get emotional. That was the other reason I wasn't driving; now that we were safe I could process all we'd done and I was starting to shake. Man, that had been super close.

Connor noticed and pulled over. He turned off the engine, unclicked my seatbelt and pulled me into his lap. 'You're okay, doe. Everything is okay.'

I nodded into the crook of his neck as the floodgates opened and sobbed as the adrenaline drained out of me. When I stopped crying, I drew back. 'How come you're not all shocky and teary?'

He smiled. 'I feel it differently to you, but I'm still affected.'

'Differently how?' I asked curiously.

A sexy smile tugged at his lips. 'After a life and death situation like that, I like to remind myself that I'm still standing.'

I cottoned on. Oh. 'And how do you do that?' I asked innocently, toying with the top button of his shirt.

His smile widened. 'You wanna have a quickie in a tree?'

I burst out laughing. When I recovered myself, I said, 'Sure, I'm game. Now?'

He undid his seatbelt. 'There's no time like the present.'

Chapter 20

When we pulled up to the Nomo's car park, April was waiting anxiously. 'What kept you?' she asked. 'Sidnee texted a while ago to say you were en route. I got worried.'

'Potholes,' Connor said blandly. 'And trouble with a tree.'

April's eyes swept over both of us, missing nothing. She grinned. 'Trees can be real pesky.'

I blushed a little. I distracted myself from the warmth in my face by picking up my sleepy feline. I carted Shadow inside. 'I'm sure Sidnee mentioned, but we're back and we found the plant,' I said quickly.

'That's great! Is everyone alive?'

'Yup!' I confirmed. 'All present and correct. How did it go here? Any trouble?'

She picked up several pink Post-it notes. 'Nothing pressing enough to require an officer immediately,' she reassured me, handing them over. She looked at her notepad. 'Liv called. She said that she interviewed everyone and no one knew anything.'

I frowned. Liv wasn't going to let us anywhere near the damned market; all we could do was hope that Jeff could somehow direct us to the curser so we could track them down and kick their asses for daring to harm Sigrid. Ahem: I meant arrest them and process them properly within the confines of the due process of the law.

Now that we had the ingredients for a possible cure, I could concentrate on finding the curser but Liv was standing securely in my way. There was nothing I could do that night, but maybe I could ferret the information out of Calliope the next day. For now, I was the only one here; April had put in ten plus hours and it was time to let her go home to her family.

'Thanks, April. I appreciate all your hard work today. I'm on shift now, so you get yourself home.'

Connor settled Shadow on his bed where my kitten promptly curled up for a sleep. I was eager to get him home and fed, but I'd deal with the calls first.

'Thanks, Bunny.' April shot me a grateful look. 'Mads made dinner today and apparently there was more carbon than meal.'

I snorted. 'Takeout?'

'You read my mind!'

So that she wouldn't think I was rushing her out while she packed up, Connor and I went into Gunnar's office. I disappeared gratefully into the oversized chair, grabbed the lever and lowered it until my feet hit the ground. I huffed: now the desk was too tall.

Connor laughed. 'Gunnar's a giant. That chair is never gonna fit you, doe.'

'I know, but I need a spot to work.' I fanned the collection of pink slips. 'These aren't going to answer themselves.' I made a show of examining them. 'Hey, look! Half of these have your name on them!' I held them out and he groaned.

I pulled back my arm. 'I'm kidding! You probably have your own work to catch up on, and I need to check on Mum.'

He nodded but made no move to leave. If he was staying, I might as well pick his brains a little. 'Apparently Liv is sponsoring the black market. Have you heard anything about it? I'm trying to find it – I need to find the curser and I have no leads until the cursed people are conscious again.'

Connor looked startled. 'Liv? Yeah, I've heard murmurings that the black market was passing through, but nothing about where. People are guarded around me. Knowing Liv, she's in this for profit. She won't risk losing money, so you won't get anything out of her.'

'Calliope knows about it, too.'

He frowned and stood up. 'Okay; now I feel left out. How about I go check in on your mother? Save you some time?'

I hesitated. If Mum got him alone, she'd fawn all over him now that she knew who he was. I couldn't let him go into the lion's den by himself. 'You know what would save me the most time?'

He lifted his eyebrows. 'Hit me.'

'If you spoke to Calliope about the market, I think she'd be more open.'

'Apparently not,' he muttered, arms folded. 'I'll definitely try and speak to her though – for you.'

'Thank you. How about I deal with these calls, run Shadow home, check on Fluffy, then we reconvene back at mine while I check on Mum?'

'Sounds like a plan.'

'Will you be okay getting around from here?'

'Margrave will pick me up.'

'Okay, see you later.' I picked up my phone to start working my way through the pink slips hoping to hell that no one answered my calls. I was crashing from the adrenaline rush and I really needed an easy shift.

Chapter 21

After I'd returned all the calls and forwarded the Nomo's office line to my mobile, I hurried home to feed my triumphant little Shadow. 'It would really be handy if you could talk,' I said to him as I drove. 'I'm really grateful for how you stood up to the beast. The only thing I can't figure, though, is if you're related and that's why he didn't wipe you out.'

Predictably, Shadow didn't reply. When I got in, Fluffy was exuberant to see us both. I could hear Mum's shower running, so I hopped into mine hoping I'd be done before Connor arrived. Naturally, I didn't make it out of the shower in time so he had to run the gauntlet alone.

I hurriedly braided my wet hair so I could go down to save him but I could hear the timbre of Mum's voice and knew that I was too late. Whoops.

'Oh, welcome, your royal highness,' she was saying. I could almost hear her curtsey. I groaned. How embarrassing!

There was a pause, then Connor's deep voice rumbled, 'Please call me Connor.'

I ran into my bedroom to get dressed, leaving the door open so I could eavesdrop as I dragged on a T-shirt.

'Please have a seat, sir.' Another pause. 'How long have you lived in Portlock?'

Poor Connor. 'I've been here about forty years.'

'Oh, how delightful.' The false tone of Mum's voice was audible and I practically ran to the living room. Fluffy met me halfway and I gave him a head rub. 'Who's the best boy?'

He wagged. He was, and he knew it. He gave me a quiet bark and leaned against my legs as I looked into the room to figure out the situation.

Connor was sitting on the sofa and Mum was on a hard kitchen chair that she must have dragged over. I was sure she wouldn't want to impose on the vampire prince by sitting next to him but it was making him very uncomfortable. He was stiff and straight backed as he held Shadow and gave him a belly rub. The cat was purring and looked ecstatic. I didn't blame him; I'd do the same in his place.

'Can I get you anything, Your Highness?'

Connor winced. 'Please, Mrs Barrington, I'm Connor.'

Mum looked horrified. 'I could never call a prince by his name...' Her hand reached up to her throat.

He raised one perfect eyebrow. 'Well, should I call you High Priestix then?'

'Gosh, no, of course not. Victoria, please.' She looked at him pleadingly.

I walked in. 'Elizabeth, darling,' Mum said wringing her hands. 'I'm glad to see you. I confess that I misplaced your cat for a time, but it's turned up again.'

Shadow had misplaced himself into my rucksack. I smiled. 'No worries. Connor, do you want some tea? I was just about to switch on the kettle.'

'Sure, let me help.' He set Shadow carefully on the couch and leapt up. The kitten curled into a ball and went straight back to sleep.

'Oh, no that won't do,' Mum said in panic as she also jumped up. 'I can't let royalty serve me.' It was like watching a tennis match in the stands at Wimbledon.

Connor gave his most charming smile and guided her back to the sofa with his hand on her elbow. That was a practised move; I gave him my impressed look and earned one of his blinding smiles.

'You sit there, Mrs Barrington – Victoria. Let Bunny and me take care of you.' He winked and she blushed. Ugh.

Apparently being princely came with some serious court manners because Connor had won her over. I wasn't sure how he did it, but somehow five minutes later he'd deposited a perfect cup of tea in her hands. Even Mum looked shocked to see it there. I grinned at him as I sipped from my own cup.

'Do you already have supper prepared, Elizabeth? If not, I'd love to take Connor out for some food.' Mum fluttered her eyelashes and looked coyly at him.

'No, I haven't prepared anything actually,' I said.

'Well, we don't have a lot of restaurant choices but the food is good and I can tell the company will be delightful,' Connor added smoothly.

Yeuch. I rolled my eyes at him when Mum wasn't looking.

She beamed. 'I would love that, Your Highness.'

'Fantastic. One small caveat – I can only take you if you call me Connor. I keep a low profile in Portlock.' He winked again, like she was in on a secret.

She was delighted. 'Of course, C-Connor.' She stumbled a bit but she was eating up the attention.

He threw me a glance and it was my turn to be on the receiving end of one of his winks. 'Something in your eye?' I murmured quietly. 'I assume you're trying to blink it out with all that winking?' He gave me a flat look and I stifled a laugh. I shouldn't have worried about leaving him alone with her; he was very good at this.

'Well, you two kids have fun,' I said. 'I'm heading back to work.' I picked up Shadow, who squeaked at having his nap interrupted, and plonked him in his pram then grabbed Fluffy's lead and left them to it.

'Please excuse me one moment,' Connor said to Mum and followed me out to the porch. He lifted Shadow's pram down the two steps for me then swept me up in a passionate kiss.

'You charmer, you,' I said once he put me down. 'I came here to save you, but you have hidden depths.'

'I can't let you know all my secrets. We need some left for fifty years down the line.'

A thrill ran through me that he could envisage our future together but I kept my smile calm and cool. 'Indeed.' I kissed him again. 'I'll let you save one or two secrets for later.'

I headed back to work. Now to solve the mystery of who had laid the curse, check on Sigrid and Stan, find out what curse my dog had and fix it. And save Jeff, too. I kept forgetting about him. I could do all that, no problem. I just needed *one* lead.

Determination poured through me. I'd find it in no time.

Chapter 22

I turned into the Nomo's building only to see that the front door was gone, not open but completely gone. The hinges had been torn off, too. What the fuck had happened here? I'd definitely locked up but it looked like someone had been unwilling to wait.

Fluffy growled and looked around nervously. The door was missing because it was six feet inside the building and the frame was bowed: something had hit it with a lot of force. Cool – rageful *and* strong, just how I liked my intruders.

Fluffy led the way inside, growling ominously. I followed him in because a) I didn't want my dog getting hurt, and b) confronting monsters was kind of my job now. I wished I had one of Thomas's machetes handy but I didn't even have my gun on me. Luckily fear had snapped my fangs down and that same fear had heat curling in my body. I was never without weapons, and that was kind of reassuring.

As I'd learned through my excursion into the mountains I wasn't the best at sneaking around so I embraced my failings and crunched through the wreckage. Fluffy got the message that we weren't trying to be subtle and started barking his equivalent of 'Come out, come out, wherever you are!'

I looked around the remains of the office in disbelief: it was like a bulldozer had been through it. Everything – and I mean *everything* – had been destroyed: my desk, Sidnee's desk, our computers, everything. Even Fluffy and Shadow's beds hadn't survived.

I scented blood in the air, too. Whoever – *whatever* – had done this had been full of rage. I rolled my shoulders. People with too much rage made mistakes, right? I needed to keep a cool head and everything would be totally fine.

It wasn't until I'd gone behind the counter that I saw the beast of mass destruction. A polar bear was lying on the ground, panting. I only knew one polar bear shifter in town although there could have been more, but my money was on Stan.

The bear had blood smeared on his fur. A quick glance showed a few cuts on him; he'd obviously gotten injured during its demolition work, but it didn't look like there were any other victims. Apart from me, potentially.

The polar bear wobbled as he heaved itself up to a sitting position. He was not feeling good. 'Stan?' I asked quietly.

He huffed and turned to look at me, eyes blazing red. In my limited experience, red eyes were never a good thing: the beast beyond the barrier had red eyes and so had the rogue werewolf that had attacked me in this very same room.

The problem was that I really, really didn't want to hurt Stan. He was cursed and his nightmares were coming to life around him. Somehow he must have broken through the stasis spell and he'd come straight here from the hospital because on some level he knew it was where he'd get help. That meant my flames and fangs were out of action. I needed to calm and disable my lumbering friend without hurting him.

I backed away until the counter was between us. The office phone rang – it was probably the sole piece of technology that had survived the rampage – but I couldn't take my eyes off of the messed-up polar bear shifter to answer it. Now really wasn't the time for a call.

Sorry chaps, there are no police officers currently available right now due to a murderous polar bear. Please leave a message after the beep and we'll help you if we survive. Beeeep.

Stan made a deep 'uuuuugh, uuuuugh' barking roar at me followed by a couple of huffs. I wasn't up on polar bear language, but it didn't sound like he was feeling friendly.

'Stan, it's Bunny. We're friends, remember?' I said in my most soothing tone.

I still had the counter in between us. Fluffy whirled around to stand in front of me and protect me. Instinct made me want to run out of the wrecked office, but that would leave a crazy polar bear on the loose.

I couldn't – *wouldn't* – hurt Stan: for one, we were friends, and for two, I'd literally risked my life trying to save his sorry arse. I wasn't going to undo all that hard work. I needed something to restrain or trap him with, or something to knock him out or bring him to his senses.

The first time I'd met April, she'd turned her hosepipe on her husband and Stan to stop them fighting and it had been surprisingly effective. There were no hosepipes lying around, so I looked for something else.

The phone kept ringing as Stan attempted to stand up and I wished it would shut the hell up so I could concentrate. The office ceiling was around eight feet tall but he was closer to twelve; he hit the acoustic tiles and predictably they broke and crumbled down on him. The metal frame that supported them bent and twisted around him, which pissed him off even more. His barking cough turned into a roar and he whipped around, ripping down more of the ceiling and tangling thin metal strips around his neck.

I backed out slowly and Fluffy followed me. I didn't have anything to use as a weapon or a restraint, so staying in the office was madness. I needed a plan. Why couldn't I think of a fucking plan?

Stan was in a blinding rage, so intent on battling the ceiling that he didn't give a shit that I was edging away. I went around the corner of the building and hurriedly pulled out my phone. It rang before I could look at it or dial.

It was Sidnee. 'Bunny! Stan's escaped. You've got to help us find him!'

'Well,' I said drily, 'we're in luck. I've found him.'

'Where is he?'

'At the office. And he is *pissed*. He's tearing it to pieces.'

'Oh shit!'

'How do we contain him? He's a freaking polar bear! A rageful one.'

'Hang on.' Silence: she'd muted me. I listened to the noises coming from the office; they were starting to fade so either Stan was lying on the floor again or he was heading out. I couldn't let that happen.

Sidnee clicked back in. 'Anissa says she's coming. She has the potion and can start the ritual. The elders are working on Sigrid right now. Jeff is already uncursed. Keep Stan there.'

Contain the rageful polar bear: sure, no sweat. 'Okay,' I said breezily. 'See you soon.' Or not, if I'd become polar bear food.

I grabbed a metal rubbish bin lid: I could whack Stan over the head with it if I got close enough, though I really didn't want to get close enough.

There was a loud cracking noise from inside the office. I stuffed the phone into my pocket and ran around the corner, brandishing my smelly shield. 'Stay back,' I murmured to Fluffy. He ignored me. Stupid dog.

I tiptoed in and Fluffy followed on silent paws. Maybe that was the approach we should have taken the first time. Live and learn. As we went inside, the cause of the noise became evident: the counter was broken in half and a groggy polar bear was draped over it. He lifted his head to look and me and let out another unfriendly noise but he didn't move. He must have worn himself out or the curse was finally taking him down.

'Stan?' I said cautiously. He growled again. Okay. Still not *my* Stan. I crept closer. I couldn't let him get out of this office – I needed to keep him there for Anissa – so my next action was for his own good.

I raised the bin lid, hit him over the head and he slumped over the counter. Oh fuck, I'd forgotten my vampire strength! I crept forward tentatively and searched his fuzzy neck for a pulse, nearly collapsing with relief when I found one. I'd never have forgiven myself if I'd accidentally killed him.

I sat by him, bin lid at the ready, and waited for reinforcements. If Stan stirred in the meantime, he was getting another bonk on the head. I was a woman with a plan.

Chapter 23

I was near the door so I could watch Stan and also keep an eye out for Anissa's arrival but Connor arrived first. The diner wasn't far away; he'd either heard some commotion or Sidnee had called him when she couldn't get through to me. My money was on Sidnee.

He saw me and relief washed over his face. 'You're okay?' He scanned me over.

'Peachy,' I promised with a thumbs-up.

'Where is he?' he asked.

I pointed inside and Connor took a step toward the door. I put my hand on his arm. 'He's unconscious now. We don't want to wake him until Anissa gets here.'

'Has Anissa prepared the cure already?' He sounded impressed.

At that moment, my mum jogged up the street, tottering on her heels. She believed a fit body equalled a fit mind and she often used the gym equipment at home, but even so I was impressed. 'Elizabeth! Are you okay?' she panted. 'What is going on? Connor said something about an out-of-control bear?'

'He's not a bear; he's a polar bear shifter. It's Stan, the shifter leader who was cursed at dinner. He's in there, so stand away from the door.' I made sure she was behind the wall.

'Anything else we need to know?' Connor asked.

'He's destroyed the office like a tornado. And,' I hesitated, 'his eyes are red.'

Connor grimaced. 'Never a good sign.'

He wasn't wrong. Luckily, Anissa arrived only a minute after Mum and Connor. However, I couldn't let her go in until I was sure Stan was staying down. It wouldn't be cool if our shaman got eaten. 'What do you want us to do?' I asked her when she joined us.

Anissa had a large bag over her shoulder stuffed full of items. She looked tired. 'I need him calm and still long enough for me to complete the ritual, and I have to get some of this potion into him.'

We looked at each other: no one wanted to volunteer to plug the bear's nose and chuck a potion down his throat.

'I could restrain him with magic, but I can't do that and the ritual at the same time,' she continued. 'We need some powerful magic users to hold him still. He won't last long if he's burning through his reserves this fast.'

A frisson of fear ran through me. I couldn't let Stan die: he was a sort of son to Gunnar and a sort of brother to Sidnee. He was the shifter leader and, for all his goofiness, he was my friend.

'He's passed out right now. Do you think he'll stay down?' Connor asked.

Anissa shook her head. 'I don't know. I wouldn't have thought he'd have the strength to break the stasis, shift and run through town – but he did. We're lucky he came here without hurting anyone or causing any damage.' She hadn't seen the office yet.

'I can hold him,' Mum volunteered.

I looked at her in surprise. 'You can?'

'Darling, I'm the High Priestix of the United Kingdom! Of course I can hold him long enough for your shaman to break the curse.'

Right. High Priestix equalled powerful fire witch. It was hard to build that into my view of my charity-lunching, social-climbing mother. The truth was that all of this was showing me that I didn't know her at all, any more than she knew me.

'How long can you hold him?' Anissa asked. 'I need at least half an hour.' She didn't seem to doubt my mum's witchy powers, which settled my nerves a bit.

Mum nodded briskly. 'I can do that.'

'What if he wakes up and fights your bindings?' Connor asked, frowning.

'I can handle it,' she said calmly. 'Trust me. But let's get a move on. It will be easier if we do it while he's unconscious.' She was right.

As we moved into the office, I stifled a curse. My trusty bin lid hadn't struck hard enough because the bear was awake.

Chapter 24

Anissa handed me the potion bottle. Great: somehow I'd been volunteered to give the conscious bear his meds. Lucky me. I hoped Mum wasn't over-exaggerating her skills. I'd been hoping for a few drops on his tongue but no: it was a full sixteen-ounce bottle's worth. Fantastic.

'I'll help you,' Connor promised as he waved Mum forward. 'Be careful and do it fast.' He looked the tiniest bit nervous, obviously frightened he was going to get my mother killed. So was I.

In her silk dress and heels, Mum looked as far from a witch as you could imagine. She took a deep breath, released it and started weaving her hands and quietly muttering what I assumed was a spell. It wasn't in English but in German.

The spell worked fast. Stan stopped making his peculiar barking polar bear grunts almost as soon as the chanting began and Connor nodded for Anissa to move in.

Stan was immobile except for his heaving chest and his blazing red eyes which were rolling around crazily in his skull, trying, but failing to focus on each of us. His limbs were locked down; he couldn't even turn his head, although I could see his muscles rippling under his fur as he tried. If Mum's spell failed, I had no doubt he'd rip us all to shreds.

She kept up her chanting and her hands continued to move in their hypnotic dance.

My teeth rattled and my skin itched – my response to witch magic. Stan had slid off the broken counter and was lying on the floor on his side. The office was completely destroycd – we'd need new computers, new everything. Even the steel filing cabinets that lined one wall were severely dented. Most of the ceiling tiles were down and the supports were wrecked and twisted. I'd never liked those soundproofing tiles; maybe we could rip them out and look at the pipes and whatever else they were there to hide. A modern commercial look.

Connor sat down and lifted Stan's heavy head into his lap. The bear's tongue lolled out the second he was moved. Connor put his fingers in Stan's mouth to open it and Stan's eyes rolled faster, his muscles nearly popping as he strained to move.

Mum's chanting became louder. She was sweating now; despite her blasé attitude, this was clearly hard work.

Connor positioned Stan's head so I could pour the potion into his mouth and I unscrewed the bottle cap. I had to go slowly so that Stan could swallow but fast enough for it not to take too long. By the time I was done, I was drenched with nervous sweat too.

Then it was Anissa's turn. She motioned us out of the way and pulled a drum from her large bag; it was a flat circle of what looked like stretched skin with a handle and a slender stick. She set the drum aside and sprinkled a mix of herbs on Stan. Next she pulled out a wooden mask, brightly painted in strips of colour and surrounded by a sinew hoop and raven feathers. She put it down and gave me the drum. As I held it, she took the stick and started a rhythmic beat about the rate of a human heart.

She looked at me. 'Can you keep that beat for me?'

I nodded, took the stick and hit the drum. It had a resonant sound, like the thrumming of a bird's wings. Anissa corrected how I struck it, waited to make sure I was keeping a steady beat, then sat at Stan's head for a few minutes.

Once she was centred, she stood and picked up her mask. Holding it in her hands, she moved it around her as she danced and chanted. Sometimes she placed the mask over her face, sometimes she looked at it, and sometimes she held it up to the ceiling. Then she danced and chanted some more. Her magic wasn't like witch magic; I didn't itch but I felt it as a pressure on my ears and a vibration in my bones.

I switched between watching her and watching Stan. Mum kept up her spell, although her arms were shaking and she was slowing down. Whilst I continued rhythmically beating, I watched her intently. Could I learn to do something like that? I committed the German phrases she muttered over and over to the plains of my memory.

I had no idea how long we worked but Anissa's chant eventually rose to a crescendo and I heard – *felt* – a snap. As I stared at Stan, the red glow in his eyes faded away.

Anissa stopped chanting. She took off her mask and snapped it in half. 'It is done,' she said with satisfaction.

Looking relieved, Mum dropped her hands and stopped chanting. The bear sighed as he was released from Mum's vice-like grip, and his body started to shift. She held a hand to her face and swayed dangerously. Connor was by her side in a flash and caught her as she slipped into a faint.

I rushed over to her. 'She's okay, just worn out,' he reassured me. 'Get her something to drink, something with sugar in it would be best.' He laid her on the floor.

I rushed to the break-room fridge. Someone, probably Gunnar, had left a sports drink in there. I rushed it over to Connor as Mum's eyelids fluttered open. 'Drink this, Victoria,' Connor instructed. 'You'll feel better for getting some sugar and electrolytes into your system.'

Mum grimaced but drank it. Once she was done, Connor helped her stand up and I righted my office chair for her to sit on. 'I'm all right,' she insisted. 'I feel better already. It's a shame we hadn't managed to eat before all this kerfuffle.' Only Mum would call a red-eyed marauding bear a 'kerfuffle'.

Stan was unconscious on the floor, buck-naked. I found a sweatshirt someone had left in the break room and laid it over his lap so we didn't have to gaze at Little Stan. Stan looked – less somehow, like his usual bulk had wasted away. He was such a big man, but lying there he looked much smaller.

'We need to get him back to the hospital for more treatment,' Anissa said. 'I'll call the paramedics to come get him.'

'How long will it be before they're all back to normal?' I asked.

She shook her head. 'I don't know. The curse was hard on their bodies and the longer they were under its influence, the longer their recovery will be. The first guy, Jeff, is in really bad shape and he'll need lots of care and potions. The doctors need to get a thorough look at Stan now he's in his human form again, but he looks like he's lost muscle mass. He's a shifter, though, so he's primed to have fantastic healing speeds. We'll have to see how he goes.'

Stan's skin was unnaturally pale and he was visibly thinner. His cheeks were sunken and I could count his ribs.

'I'll call the ambulance.' I pulled out my phone and dialled. With that sorted, I started moving the rubble so that the medical team could reach Stan a little more easily. It wouldn't be easy to get him out with all the detritus underfoot.

'How's Sigrid?' I asked. 'Is she like this?' I gestured to Stan.

'She didn't burn as much energy by shifting and going berserk – but honestly? She looks like she's laid low. They're all still very sick,' Anissa said sombrely. 'And unlike Stan, she doesn't have any extra healing skills in her back pocket.'

I felt sick thinking about it. If we hadn't found that plant, would they have made it? We needed to find that damned curser and stop them from doing this to anyone else.

'How much of the plant did you use?' I asked. I didn't want to go beyond the barrier again any time soon.

'Most of it,' she admitted. 'We probably have enough for one or two more doses.'

Connor and I exchanged glances; we were both thinking the same thing: if more than two more people were cursed, they would probably die.

Chapter 25

Connor took Mum home and Anissa went with an unconscious Stan back to the hospital. I was left to pick up the pieces at the office.

I looked around in despair before shoving the feeling down. Despair achieved nothing but atrophy; I'd feel better after I'd made inroads into this mess. I needed a shovel and a commercial bin not a few flimsy rubbish bags, but they were all I had so I started to work.

Connor was smarter. After he'd settled Mum, he came back with several commercial waste bags and a shovel. I held the bags as he shovelled broken ceiling tiles and computer pieces into them. We filled six bags and stacked the rest of the rubble – the broken counter and desks – against a wall. There was only one office chair that wasn't broken, the one that Mum had sat in to recover.

The only other thing that wasn't broken was the office phone. I stared at it: it should have been destroyed, too, but it had survived against all odds. In honour of Tom Hank's film *Castaway,* I dubbed it Wilson.

When we were done, we were in an empty room with a line of dented file cabinets, one chair and Wilson. Wouldn't Gunnar, Sidnee and April be surprised?

The file cabinets, although they only looked a little dented, were actually totally fucked. The drawers had jammed and I had to use vampire strength to force them open. After that, I couldn't close them again. Excellent.

Connor used one of Gunnar's many pre-cut pieces of wood to board up the front door, so at least the office was secure even if it was in tatters. Luckily the side rooms, interview rooms and the jail were all untouched, though Gunnar's office was now the only functioning office space. Regardless, I felt like we were lucky that somewhere in Stan's affected brain he'd associated this place with safety and not gone somewhere public where people could have been hurt. This was all *stuff*; although it would be expensive to replace, no one was hurt. We really had been lucky.

Even with all our hard work, the main room looked shambolic. Connor pulled me down with him into the single remaining chair and we sat in the moonlight – Stan had destroyed all the lighting. He kissed my neck. 'Don't worry. I've already informed the council and funds will be released to get this fixed. I've got Margrave ordering new furniture and computers. Anyway, it will give us a chance to update the system.'

Some of my stress dropped away. He was a godsend. 'Thank you so much.'

'You're welcome.'

The phone rang loudly. 'At least Wilson is okay,' I said as I answered the call. It was someone complaining about a noise disturbance. I told them that we were short staffed and to use earplugs. Policing at its finest. I hung up.

'Wilson?' Connor asked curiously.

'You ever see that Tom Hanks' film *Castaway?*'

He grinned. 'You named the phone after his volleyball?'

'Yep. It was a real survivor.'

His grin widened. 'Wilson dies in the end.'

'Well, yeah, but Tom Hank's character was named Chuck and I think that would cause confusion. If I yelled "Chuck" in the office, Sidnee would start lobbing things at me.'

He burst out laughing.

'You've got to think these things through,' I tapped my head. 'No grass growing here.' I let my bout of whimsy fall away. 'We should check on Sig and Stan.' I did want to see them but I was bone tired.

'Yeah, but it's very late even for vampires.'

He was right. 'I need to check on my mum, too.'

'She was taking a shower and going to bed. You'll disturb her if you bother her now.'

I chewed my lip. 'What about Fluffy and Shadow?'

'Fed and also in bed.'

I melted against him. 'Thank you so much, Connor.'

'You're welcome, doe. I'm taking you home. You're exhausted, and to be honest we both need a shower.'

I looked down: my shirt was torn and I was covered in dust and sweat which had turned to mud in places. And I was tired to my toes. Braving the beast beyond the barrier seemed like a lifetime ago, but it was only a matter of hours. It really had been a long-ass day.

'I hear you,' I sighed. 'But I don't want to go home.' I didn't want to wake up to Mum's judgement though admittedly, bar one or two off comments, she hadn't been as bad as I'd expected.

'My home,' Connor offered softly.

I looked at him. He smiled and I wrapped my arms around his neck. 'Do I have to come back to this dump?' I whined.

'Not for a good eight hours,' he promised.

'Sounds like heaven.' I kissed him and felt his smile beneath my lips. 'Let's blow this joint. That's what you Yanks say, right?'

He swept me into my arms and stood up in one smooth motion. I squealed, even though Mum had taught me that a lady shouldn't squeal because it was unbecoming. I decided right then and there that it was a stupid rule that was definitely meant to be broken when sexy vampire men were involved.

I looked at him and his eyes darkened as he looked back. I wanted food, a bath and Connor in that order. He needed to move faster – now and later – because I wasn't in the mood for slow. Some of the heat in my stomach must have reached my eyes because he hustled us out of the back door and into the car park.

He set me in the passenger seat, belted me in and turned on the heaters. The warmth, combined with the scent of him and the rocking of the truck, sent me straight to sleep. I'm a *fabulous* date.

I woke up in Connor's glorious bed – alone. I reached over to make sure: no, he wasn't there. I groaned and grabbed my phone from the nightstand to check the time. It was early evening and I had to go to work soon. At least I felt rested and mostly recovered from yesterday in my body, if not my mind. The more interaction I had with the beast beyond the barrier, the more scared I became. It was some sort of giant cat doused in shadows that acted like acid. Learning that had been more fodder for my nightmares.

And how was I going to save Fluffy? He wasn't cursed in the same way, but would the left-over azalea be enough to save him? Hopefully now that Anissa had broken the curse on the others, she'd help me with my boy.

I was about to get up when Connor appeared balancing a tray in his hands. I hurriedly pulled the covers back over me and sat up. 'You brought me breakfast in bed?' No one had done that for me except my nana when I'd been ill.

Thinking about that stirred a lot of childhood memories. I was sick or injured a lot as a child and it was always Nana who looked after me, her blue eyes flashing with rage because she hated it when I got hurt.

I'd been a really clumsy kid, which was another reason I hadn't got many friends because I'd taken lots of time off school while I was healing. Only my excellent memory had kept me from falling behind.

Connor placed the tray on my lap and raised an eyebrow. 'Are you going to share with the class?'

'Just remembering some childhood stuff. I was a sickly, clumsy kid. Luckily I grew out of it, though I did get hit by a bus once. It's ridiculous – who gets hit by a bus?'

'How did the tray make you remember that?'

'My nana used to bring me breakfast in bed when I was sick, and one of the times was the bus thing.'

Connor was frowning. 'Talk to me about the bus,' he said tightly.

I didn't understand why he was looking so upset because it had been years ago. I grabbed a piece of perfectly crisped bacon and nibbled on it, but a lurch in my stomach reminded me I needed to have blood before food. I took the glass, plugged my nose and downed it in a few swallows, then happily tucked into my bacon.

'American bacon is so much better,' I said happily. 'You have streaky bacon but in the UK we mainly eat back bacon. It's a lot meatier and not half as crispy.'

Connor's eyes were still intense. 'The bus, Bunny.'

I rolled my eyes. 'It's not a big deal. I was twelve. I was crossing the street in London. I'm not sure what distracted me – the bus sort of wiped that out of my memory.' He was listening intently. 'Do you know those large red tour buses we get in London? Double deckers? Well, one of them came out of nowhere.'

I frowned as I tried to recall it. 'It was weird though, because you really can't miss them,' I said slowly. 'And they don't move fast because of the traffic, but I swear it wasn't there one minute and the next it was. Bam.' I winced as remembered pain flooded me and I absently rubbed my leg. 'Luckily, it was a glancing blow, though it broke my left femur. I was in hospital for a while. I guess they brought me breakfast in bed, too.'

I picked up a slice of toast and bit into it. It was delicious and all of a sudden I was ravenous.

Connor's eyes narrowed. 'It's odd that you missed seeing a bus because you're very aware of your surroundings.'

I shrugged. 'Yeah, maybe. I was probably thinking about something and not paying attention. My memory is weirdly hazy about the whole thing. I guess it was the pain – I remember the pain.'

'What else? You said you were sick and injured a lot?'

'The usual childhood things – colds, flu, food poisoning, measles. I fell out of a swing and broke my arm. I tripped on a log in the back garden and rolled down a hill and fell into the pond. I nearly drowned that time.' I brightened. 'One time there was even an escaped lion.'

His jaw clenched. 'A lion?'

'One of our posher neighbours had exotic animals in a private menagerie. They had an African lion that got loose and onto our property. I was playing in the garden and it scared me so badly I peed my pants. It stalked towards me growling and I thought I was a goner, but then it went away, thank God.'

Connor licked his lips. 'Bunny, honey, those weren't normal childhood problems.'

I shrugged. 'I had a privileged childhood. It came with some weirder problems, I guess.'

'Who was watching you when you were growing up? Who was supposed to keep you safe?'

'The staff – nannies and tutors. I had a lot of free time to play, too.'

He shook his head. 'Your parents should have taken better care of you.' Anger was crackling on his skin and he was struggling to keep calm. He blew out a breath then studied me intensely. I knew that look: he was weighing something up.

'What? Tell me,' I insisted.

His frown deepened and he hesitated for a second before taking my hand. 'Bunny, I've heard tales from the supernat community. Most magic users manifest their magic when they're afraid.'

A cold chill ran down my spine and I swallowed hard. 'You think these events were manufactured to get my magic to manifest?'

'Two strong witches expect a strong witch daughter.'

'And they got a ped,' I whispered.

'They got you,' he snarled. 'And they should have been fucking grateful!'

'But they weren't.' The words were pulled from me and my heart started breaking all over again. Mum hadn't told me that she was a witch and that had hurt, but this...? They'd allowed me to get injured. How could any parent do that? Bewildered, I looked at Connor. 'How could they?'

'It's conjecture...'

'It is, but it's solid. The wild lion ... it was a shifter, wasn't it?'

He nodded. 'I think so. That cinched it for me because it didn't attack you, it just scared you shitless.'

I didn't know what to say, so I did what any good Barrington did: I shoved it deep in a box to deal with another day. 'I need to go to work.'

'Bunny...'

'Give me time, Connor. I need to process this.' I paused. 'Don't talk to my mother about it, not until I've had a chance to speak to her, okay?'

'I wouldn't trust myself around her right now. I'd rip her head off.'

I shot him a bittersweet smile. 'You say the nicest things.'

Chapter 26

I let myself in through the back door. Connor had dropped me off and he said he was going to a library for some light reading, though his tone had suggested the reading would be heavy and boring. As he kissed me goodbye, I cursed myself for falling asleep so early last night.

I heard a noise in the office and I froze. 'Hello?' I called.

'It's me,' Gunnar called. 'I see you rearranged the place. Very Marie Kondo.'

I joined him. 'I cleaned up. Stan did the rearranging.'

'I heard. I came to survey the damage. The council has already released funds. I wanted to check on you.'

'I'm fine, just tired. How're Sigrid and Stan?' I should have added Jeff too but I didn't know him. I cared about what happened to him, but not in the way I cared about Sigrid and Stan.

'It's going to be a long road but they're finally showing signs of recovery. I'm heading home to shower and change, plus Loki is lonely and sad that we're both gone. I should spend a little time with him.'

'Yeah.' Gunnar had enough on his plate but he was always urging me to share, so I said, 'Since we're talking pets, I'm really worried about Fluffy being cursed. I know Anissa said he's not in pain but it's obviously doing something to him.'

His eyes softened. 'Of course you're worried. Did Anissa mention any way to break the curse?'

'She said she'd look into it after she'd dealt with the cursed people.'

'You should have told her Fluffy is family. She needs to prioritise him, too,' Gunnar growled.

'I'm sure she will, but the humans were far sicker.'

Gunnar grunted. 'She did all of us a great service. I'm very grateful to her and I'm incredibly impressed with her skills. I'm sure she can help Fluffy.'

'Yeah, me too. But we still have no idea who's laying the curses. Has Jeff come round yet?'

'No, he's still out – his curse was the worst by far. They're still not sure he'll make it.'

'Fuck.'

'Speaking of the curser, for once *I* had an out-of-the-box idea,' he said.

I smiled. 'I'm impressed! Hit me!'

'Well, wait until you hear it before you applaud me,' Gunnar said drily. I grinned; he had a point. 'I feel bad about even suggesting this,' he admitted. 'Liv came to visit Stan and Sig in hospital – maybe she's not all bad. Anyway, she's the closest we have to a lead on the market and we can't let feelings get in the way. This will bite us in the ass if she ever finds out, but I think I can use her phone to pinpoint where the black market is, or at least narrow down an area.'

'How will we know when she's there?'

'That was the extent of my idea,' he confessed. 'And we'd need two council members to sign off on using her phone to triangulate her location.'

I frowned. 'Two people to sign off on it and not tell her it's happening. Calliope would do it but I think she'd tell Liv.' I leaned forward. 'The alternative is to follow her,' I said dubiously. Liv would kill me if she knew I was tailing her.

'But first you'd have to find her,' Gunnar pointed out. That was true; Liv and I weren't phone buddies so I couldn't just ring and ask casually where she was.

'I could stake out her house.'

'Out there in the middle of nowhere? She'd see you.'

I grimaced. He was right. 'Let me think about it,' I murmured. 'Tailing Liv is workable but we need to sort out the logistics.'

'Agreed. Thanks for holding down the fort, Bunny Rabbit.'

'I'd do anything for you and Sigrid,' I said awkwardly. 'You know that, right?'

'Kid, you went over the barrier for us. I won't forget that for as long as I live.' Gunnar looked away and cleared his throat, hoping I hadn't noticed the tears in his eyes. I swallowed hard against the lump in my throat.

'I'm going,' he said abruptly. 'I need to see Loki and to get back to Sig. You've got everything under control.'

'Did you doubt it?'

He smiled. 'Not for a second.'

Gunnar went, leaving me alone with my thoughts and very little to do. I was making a cup of tea when April sneaked in through the back door. 'Oh my God,' she said, eyes wide. 'It looks like a whole family of bears had a brawl in here.'

'Only one polar bear,' I said wryly.

She shrugged. 'There's a reason Stan's in charge, I guess. That man can open a whole can of whoop ass.'

'And boy, was he pissed,' I agreed.

'And you didn't have a garden hose,' she said sagely, making me grin.

'Yeah, that was a bummer.'

'No doubt.' She flashed me a smile and rolled up her sleeves. 'I'll grab the vacuum and we can get this place looking a little more respectable.'

I was pretty sure respectable had left the station but we could aim for not covered in dust and grime.

Connor and I had cleared away a lot of the big-ticket items but the place was far from clean.

'I'll help,' I offered. I went into the break room to snap on some gloves and grab a bottle of cleaning fluids. Time to make this place sparkle.

Chapter 27

All that cleaning left my hands busy and my brain free, so I mentally wrote a pros and cons list. By the time I was done, the pros had it. I picked up Wilson and called Liv. 'Gunnar,' she purred.

'It's Bunny.'

'Oh,' she said flatly, her disappointment clear. Burn.

'Gunnar is still with Sig in hospital. I need to talk to you about your interviews with the black market people. Can you come in?'

She harrumphed. 'I've already told Gunnar that no one knew anything. Besides, I'm busy.'

'I don't have any leads, so I'm asking you as a councillor to please come in. Maybe if I ask you some questions, it will trigger a memory or something that will help our investigation.'

She sighed audibly. 'Fine. Give me an hour.' She hung up. Did no one in this town say goodbye?

There was a knock on the back door; it was Ernie, the owner of the hardware store-slash-café. I opened the door with a smile. 'Hey Ernie!'

'Hi, little lady. I've got a new front door for you. Just wanted to give you the heads up before I rip that wooden travesty off.'

'Thanks, Ernie, you're the best.'

The old man grunted and thrust a paper takeout cup at me. 'Chai latte,' he said, scratching his head awkwardly.

My eyes lit up. 'Thank you!'

'If you cry—' he started.

'—you'll leave. I remember. No tears, I promise.'

'Some people got no respect,' he complained. 'Doing this to the Nomo's office? You wouldn't have gotten such disrespect in my day.'

I wondered when *his* day was. Ernie could have been anything between sixty and a few centuries; with a paranormal town, you never quite knew.

'It wasn't his fault,' I said vaguely. 'Extenuating circumstances.'

'It ain't right,' he groused. 'We'll see you fixed up.' He touched a hat he didn't have and went to start work on the front door. Banging and clanging commenced and I winced. I wasn't going to be able to hear Wilson over all this racket.

I went back to my cleaning as I waited for Liv. By the time she swanned in, Ernie had hung the door and left. She arrived fifteen minutes early but I was prepared. She liked people off balance, especially me. Well, two could play that game.

'I like what you've done with the place,' she said drily, looking around the empty office space with its lonely phone and single chair.

'We had an angry polar bear stop by.'

'So I heard.' She looked amused. 'He's been a very naughty boy, but at least Gunnar will finally have to redecorate this monstrosity.'

'I liked it the way it was.'

'Of course you did.' She waved a hand imperiously. 'You have no taste.'

'Hey!' I objected, more out of principal than because I thought she was wrong.

Rather than ushering her into the interview room, I took her to Gunnar's office. Two friends shooting the breeze. I sat in his big chair and she took the one across from his desk. 'I don't know what I can add,' she said dismissively.

'Tell me about who you interviewed and what they said. Anything that might help.'

'Most of the vendors aren't from here, so out of respect I won't give you their names.'

I wanted to yell at her for being evasive but she was a councillor and I couldn't afford to alienate her. 'Any hints whatsoever?' I asked.

'None. The ones that saw the vendor get sick said he was fine one moment and collapsed the next. No one saw anyone cursing anyone else.'

'You still won't tell me where the market is so I can interview people myself?'

She scoffed. 'If I did that, they'd never come back and several of us would be without an opportunity to procure items we need for our magic. So no, I will not.'

'Liv, the cursed people almost died. Two were from our community. We have to protect our own.'

She fixed me with a condescending look. 'And that's why I interviewed everyone.'

'But you aren't a trained interviewer,' I pointed out.

'Bunny darling, neither are you,' she laughed.

Touché. Annoyingly, she was completely right; I was due to go to the police academy in Sitka for training at the end of the month, but all I'd had was on-the-job training with Gunnar. 'I have plenty of experience,' I pointed out.

'And so do I. Are we done?' She stood up.

'Are you meeting my mother later?' I asked casually. If she came to pick up Mum, I could tail her to wherever they went.

'Yes,' she said impatiently, 'and the other three witches. We need to sort out the gems because they're dangerous.' She looked at me intently. 'As I said, I'm busy. I have to go.'

'Fine. Thanks for coming in,' I said begrudgingly.

She nodded curtly and left in a swirl of hot desert air, her way of punishing me, I guessed. The joke was on her because I loved the heat.

And things were about to heat up even more because I was going to follow her snooty ass.

Chapter 28

I dived into the car park. The Suburban was there, as was Sidnee's car. She'd been sharing some lifts around town with Thomas and evidently hadn't been in yet to fetch her car. She always left a spare key on the front tyre so that I could borrow it if I needed to while she was stuck in the office.

I cranked the engine then followed Liv as she drove to the only hotel in town and on to my house. With a car full of witches, she drove off again. Annoyingly, the destination was the one place I was pretty sure *wasn't* holding the black markets: her funeral home.

I needed an inconspicuous spot to park so she wouldn't notice me and I found one on the street, where it looked like I could be in any of three different businesses. As I sat back to wait, I texted Sidnee to let her know I'd borrowed her car to search for the black market.

I had no idea how long the witches' meeting would go on for or what they were discussing other than something to do with the gems. I watched and waited for two bum-numbing hours, during which time Sidnee texted back and confirmed she was more than happy to lend me her car.

I was about to sneak out to see if Ernie had any more chai latte when I saw my mum and the others emerge from the funeral home.

Mum turned to walk back towards home, thank heavens: I didn't need her coming over and noticing me. No doubt she was missing the gym, so she'd get her steps in when she could. The other witches climbed in Liv's car. I'd have to be careful tailing her because she'd be dropping them off first – unless they were all headed to the black market. Could it be that easy?

I waited for her to drive onto the street then pulled out. She headed down the road that went to Kamluck Logging, ten miles out of town. She didn't turn again until we were at South Harbour where the warehouses were. She wasn't dropping the witches off at their hotel, so the chances were good she was taking them to the black market to purchase some of those 'hard to get' items she'd mentioned earlier. I'd probably been close to the market when I last searched here and hadn't got far enough down the line of buildings.

Sure enough, Liv stopped in a busy car park outside the furthest warehouse from town. It was quite small and run down; I'd thought it was abandoned since I'd never seen cars there before. Bingo.

I pulled in next to another plain sedan and got out. Liv and her three witch friends were chatting as they headed for the warehouse.

I really needed a disguise. I thought for a moment then got back into the car. Now I knew where the market was, I could take a minute and put together something that would help me to sneak in. No one would talk to me if they knew I was the law, and I also had to avoid Liv, Laura and anyone else who might recognize me. I needed to hide my hair and maybe wear sunglasses. I was already dressed close to the local norm, but I was wearing a button-up shirt and my nicer boots so I needed to run home and change. I had time: the market wasn't going anywhere.

I raced home a shade over the speed limit, parked up and texted Sidnee to let her know I was still using her car but wouldn't be too much longer. Then I barrelled into my house, to greet my pets. 'I missed you guys,' I said as I cuddled Fluffy and stroked Shadow as much as he would allow.

I could see from the tins on the counter that Mum had already fed them, so I opened the back door and let them out while I got changed. I found a baseball cap and sunglasses, then realised I'd look suspicious wandering into a dark warehouse with those on. Instead, I applied some fake eyelashes and a heavy dose of makeup.

I tied my long blonde hair into a bun and secured the cap then admired the effect: not bad. I put my badge in my pocket, changed into grungy jeans and pulled on my XtraTuf boots. Disguise complete, I was good to go.

'You guys stay here,' I said to my animals as I locked the back door. 'I won't be long but taking you would kind of undo all my disguise work.'

I headed to the front door – and that's when Mum walked in. Everything in me froze. 'Elizabeth? I thought you were at work,' she said.

And I thought you weren't a monster. I didn't say it, though I wanted to. I was on my way out: now was *not* a time to pick a fight with my mother. 'I am. I had to change. I'm going on a stakeout,' I managed.

'That sounds exciting. Can I come?' She looked genuinely excited and I felt conflicted. It was nice that she was taking an interest in my work, but at the same time ... the bus thing.

'You want to go on a stakeout?' I asked slowly.

'It sounds more exciting than watching TV, and we'd get to spend some quality time together.'

I realised that no one would expect Officer Barrington to come in with anyone other than Sidnee or Gunnar; shopping with my mother was actually the perfect cover. Even so, she deserved to know what she was walking in to. 'I'm going to the black market to interview people and try to pinpoint the curser,' I said firmly, looking to see if I'd scared her off.

'Oh. Liv invited me but I declined. The High Priestix can't be seen in such places.'

A wave of relief flowed over me. Good. But she wasn't done. 'Still, I think it will be fun. If anyone finds out, I can tell them that I was helping with a police sting operation.'

I weighed up my options. We could pretend to be shopping and she was good at shopping, plus I needed her because I hadn't got the slightest clue what anything was. I'd probably give myself away in a minute. 'Okay – but Liv and the other witches can't see us or we'll get thrown out. I need to talk to people and no one can know I'm a cop.'

'Of course.'

I eyed her. 'Mum, you can't go dressed like that. You'll stand out like a sore thumb.'

'Well, I don't have anything like *that*.' She gestured disdainfully at my ensemble.

'Did you bring jeans?'

'Of course not.'

I didn't have jeans that would fit her but I had plenty of baggy sweatshirts she could borrow. 'What trousers do you have?' I asked.

'None,' she sniffed.

I had leggings; she'd be horrified, but that was all I had, plus they were stretchy so she'd fit into them. 'It's fine, you can wear my leggings and spare boots.'

'Boots like those?' she pointed at my feet and wrinkled her brow.

'Nope, these are my nice pair.' I smiled wickedly.

She took the leggings and sweatshirt and went to change. When she came out, her face was scrunched up in a rictus of distaste. I handed her Sigrid's old brown boots and she put them on. Her hair was still twisted up in a chignon. That wouldn't do. 'Do you mind if I fix your hair?'

'What's wrong with my hair?'

'It's too nice.'

'Fine,' she grumped. A lot of the excitement had faded now that she realised she had to dress like a commoner.

I pulled out the pins and finger mussed it until it looked like she'd been out in the wind. 'Ow,' she complained.

I wasn't feeling especially charitable. If Connor's supposition was right... *Not now, Bunny.* 'There,' I said gruffly.

'I'll go and look in the mirror.'

'No! Trust me, you don't want to look. Let's go.'

I picked up Arabella and put her in Mum's room, turned on the TV for Fluffy and hurried my mother out of the door.

We were going on a mission – and I didn't trust her as far as I could throw her.

Chapter 29

I drove quickly to the warehouse and found another inconspicuous parking place. 'Remember, we are not going to draw attention to ourselves,' I said. 'If you see anyone you know, hide. Pick up a book or bend down, something subtle like that.'

'Okay, darling.'

Mum's colour was high; she really was finding this exciting. If I hadn't been thinking that she'd quite literally had me shoved under a bus, I might have been too. I'd been itching to have a real look around the black market; the brief glimpse I'd seen before had been tantalising.

There was a handwritten piece of laminated paper taped to the door with an arrow: *Enter around the side*. At least they had signs this time; the organisation had obviously improved. We went to the side door. It was hidden from the road since it was at the end of the warehouse row. No one would see people using the side entrance. Clever.

When we walked up to the door, Mum stopped me before I felt the buzz of magic in my teeth. 'There's a ward around it. Hold on.'

Great. Would we be denied entry because we didn't have a password or a spelled item?

She closed her eyes and muttered for a moment, weaving her hands in the air. After a few seconds she said with satisfaction, 'Got it. Hold my hand and we'll get through.'

I grasped her hand and she pulled me forward. As before, all was silent until the door opened and then the roar of many people in a small space rumbled over us. Mum closed the door. We were in.

I scanned the crowd and saw some familiar faces but no one I knew well. Nobody was looking at me but even so I pulled my cap down a little further.

We started to work our way up and down the rows. The first booth had nothing but packaged herbs. I had no idea what they were for, but Mum exclaimed when she saw something. 'Oh my, how much for this?' she asked the vendor.

The vendor squinted at it. 'Balm of Gilead is forty.'

Mum reached into her pocketbook and pulled out two twenties.

The vendor's hood fell back as he took the money. 'Hey, you look familiar,' I said, trying for casual. 'Do you know Jeff?'

'Not well. Jeff keeps to himself.' The answer was terse and abrupt, not inviting any further conversation.

We walked to the next booth. 'This was incredibly cheap,' Mum said happily. 'It grows in North America, so it's twice as much at home.'

'Good stuff,' I said aloud. *Did you push me into a bus?* I said in my head. It was harder to concentrate than I'd thought it would be and I railed at myself. I had to focus for Fluffy's sake. We needed to find the curser and stop them. If anyone else was cursed, they'd get the remaining alpine azalea and Fluffy would be shit out of luck.

The next few booths were also dead ends but the corner booth was selling grimoires like Jeff's had. Mum started examining the volumes, which gave us an excuse for loitering. 'Hi,' I said to the stallholder. 'I was here the other day looking for a grimoire at Jeff's booth. I wasn't sure about buying it, but now I can't see Jeff anywhere.'

'What was the grimoire?' The vendor looked at me suspiciously.

I quickly accessed my memory. '*The Arrowheads Grimoire*,' I said promptly. 'I think its latest owner was R. Wylor-Owen.'

Mum, who was scanning through a book, slammed it closed. The seller and I both jumped. 'This is a fake grimoire!' she protested loudly, glaring at the man. She wagged her finger at him. 'You shouldn't sell false wares – they could be dangerous to the uninitiated.'

'Keep your voice down, please,' he hissed as he looked around. 'It's not fake. All of my stock has been verified.'

'By whom? An internet witch? Hmph.'

'It's okay, Mum, there's another seller on the other side of the room. We'll check there,' I said, trying to prevent a scene.

'Hold on,' the man said. 'Jeff isn't here, I don't have that particular grimoire, but if you tell me what you're looking for, lady, I'll give you a discount. Just keep your voice down,' he pleaded again with Mum.

'So you do know Jeff?' I asked quietly.

He nodded. 'Of course. We all know each other here and most of us live together. Sometimes we're joined by local sellers, but Jeff is one of us.'

'What happened to him? He was here the other day.'

He lowered his voice further. 'Rumour is that he was cursed.'

'Cursed?' I grasped at my non-existent pearls like I'd seen my mum do many times. 'Is he all right? Who did that to him?'

The guy looked around again. 'I heard that he pissed off a local. Didn't pay the protection fee.'

'Protection?' I asked dumbly. Portlock didn't have gangs or mafia that I knew of.

He shrugged. 'That's what I heard.'

'Gosh,' I said, wide eyed.

Mum had been looking at the books while we spoke. When it was clear he had no more information to offer me, she thrust an old and dusty tome at him. 'We'll take this one.'

The man blanched. 'This is over a thousand years old. I didn't intend for it to be out on the table...' He frowned. 'How did it get there?'

'How much?' Mum insisted. 'Or I can talk louder about that fake grimoire.'

He gulped and looked shifty. He was going to quote something outrageous. 'Ten thousand.'

'And with discount?' She was ruthless.

'Uh, $9,800.' Now he was sweating.

'Do you take Visa?'

He blinked. 'It's cash only.'

'Well, I have cash, but pounds rather than dollars.'

'That's fine,' he said faintly.

'Nine thousand eight hundred dollars is about £7700 pounds sterling, yes?' Mum said briskly. The man nodded again. She pulled out a thick wad of notes and I gaped. Who knew her ugly bag held that much moolah?

The dealer took the money, placed the ancient book in a bag and handed it to her. Mum gave him a curt nod and power-walked away. Once we were out of earshot, she let out an excited squeal that was *definitely* unbecoming in a lady of her station. 'There are only two known copies of this book in the world. I can't believe I bought it for $9800 dollars – it's worth several hundred thousand pounds, maybe even a million. And it was just mouldering away at the bottom of the pile! Unbelievable! I am *so* glad I came with you.'

'I think I got a lead, too. I need to ask a few more vendors to verify it.'

'Go ahead, dear. I'm having so much fun. This has been eye-opening. Perhaps I should visit some black markets in the UK.' I grimaced. I didn't want to have accidentally started my mother on a life of crime.

As we wandered around, I whispered conspiratorially with a few vendors about Jeff not paying protection money. Their reactions verified the story, but no one would say *who* they'd paid money to.

We didn't spot Liv or the other three elemental witches, but by the time we left Mum was laden with packages. I had no names but at least I had *something*: the curser was almost certainly the one running a protection racket. No one knew anything about Stan or Sigrid, and they all thought the racketeer was a local.

I'd narrowed it down to the magic users. Liv would be furious that I was 'picking' on her precious magic users again but it wasn't my fault that they were all dodgier than two-day-old raw chicken left in the sun. I followed where the evidence took me – and the evidence was pointing me towards some naughty shamans or witches.

Chapter 30

I dropped Mum off at home and went back to the office to return Sidnee's car. She looked up expectantly as I walked in. 'What happened?' she asked eagerly. 'Did you find the black market?'

'I did.' I sat down heavily on one of Gunnar's visitor chairs. 'It's at one of the warehouses on South Harbour, just up from AML.' From the outside the warehouse had looked like a wreck but inside it hadn't been so bad. I wondered whether the Grimes brothers had been up to their illusion magic again to make the place look ramshackle.

'I found out that someone is demanding protection money from the vendors. Apparently Jeff didn't pay up. No one identified the person, but they all agreed it was someone local – and it's someone with the power to curse their victims.'

'A magic user,' Sidnee murmured.

'You know what that means?'

She grinned. 'Liv is gonna eat you for lunch if you start interviewing her magic users.'

I blew out a breath. 'Yup. But did you know that she visited Stan and Sigrid in the hospital? She does have a heart somewhere.'

'Buried deep, deep down,' Sidnee snorted. 'Anyway, it's a start, though I honestly have no idea who would run a protection racket in this town. Threatening people here can go very badly for you.'

'I guess that's why they came down so hard on Jeff – you can't let anyone buck the rules. Do you know anyone who has tried this before? Any complaints about people around town demanding protection money?'

She frowned. 'Nothing springs to mind but I can search the database.' Gunnar had a computer at his desk but we didn't have his password. 'Um, when are our new computers coming in?'

'I have no idea. I'll text the boss for his password.'

She smiled. 'Don't bother, it'll be written down on a sticky note in his desk.' She started pulling open drawers.

'While you look, I'm going to call my favourite council member and see about our computers and office furniture. He was sorting it out for us.'

She grinned. 'Buying your love?'

It was terrifying to admit to myself that he didn't need to because he already had it for free. My commitment-phobic thoughts washed in and the urge to dump Connor and run for the hills was strong, but I told it to piss off and took a steadying breath. I was worthy of love, of being loved. I could do this.

I dialled Connor, my heart and mind a maelstrom of emotion. His phone rang for a long time and I nearly hung up before his husky voice filled my ear. 'Bunny,' he answered warmly.

'Hey,' I said happily, my emotions settling in an instant. Something about him grounded me in the very best way.

'I'm down at the docks. Edgy is flying me to Homer – I'm heading to Anchorage to pick up the computers for your office.'

'Oh.' I was sure he could hear the disappointment in my voice.

'I wish we were making the trip together but I know you're busy, and the sooner I get these the quicker you'll be back in business.' He paused. 'I don't want to raise your hopes, but there's a book in Anchorage that might have some answers as to what you are. That's why I'm going myself rather than sending Margrave. This is too sensitive to farm out to anyone else.'

My heart swelled. 'Thank you, Connor. And you're right – we do need those computers and I need to do some research.'

'Exactly. This way, I'll have more time with you.'

'I'll miss you,' I said in a small voice. It was hard to admit but it was undoubtedly true.

'I'll miss you too, doe. I'll make up for it when I'm back home. I've gotta go. Edgy is ready.'

'Okay, be safe.'

'Back at you.'

We hung up. At least I had the answer on the office equipment. Connor had told me that no one would ship electronic items here directly; you had to arrange delivery with a pilot or go yourself. With the book coming into play, Connor had assigned himself the role.

I couldn't suppress the fizz of excitement that ran through me at the thought of finally getting some answers about what I was. He'd told me not to raise my hopes but it was too late: they were already sky high.

Sidnee was clacking away on Gunnar's computer. I popped my head around the door. 'Connor is leaving now to go get us some more computers.'

'Yes!' she said giving a triumphant fist pump. 'Gunnar's computer is so slow it's driving me wild – but I'm determined.' She went back to clacking on the keyboard.

I waited a few minutes, trying to be patient. After another minute I asked, 'Any luck?'

She looked up and gave me a wry look. 'Not yet, Bunny. I barely got into the program.'

'Right, of course. Sorry.' I swung my legs whilst I waited.

She grinned at me. 'You are terrible at being bored.'

I really was. I was rarely bored: I usually had work or I was home doing chores or watching TV, or I was with Connor. I preferred it that way; idle hands do devilish things.

Shadow chose that moment to jump into my lap from out of nowhere. I jumped and earned a firm set of claws in my thighs. 'Ow, you son of a bitch!' I yelped.

He relaxed and started kneading my legs. 'Gently!' I chastised and he retracted his claws. I swept my hand down his silky kitten fur and noticed that he had grown again. I stared at his shadowed coat and wondered yet again what the heck he was. Whatever he was was key to whatever the beast was, and once you knew your enemy you could defeat it. Or bribe it – I'd be totally happy to end the beast's years of terror with a little well-placed bribery. My mother had taught me well.

Fluffy whined at me pointedly and I reached down to rub his ears. 'You're right,' I said to him. 'I'll text Anissa and see if she's ready to help you. The worst thing she can say is that she's busy.'

I started to text: *Anissa, when you have a moment, I'd really like you to take a thorough look at my dog to see about getting the curse taken care of. I do appreciate all you've been doing, but please let me know when you're free. Thanks.*

I watched the phone for a few seconds but there was no response; she must be busy or at work. I patted Fluffy again. 'Maybe we can go talk to John while Sidnee is collecting records on potential racketeers,' I suggested. She was still typing away. 'The rabble and I are heading out to talk to John. Are you good?' I asked her.

She nodded then pursed her lips. 'Maybe leave me Shadow?'

'Sure. He's great company.' And a liability when he was out and about; as his little battle with the beast had shown, he did *not* listen to me.

Shadow obligingly stayed with Sidnee, padding over and lying on the desk so she had to type over the top of him. Typical.

I placed her car keys on the desk in front of her with a muttered thanks and went to the car park to the Suburban. Fluffy jumped in with me. I was halfway to Kamluck, where John was bunking down, when Anissa called me.

'Hi, Bunny, it's Anissa. Sorry for the delay in getting back to you, I was putting the baby down. I'm free for a few moments now if you can bring your dog by. We can look at him while the baby naps.'

'Yes! I'm on the road now. I can be there in five minutes.'

'Perfect. I'll watch for you so please don't knock. If you wake the baby, I'll have to kill you and I'm all out of hiding places.' She sounded like she was only half-joking.

I laughed. 'Sure, of course. I'll be as quiet as a mouse.' I pulled over, waited for a car to pass then did a U-turn. I drove quickly to the old-fashioned, sod-roofed cabin and Fluffy and I walked up to the front door. 'Be as quiet as you can, boy. The baby is asleep and we don't want to enrage Anissa before we get some help.'

He flicked his ear at me to show he'd understood. His body was taut and alert; he was excited – or at least intrigued.

Anissa opened the door of her cottage as we approached and quietly invited us in with a warm smile. 'Is your mother here?' I asked, more to set her at ease than out of any genuine curiosity.

'Yes, but she's having a lie down. She watches the baby for me when I'm at work, so she likes to grab a nap when she can. She's actually my grandmother but she raised me, and I've always called her mother. Please have a seat. I'll get my drum and see what I can see.'

The drum? I blinked. 'Er, won't the drum wake the baby?'

'No – it's what we use to put her to sleep on bad days. She loves the rhythm.'

'Oh.'

Anissa laughed. 'It's part of my shamanic tradition and the baby will probably have the power, too. It often runs in families.' *Like mine did*. I pushed the thought away. Now was not the time to think about my mum and the bus; I was here for Fluffy.

Anissa sat on the floor with her eyes closed to centre herself then she picked up her drum and started beating a rhythm. She was chanting in a language I didn't recognise, and she started to glow slightly. When she called Fluffy, he looked at me and whined a little but then stood in front of her. As she looked him over, the glow extended from her to my dog.

Finally, after at least ten minutes, the drumming stopped. Anissa stood up, replaced the drum in its spot next to the playpen and sat on the couch next to me. She sighed. 'That is one complex curse.'

My heart sank. 'Does that mean it can't be removed?' I buried my hands in Fluffy's fur to reassure him – and myself.

'I really don't know. I'm good with curse breaking but I'm not a world-class expert. It's only one aspect of my work. Honestly? Your best bet would be to find whoever laid the curse.'

I watched Fluffy droop. 'We don't know who did it and even if we did, it was almost certainly done back in London. You said it was old?'

'I'd say a good two or three months. I'll speak to the elders, they might have some ideas.'

'I'd appreciate it.'

'I can tell you one thing, though. The curse involves an element of transformation. Do you know anyone who specialises in that?'

I didn't but Connor knew people – and Liv *definitely* knew people. 'Does anyone in the magic user's group besides you specialise in transformation?'

'Some of the elders do, and I can certainly look into it for you, but it'll take time,' she said apologetically. 'I'm not saying I can't do it, but I'll need to do some research first.'

I tried to keep my disappointment out of my voice as I thanked her. Fluffy seemed dejected as he jumped in the SUV. He immediately lay on the back seat with his head on his crossed paws and stared at the fabric.

I felt bad for him. We'd both had high hopes that Anissa could remove the curse but instead we had more questions. And I had no answers.

Chapter 31

I turned the vehicle back towards Kamluck Logging. Until the cursed vendor, Jeff, came round, I was still waiting on Sidnee's research so I might as well continue with my other task of speaking to John. I'd put him off for days and now it was time.

I didn't want to hear whatever message he was here to deliver, but avoiding it wouldn't make it go away. I wondered if Octavius was going to use threats or bribery and braced myself for both.

I pulled into the main car park by the warehouse. The bunkhouse was back there somewhere; Connor had told me about its existence, though I'd never been there. Fluffy followed me, still visibly moping.

I found what I thought was the right building and knocked. I heard steps approaching and the door opened. 'Bunny!' John said with surprise. I probably should have texted and let him know to expect me.

'Hi. I hope you don't mind me dropping by but I feel bad that I've put you off again and again. I was close by so I decided to stop in.'

'No, it's fine. Come in.' Even as he said it, alarm bells were ringing. John did not look fine – he looked wrecked. His hair was lank and greasy, and he looked exhausted, which is pretty hard for a vampire to do. I'd gone days with hardly any sleep and I still looked fresh-faced and ready to go. Vampirism had some upsides.

'Good to see your dog looking so much better than he did in London,' he commented, looking at Fluffy. 'He was in a complete state.'

I grimaced. When I'd rescued Fluffy from a bin near my house in London, I'd lied to John and told him I'd had my dog for years. Obviously I'd been talking out of my arse: firstly, Fluffy was young, and secondly, he was visibly undernourished. No pet of mine would ever be in that state. John had let the lie go, though he'd obviously not bought it.

He led the way into the barracks and Fluffy and I followed. The building was basic but useable: there was a common area with a kitchen, sofa and TV, and some doors off the corridor led to bedrooms and bathrooms. It wasn't a place you'd want to stay for long, but it was better than nothing. And there were no windows, so it was far safer for a vampire than the Portlock Hotel.

John ushered me into the communal living area. I sat on the sofa and Fluffy sank down at my feet. As John took a seat, he seemed to fold in on himself. I looked at him, alarmed. 'Are you all right, John?' I asked with concern.

He smiled wanly. 'I'm fine.'

He was far from fine. Guilt coiled in my stomach; he'd been trying to see me for days. 'I know I've been putting you off and I haven't been a good friend, but I'll never forget what you did for me. You helped me when no one else would. Whatever you need, I'm here for you.'

That seemed to flick a switch in him. He leaned forward, put his head in his hands and started to cry.

Crap. I was so not the person for this: I was terrible with *my* emotions, let alone someone else's. I walked over, perched on the arm of his chair and rubbed his back. 'Let it out,' I murmured.

He shoulders shook; whatever was wrong, it was breaking his heart. It was several minutes before he brushed the tears from his cheeks. 'My wife died,' he said dully.

'Oh God, John. I'm so, so, sorry. Was it sudden?'

'Sudden, but not wholly unexpected, I guess,' he said. 'She'd been ill for a long while. Gwen was human. She had cancer so they couldn't turn her, but as long as I obeyed the king he kept her in cutting-edge trials and programs. She didn't have much of a chance and it killed her to see her illness being used to make me do things I wouldn't ever do otherwise. Horrible things. I think I'd reached my limit when I met you. I needed to know I wasn't a monster, even though I felt like one. Saving you was saving me, too.'

I squeezed his arm but didn't interrupt. He was silent for a moment before he continued. 'Gwen could see that it was killing me too, I guess. I loved her enough to do heinous things to keep her alive, and she loved me enough to do a heinous thing to stop living.' His voice caught. 'Yesterday she took her own life to free me from Octavius. Now I have no reason to go back.'

'God, John, I'm so sorry.' I had nothing but the empty platitude to offer. I tried to imagine it, tried to imagine doing dark things to keep Connor alive. I'd do them, I realised, like John had.

He looked at me with haunted eyes. 'I didn't get to say goodbye. I wasn't by her side, and I'll never be by her side again. And if I go back for her funeral, Octavius will get his claws into me. What do I do?'

I bit my lip. Gunnar could do some paperwork like he had for me and get John transferred to Portlock. Connor would take him in, no questions asked. Maybe Connor or Gunnar knew someone in London who could pull strings to get Gwen's body here for burial. I didn't want to make any promises, though. 'Leave it with me. Maybe I can help.'

John nodded but his eyes were still dull and lost. Abruptly they fixed on me. 'I don't know what's best,' he said finally, somewhat cryptically.

'Best for what?'

'For you,' he admitted. 'I was sent here with instructions from Octavius to tell you something. I verified it and it's true, but telling you ... it's cruel.'

Fuck, that sounded ominous. Did I want to know whatever truth Octavius had sent John with? After all, ignorance was supposed to be bliss. I weighed it up. The problem was that I was curious – and although curiosity killed the cat, it might make the bunny stronger. 'Tell me,' I said finally. 'If it's true, then tell me.'

John studied me before nodding. 'You know Franklin was paid 50,000 pounds to turn you?' he said.

I knew that because Franklin himself had told me. I was suddenly sure that the secret Octavius had sent with John was the truth about who had instructed Franklin. Suddenly, I wasn't so sure I wanted to know; did I really want to solve the case of my death?

John looked away and shook his head. 'This is hard.'

My blood ran cold. 'Tell me,' I whispered. I had to know the truth even if it broke me.

He stared at me for a moment, opened his mouth and slayed me all over again. 'I'm sorry. I double-checked. The money ... it came from your parents' bank account.'

Chapter 32

Fluffy was barking wildly but I barely registered his agitation. *My parents.* My mother, who was currently pottering around my house, who I was pretty sure had shoved me under a bus. My mother, with her worthless ped daughter. Well, I wasn't ped now, was I? Finally, they could be open about magic with me. They'd wanted me to stay in London in Octavius's conclave for a hundred years and instead I'd run all the way to Portlock.

I gave a dark smile. I was their useless ped daughter and yet somehow I'd still managed to fuck up their sick plans. It gave me a sense of grim satisfaction.

'Bunny?' John said softly, looking concerned.

Ah – I was smiling. That probably wasn't a normal reaction to being told your parents had paid someone to attack and kill you. 'I'm okay,' I said evenly. I wasn't, but John had enough shit on his plate without me adding to it.

If anything, he now looked even more distressed. 'I struggled with telling you, and I'm still not sure if it was the right thing to do. The fact that Octavius wanted me to tell you should have been reason enough to keep quiet, but if I were in your shoes I'd want to know.'

'You did the right thing,' I reassured him. 'I needed to know and I'm going to handle it. The truth always comes out. Thanks for telling me – I really do appreciate it. I should go, leave you to your grief.' And me to mine.

I stood up. 'I'll speak to Connor about getting you a job and a visa or whatever we need to keep you here. Don't worry on that score. I won't let Gwen's sacrifice be for nothing. Octavius doesn't get to keep you.'

He pulled me in for a hug. 'Thank you,' he murmured.

'I've got you,' I promised, patting his back.

He showed me to the door and I kept my composure, even managing a jaunty wave as I walked to the SUV. He wouldn't buy it, of course, but mother had taught me to care about appearances. One shouldn't bawl in public.

Fluffy and I jumped in the SUV. He kept looking at me as if I was about to explode and he wasn't far off the mark. The punch of knowing that my parents had paid money to sacrifice me, the despair that they had never truly loved me, and the rage that they had made such a huge decision for me, boiled inside. The fire I carried within me was reacting to the maelstrom of emotion and I was sweating with trying to contain it.

I drove out of Kamluck and headed straight to the water. I'd have to let the fire go and I couldn't do that in a heavily forested area. I drove erratically, barely conscious of the road. Finally I stopped the car, jumped out, slid down the embankment and ran onto the beach, Fluffy by my heels.

I had the presence of mind enough to check for witnesses or boats but, seeing no one, I pulled the fire from my chest and let it go with a guttural scream. The fireball that launched out of me looked like a nuclear flash but it totally emptied the rage from my body. Emptied *me* completely.

I stood with my hands on my knees, panting. No wonder I demanded that people call me Bunny; on some level I had known that my parents were keeping something from me. They didn't have my trust or love any more than I had theirs, which was why I'd rejected the name they'd given me. They hadn't deserved to carve their mark on me, and that was why I clung to the name my nana had given me. *She* had loved me, of that I was sure.

My parents had ordered me to be turned into a vampire without my knowledge or consent. It would take a long while for me to absorb that.

My phone rang. I pulled it out of my pocket and saw that Connor had rung repeatedly; in my daze, I hadn't even registered its blare. I answered the call.

'What's wrong?' he asked instantly.

'Did our bond tell you something was wrong?' I asked curiously, instead of answering. I felt strangely numb.

'It feels like I can hear someone scratching nails on a chalkboard. Talk to me, honey.'

'My parents were the ones who paid Franklin to turn me,' I said dully.

'Are you sure?' he asked tightly.

'John followed the money trail. I need you.'

'I'm on my way back, doe. I'm hurrying but I'm a few hours' drive out of Anchorage, then I need to fly to Homer and then back home. I'll be there as soon as I can but it won't be soon. Even so, you don't have to confront your mom alone. Wait for me,' he urged.

'I appreciate the thought, but I do. I need to do this by myself because otherwise it'll break me.'

'It won't,' he said fiercely. 'You are so strong, Bunny, stronger than you know.'

'The book,' I said suddenly. 'Did it tell you who I am?'

'I don't need a book to tell me who you are,' he said. 'I know you.'

'Not *who*, then, but *what*.'

He hesitated. 'I have some information. Let's talk when I'm home, okay?'

I accepted that; besides, I'd probably had enough answers for one day. 'Hurry,' I said softly. I hung up, then I sank to my knees and cried.

Chapter 33

I pulled into my driveway and sat frozen for a moment. I wasn't ready for what was coming but I couldn't avoid it any longer. I climbed out of the car, Fluffy following anxiously. I could feel his concern like it was my own.

It was nearly morning and Mum was up, sitting at the kitchen table drinking a cup of tea and eating a piece of toast. She looked at me as I came in and gave me a warm smile. It stabbed me; she had never before looked at me with such warmth. Somehow by coming here, living with me, capering in black markets together, she'd finally connected with me. Now that I wasn't ped, I guessed.

My face must have shown the mess of my emotions because she stood up, alarmed. 'What's wrong, Elizabeth?' she asked. Fluffy moved in between us and growled loudly. 'Stop that, you brute,' she grumped at him.

That was it. Connor called Fluffy 'Brute' with affection, but I wouldn't stand for my dog to be mocked or belittled, not after all he'd been through. Not when he was protecting me. 'No. *You* stop it, Victoria,' I snarled.

She stepped back as if I'd slapped her. I'd always been respectful to her, despite all her put downs and pushiness.

'I know,' I spat. 'I know what you did to me. You'd better tell me why or you are leaving Portlock and I'll *never* talk to you again.'

She sat down hard. She didn't ask what I knew; she read the rage in my face and connected the dots. To her credit, neither did she try to deny it. 'I can understand why you're distressed,' she said. 'But he did it to *help* you, darling.'

'Help *kill* me, you mean?' My voice was ice. Then I realised what she'd said: not *I* or *we*, but he.

Mum looked horrified. 'No! He was trying to help you! And the business,' she conceded weakly.

The business. Dad? *Dad* had done this to me? But with or without Mum's knowledge? 'Did you know?' I demanded. 'Did you know what he'd planned for me?'

'No! I swear I didn't know. You saw how shocked I was that day!'

I replayed the memory.

'Those marks on your neck, are they ... love bites?' she asked, horrified. The truth was going to horrify her more.

My hand leapt up to my throat, covering the two tell-tale pricks in my neck. 'No!'

She stood up and reached out to pull my hand and the jacket collar away, displaying the bite in all its vampiric glory.

'Is that...?' She trailed off looking shocked and dismayed, then shook her head. 'No, that's silly. They wouldn't dare...'

I looked at her, seeing the fear in her eyes. There was no point trying to hide it. Her long association with Dad's business meant that she knew what it was as surely as I did, for all she was practising denial right now. It wasn't a river in Egypt.

I decided to say it quickly, like ripping off a plaster. 'I've been bitten, Mum. I'm a vampire.'

She clutched her pearl necklace and sat down heavily on the sofa. 'No,' she whispered.

'You were shocked,' I conceded slowly. Something in me eased and I sat down. 'You didn't know.'

'I swear I didn't!' she repeated desperately. 'After I saw the marks, I went straight to talk to Cyril, to demand that Octavius find whoever had done this to you and punish them.'

'But Dad wasn't shocked,' I said faintly.

'No,' she agreed grimly. 'He wasn't.'

Mum may not have been responsible for turning me into a vampire, but she wasn't without her sins. 'And what about the lion and the bus?' I asked tightly. 'You were trying to make my magic come out, weren't you?'

Her eyes filled with tears. 'It was common practice in the magic-users' community. Most kids only needed a little scare. I was *sure* you had magic and I kept thinking that if I scared you a little more...'

She covered her mouth and gave a sob. 'Your nana told me to stop – she said I'd get you killed. She had me taken to a doctor. I'd been suffering with undiagnosed post-natal depression and never connected properly with you. I've been in counselling ever since, and I'm medicated too. That's not an excuse for my behaviour but an explanation. I swear it was normal amongst witching families to bring magic out like that. I wanted magic in your life for you.' Her voice was full of tears. 'I'm sorry. I'm so sorry.'

She shook her head. 'I know there's nothing I can do or say to undo it, but Elizabeth – Bunny – I am so damned sorry. It will haunt me for the rest of my life.'

'I don't know if I can ever forgive you,' I admitted in a small voice.

She flinched. 'I understand. Her voice wavered. 'But I swear I didn't have anything to do with you being turned.'

I nodded. 'I believe you. Tell me what Cyril said when you spoke to him.'

'Your dad and I have worked hard our whole lives, not for ourselves but for you. We wanted you to have everything you ever wanted. For me, that was for you to have access to your witch power, for your Dad it was his business.'

I gave an unladylike snort.

'You should have been the most powerful fire elemental witch in centuries,' my mother went on, 'so I was shocked when at age five you'd never even showed a spark of power. When we had you examined we were told you were a fire elemental, but nothing happened. I resigned myself to you being pedestrian, but your father ... I don't think he ever accepted it.'

'He couldn't make me a witch so he made me a vampire instead.'

She looked lost. 'I didn't know until afterwards. Dad thought that you being in the conclave would give you the things that we couldn't – immortality, for one. You'd be in an amazing position to take over the company when we retired because you'd already have a relationship with the king. And I think he hoped the attack might trigger your powers, even if it meant you couldn't then be turned.'

I frowned. 'What do you mean – couldn't be turned?'

'Witches can't be turned into vampires because the two magics aren't compatible. A witch attacked by a vampire inevitably heals or dies. They don't turn.'

Except that I had. I didn't say that to Mum, though, because I didn't think she deserved to know the truth. Not now, maybe not ever. 'Dad wanted to give me to the king?' I scoffed. 'Octavius only wanted to control me, to use me. He's a freaking psychopath.'

She shook her head. 'At the time, your father thought the king had your best interests at heart. He and Dad had a great relationship. I know Octavius has a harsh reputation, but he had never been less than generous to our family.'

'You don't know the truth,' I said grimly. 'He's playing you both. He gave me to his son to be some kind of slave. The king was going to use me against you!'

She shook her head stubbornly. 'No, darling, don't be absurd. Your father was trying to help you. You'd left home and you were struggling so much. Then you started waitressing! You had a university education, powerful witch parents – and a dead-end job. You were wasting your life. Dad wanted you to fulfil your potential.'

'It was my life to waste!' I protested. 'As for fulfilling my potential? I was *trying*! I had zero skills and the most worthless degree ever, but I had plans! I needed time. I'm only twenty-three! And now I'll be that forever, thanks to Dad!' I was shouting. I rarely yelled: usually I ignored a lot of things and did my own thing quietly, but now I was done with being diplomatic.

'I know, I'm sorry. After I saw the...' she gestured to my neck, 'I spoke to you father. He realised it had been a mistake, but it was too late. Octavius tried to strongarm your dad using you as leverage, which was why we couldn't help you escape. Octavius said he could have you killed and remain within the law if he did.'

I shook my head. Mum clutched my hand, forcing me to look at her as she continued. 'If you want the truth then you need it all. There was a prophecy about you, which was why I tried so hard for all those years to raise your magic. The prophecy told me you had magic. I knew you had to have it to survive what was coming.'

I snorted. 'I don't believe in prophecies.' Though my connection with Connor had forced me to accept that fated mates were a real thing. And if fated mates were real, was the idea of a prophecy so far-fetched?

'Believe in them or not, official prophecies are recorded with the coven. This was made when you were born – you can check the records.'

'Fine.' I folded my arms. 'I'll bite. What did it say?'

She licked her lips. 'It said: *When the flame-born guardian descends to the night, the veiled city's mysteries will unfold. Thrice shall the cursed wolf's mournful howl sound, heralding the coming of the shadow beast. Love shall be her beacon and with its power, the city might endure the destruction that comes.*'

The veiled city probably referred to Portlock – though it was definitely a *town* not a city – and the shadow beast almost certainly referred to the beast beyond the barrier. I blew out a harsh breath. Okay, maybe I *could* believe in prophecy, in which case 'the destruction that comes' didn't sound all that good.

'Your father became convinced that "descending to the night" meant you became a vampire. When it didn't happen naturally, he engineered it.'

I shook my head at his sheer audacity. 'And he gave a shit about Portlock because…?'

My mother gave an unladylike snort. 'He doesn't care at all about Portlock, but he did want his daughter to be a "flame-born guardian" with power enough to protect a whole city.'

'And you? What did you think of the prophecy?'

She hesitated and looked at Fluffy. 'Once you became a vampire, I worried that your dad had forced the prophecy on you. I returned to your flat later on that day to see a bloody werewolf prowling around outside and I *knew* it was there for you. Something told me that the werewolf was important. And I knew the prophecy – I knew you needed a cursed wolf by your side. I carry a safety curse on me, a shamanic one designed to downgrade any threat. So a cursed vampire might become a mosquito, and a cursed werewolf...'

'Might become a dog,' I whispered, my eyes wide as I stared at Fluffy. He gave a bark. I swallowed hard. 'You're the one that cursed Fluffy. You turned him into a "cursed wolf".'

She folded her hands primly on her lap. 'I did.'

Outrage roared through me. 'And you put him in a *bin*!'

She sighed. 'You collect strays, Bunny, you always have. Yes, I locked him in the bin, but I knew you'd rescue him.' She spoke patiently, like she was talking to a slow child.

'How?' I demanded. 'How could you possibly have known that?'

She raised an eyebrow. 'When I visited your flat that day, your waste bins were overflowing. I knew it wouldn't be long before you put the rubbish out, found him and took him under your wing. If your father wasn't above a little manipulation to make your prophecy come true, then I decided I could do the same.'

I felt sick. She'd risked Fluffy's life on my cleanliness? We were lucky he hadn't died. 'He was so thin, Mum.'

She grimaced. 'As I said, the curse downgrades the threat. Big strong werewolf, little thin dog.'

'Fluffy is a werewolf.' I shook my head in disbelief. It was too much; all of it was too much. Still, if Mum had made the curse then she could undo it, like Anissa had said.

'Undo the curse,' I ordered.

Mum blinked. 'It's not that simple. It's not *my* curse, it's a shamanic one – one I bought from a market.'

Fluffy leaned hard against me and I finally realised that all along he'd been telling me not to trust my mother. He had growled at her from the moment he'd first seen her; his dislike had nothing to do with her irritating Pomeranian but the fact that she had cursed him.

I couldn't look at her. 'I need time to process all of this.'

'Bunny—' she started.

Hearing my name on her lips somehow made me angrier. 'I need to go to work,' I snapped. 'Don't be here when I come home.'

I stormed out and I didn't look back.

Chapter 34

I took the Suburban back to work. Work was my salvation; I needed to keep busy until Connor was home, then I could fall apart with him.

I walked into the office and sat heavily in Gunnar's spare chair. Sidnee was still on the computer, leaning forward, her chin on one hand and typing with the other hand. She didn't look at me as she shoved a sheaf of papers towards me. 'These are the people who've been known to hustle others. It's been slow going but we're getting there!'

When I didn't take it or say anything, she looked up at me. Then, in an alarmed voice, she demanded, 'What's wrong? Is it Sig?'

I shook my head and sighed. 'No, she's fine as far as I know. It's my mother.'

'What's wrong? Is she cursed too?'

'Ha. I wish,' I said drily. But I didn't, not really. After everything she'd done to me, I still couldn't bring myself to wish her harm. I was the most pathetic vampire on earth.

'What happened? Bunny?'

I rubbed a hand across my face. 'My father was the one that paid the vamps to turn me. And Mum deliberately caused accidents that hurt me during my childhood to awaken my magic. Oh, and she's the one who cursed Fluffy. Can I come stay with you until Connor gets back?'

'Oh my God, Bunny. That's a lot for you to deal with, hon. Of course you can stay with me. Any time, you know that.' Her eyes looked a little wild; I think I'd shocked her.

'Thanks. I did tell her to get out of my house, but I don't want to be there right now.'

'She can stay in the hotel,' Sidnee agreed. 'And you can stay with me as long as you need.'

'It probably won't be long. Connor should be back soon. I don't want to be alone.'

Fluffy whined and I stroked his head. 'I know I'm not really alone when I have you,' I said to him. 'But it's not quite the same. In this form, you can't talk to me, you know?'

Sidnee watched, eyes wide. 'So what did she curse Fluffy with?'

'Oh, apparently he's a werewolf. Mum transformed him into a "lesser threat", which was a skinny, underfed German Shepherd.'

She shook her head as she took it in. 'Fluffy's a werewolf? Under all that fur is a human trapped in dog form?'

I nodded. 'Yeah.'

'That's awful.' Sidnee looked horrified and I couldn't blame her; I was horrified too. She turned to Fluffy, 'I'm so sorry, dude – whoever you are.'

'I honestly can't get my head around it all. Do you want to take a break? You've already been here for hours and your shift has barely started. Wanna grab some food then go see Sigrid and Stan together? I need to do something.'

'Yeah, let's do that,' she said too quickly. She was worried about me. 'It's been slow. I'll put up the sign and see if April wants some extra hours. Hold on.'

She texted April then finished what she was doing on the computer. We left Fluffy and Shadow to man the fort, mostly because the Garden of Eat'n didn't love it when you brought in your pets. Also, I wasn't sure how I felt about Fluffy. He wasn't a smart, loyal dog – he was a werewolf, cursed by my mother. It was a wonder he'd shown me such compassion over the last few months. Now I didn't quite know where I stood and I needed space.

I shot him an apologetic look as we locked the brand-new front door and put up the 'gone to lunch' sign. Just before we walked out, Sidnee checked her phone then looked relieved. 'April texted that she can come in at ten. I'll work until then and turn it over to her.'

'Great.'

We headed to the diner and sat in our usual booth. After we'd eaten, we went to the hospital. The patients both still needed lots of potions daily to help them regain their strength and heal their cursed bodies.

When we checked in to see Stan, he was dozing. His colour was up and he looked a lot more solid. Jeff was in the room next to him looking like skin and bones and not much else. It felt like the Grim Reaper was loitering in the corner of his room and I could see why Anissa had said it was touch and go if he would live.

I was desperate to see Sigrid; I hoped she was on the way to recovery like Stan, but she was no shifter.

She looked washed out but at least she was sitting upright. 'Bunny, Sidnee!' She greeted us with a huge smile. 'My gorgeous girls.' She was super thin and gaunt, but she was on the mend and we had to focus on the positives.

Sidnee rushed to her and gave her a gentle hug, and Sigrid squeezed her back. Gunnar was relaxing in an easy chair next to the bed.

'How are you feeling?' I asked Sigrid.

'Much better, thanks, Bunny. They might release me early,' she said eagerly.

'That's great news!'

'She's weak as a kitten,' Gunnar rumbled.

'Oh, nonsense,' Sigrid protested.

'They have her and Stan up and walking and doing PT several times a day. She can barely make it down the hall,' he continued. 'Stan's zonked after his session. She's not much better.'

'I'll be better at home,' she said. Gunnar threw up his hands.

'You need to go back to work,' Sig said to him, which was a different tune from the one she'd been singing when *he'd* been ill; then she'd insisted he rest or stay home. She widened her eyes and jerked her head at her husband.

I grinned then turned to my boss. 'I'm rather stalled on the investigation into who cursed them. We could use another set of eyes. Sidnee's put together a list of people who've attempted to run a protection racket, but there are quite a few names. We could check through them together.' I was hoping to engage him and get him out of the hospital for Sigrid's sake.

'I can do that. I'll come in tomorrow.' Gunnar sounded eager; he must have been missing work as much as we missed him. We'd be back to three people in one office, but hopefully Connor would be back later today or early tomorrow with the computers. We could bring in some folding tables to work on; hell, I'd have worked on the floor at that point.

I got my own cuddle with Sigrid but, as always, she saw too much. 'Everything okay?' she whispered.

I smiled. 'Everything will be fine.'

'That's not the same thing.'

'No,' I agreed blandly. 'It's not.'

She fixed me with a firm look. 'You talk to me or Gunnar when you're ready.'

I nodded. We talked for a few more minutes but it was obvious that Sigrid was wracked by exhaustion, so we soon made our excuses and left.

Sidnee set me up in her house then went back to work. I took my list of racketeers and started making appointments to see them during my next shift; it wasn't the most exciting part of police work but it might help me to find the curser.

I wished I'd bought my fire elemental tome with me because it would have been the perfect time to look through it. I watched TV for a bit, then finally crawled into Sidnee's spare bed and fell into a restless sleep a couple of hours later. Before my eyelids closed, I wished I had Fluffy with me.

Chapter 35

I was awoken rudely by the ringing of my phone. I stared at the screen blearily: Liv. I swiped to answer, still yawning. 'Your mother isn't answering her phone. I need her to meet us at the first gem site,' she said without preamble.

Liv's wasn't the voice I wanted to hear when I woke up, but I got it. Mum must have either crashed hard after our fight or had turned off her phone. 'I'll find her,' I promised grimly. After all, the gems were the *real* reason she'd come to Portlock. 'When and where?'

Liv had changed the rota of elemental witches who were in charge of the gems and was keeping them warded. Although I'd known all of the previous gem custodians, I didn't know the newly appointed ones.

'Water. Dakota Caples, 666 Nordic Ave.'

'Six-six-six? Really?'

She huffed. 'Really. Then we'll go to the fire gem. I need your mother in two hours.' She hung up.

I sat up in bed. I didn't want to talk to my mother but at least the phone was a good buffer. I dialled her number and let it ring. Nothing. For fuck's sake. I Googled the Portlock Hotel's number and rang it. It was the only hotel in town so if Mum had actually left after I'd chucked her out of my house, that's where she would be.

When the phone was answered, I asked to be put through to her. There was a bemused silence before they confirmed that they didn't have a Victoria Barrington staying with them. Concern wormed its way into my heart; I was a soft idiot.

I hung up and threw off the covers, then dressed and marched the short distance to my house. She'd better damn well be there.

She wasn't. One of her fancy bags sat on my porch but there was no sign of the woman herself. Instead, a note was flapping on my door in the gentle breeze – and I could smell blood. The note said: *Bring all four barrier gems to the following location.* That was followed by a string of numbers that had to be GPS coordinates. *You have 24 hours, or your mom gets it.*

As I ripped off the note, the rhythm of my thudding heartbeat was almost human. I twisted the door knob. Locked. I unlocked it and peered inside. The house was quiet. I raced through it but there was no sign of Mum – and no Arabella.

After I'd searched the whole place, I returned to the porch and opened Mum's bag to search for clues. As I unzipped it, Arabella's fear-filled eyes met mine; her mouth was duct taped shut. 'Hey now,' I greeted my nemesis softly. 'It's okay. Let's get you out of there.'

Apparently the kidnappers hadn't been in the market for a yapping dog. I removed the tape as gently as I could but even so she whimpered and trembled as I apologised profusely. I looked through mum's bag; she'd only packed a few things so she'd obviously expected to be invited back to mine fairly quickly, but she *had* been moving out like I'd asked.

And someone had snatched her right off my damned porch.

Chapter 36

I wanted to scream or cry, to do *something*, but I stood frozen with the bloody note in one hand and a terrified Pomeranian in the other.

When I set Arabella down, she raced into Mum's room and went directly under the bed. I didn't blame her. I pulled out my phone. I needed all hands on deck, but first I had to tell Liv that Mum wasn't going to make her party.

She answered with an impatient, 'What?'

'Liv, my mum's been kidnapped.' I figured I'd be blunt; she understood blunt.

She was quiet for a moment. I think I'd actually managed to shock her. 'Oh.'

I was equally shocked when she asked, 'What can I do to help?' Normally Liv's 'help' came with snark, reluctance and a bill.

'I don't know,' I said. 'But the kidnapper demanded I take all four gems to a specific location.'

'If you do that, the barrier will go down.'

'I'm aware,' I said drily. 'Any ideas?'

'I'll think about it.' Click.

I loved her goodbyes. I called Gunnar and Sidnee next and they said they'd pull together a search party while I came up with a plan. I checked the time and saw I had a text from Connor. I could breathe again.

Just landed. Floating into North Harbour. Finally North Harbour was bringing me something good. I sprinted out of my house to meet him; I needed Connor like I needed air, and I doubly needed his solid presence to get me through this.

He was helping Edgy unload when I flew down the ramp. He looked up, his smile like sunshine that warmed every part of me. He put down the box he was holding in time to catch me as I launched myself into his arms. 'Hey, doe,' he said before wrapping his arms around me.

'Connor, someone kidnapped Mum.' The tears began. Part of me was shocked at how I felt; after all she'd done to me, I shouldn't have cared that she was in danger. She was a *stranger* in a lot of ways; she'd hurt me many times through the years and she'd even cursed Fluffy. I should hate her, but at the end of the day she was still my mum.

He clutched me tighter. 'We'll find her, don't worry.'

His words calmed me immediately. I knew Connor wouldn't stop until he'd fulfilled his promise. I clung to him for a minute more, then it was down to business.

We carried the boxes for the Nomo's office and put them in Margrave's idling truck. Connor hadn't just brought back computers but also two desk chairs. Desks were being made in town with some lumber he'd donated; in the meantime, someone from the mayor's office was bringing in folding tables and chairs for the tiny 'lobby'.

Connor took me to the office. Sidnee was already in, Fluffy was gambolling around her heels and Shadow was giving a lazy stretch. Sidnee had only left for the office when she'd received my panicked call, and considering she was pulling back-to-back shifts, she was looking great. Better than me: I hadn't showered or combed my hair. I must have looked like a madwoman flying down the dock at Connor but I'd had more pressing concerns.

'Bunny, how are you holding up?' my friend asked anxiously.

'I'm all right,' I lied. 'Thanks for helping.'

'Gunnar has started calling people to help search, and I'm making a list of possible suspects – mainly barrier protestors and the old gem witches. Someone wants our barrier down.'

I nodded, suddenly exhausted. The constant fear about the barrier, my mum and her revelations, and the problems with the gems was wearing me out. I'd solved who'd stolen the gems a week earlier but the problem was still going on. There had to be another way forward that meant we weren't dependent on those cursed things. Curses here, curses there, curses everywhere.

I sat down heavily on the floor – and suddenly I couldn't get up. Fluffy barked loudly, and Connor and Sidnee were looming over me. 'What's going on?' I asked. 'Why can't I move?' But then I couldn't talk.

Connor snatched me up and ran through the front door. That was the last thing I remembered.

Chapter 37

I woke up to see Anissa's face leaning over me. I gasped and tried to move back, but I was lying on a bed and couldn't go anywhere. 'Drink this, Bunny.'

She was holding blood in a hospital cup with a straw. Well, that would be a new experience. I tried to push it away.

'Drink it, Bunny, dammit,' Connor growled from my other side. I turned my head and he was standing over me as well. I realised it wasn't anger that had sharpened his tone but fear, and that scared me enough to drink.

I drank the blood fast even though I couldn't hold my nose – and there was no point when you were drinking through a straw. I finished it with a grimace. 'What happened?' I asked. My head felt muddled and hazy.

'You were cursed,' Anissa said grimly.

'Was it the same curse?' I looked down at my limbs but it didn't appear that I had started wasting away. 'How long have I been here?' My voice cracked.

'An hour,' Connor answered.

Relief filled me. I hadn't let my mum down; I still had time to find her.

'Not the same curse,' Anissa confirmed. 'It seems to be a curse to send you to sleep, sap your energy.'

That's how I'd felt: sapped, limp, wrung out. I'd experienced true weariness since I'd been turned – daylight exhaustion was a real thing – but this tiredness was far greater.

'It has to be the kidnapper. They don't want you on their case,' Connor snarled.

'Why give me an ultimatum that I can't follow?' I asked, confused.

'Did you touch anything, or eat or drink anything new or strange?' Anissa asked.

'No, nothing. I—' That bloody note. 'I touched the note that was on my door,' I groaned. 'It's in my jeans' pocket.' I hadn't worn gloves, a rookie error.

Anissa retrieved a plastic bag full of my clothes from next to the bed then pulled out my jeans and waved a hand over the pockets. 'This is the source.' Her hand blazed brightly for a moment and I felt pressure in my ears. 'Not a strong curse, but effective. I've neutralized it.'

'Thanks, Anissa,' I said. Connor's statement about the kidnapper had started my brain racing. 'If mum's kidnapper is cursing me, that probably means the kidnapper and the curser are the same person – or two people working together,' I mumbled. I scooched back in the bed and sat up. 'I have to get out there. Time is ticking.'

'No,' Connor said firmly. 'You need to stay here until Anissa clears you.'

I looked at Anissa. 'Am I curse free?'

She nodded. 'But you're going to need more blood and some rest or you'll be in here a lot longer than a few hours.'

'Hours?'

'Hours to heal up is better than days, so lie back and relax. I'll bring you more blood in thirty minutes.'

I felt the first stirring of panic. Mum had less than twenty-four hours and I had to find her. Connor, brilliant as always at reading me, said, 'Gunnar has a search party out. They're looking everywhere – homes, businesses, the woods. They'll find her.'

'If it's the curser, we'll never find her. We don't have any clue who it is!' I protested.

'Sidnee has a list of possible suspects. Whoever this is, they made a mistake when they asked for the gems. She and Gunnar have narrowed down our list to people who are against the barrier.'

I shook my head and started to swing my legs over the edge. 'No, no! This is like before! Because it seems to be about the barrier, doesn't mean it is. The gems are valuable and powerful, and they're also possessed and evil. Check the new gem witches first. Maybe they're being possessed like Wintersteen was.'

Connor picked up my legs and swung them back into the bed, then whipped out his phone and texted someone. He waited a second until his phone vibrated with a return message. 'Sidnee is on it and Thomas is helping.'

That calmed me a little; Sidnee would do anything to help my mum because she was my mum, but Thomas was a true hunter. If anyone could track her down, my money was on him. 'Okay, thanks.' I looked around. 'Where's Fluffy?'

'Sidnee has him and Shadow at the Nomo's office.'

'I talked to Mum,' I blurted out. 'She told me everything. You were right about the bus.'

Connor's jaw worked but he held his silence as I continued. 'My dad ordered me to be turned into a vampire, and my mum cursed Fluffy.' I turned to Anissa. 'She said it was a transformation curse to change a threat into a lesser one. She said it would turn a bloodsucking vampire into a mosquito, or a werewolf into a dog.'

I continued. 'She can't undo it. She said she's not a curse breaker, nor was she its maker. If she can get the spell from the person that designed the curse, do you think you could break it?' I asked Anissa. My heart was in my throat.

She cocked her head as she thought about it. 'If we have the original spell, or better still the curse-breaking spell from the person who designed the curse, there's a good chance I can end this.'

I closed my eyes: a good chance was better than the chance Fluffy had now. Even if I lost my dog because he turned back into a werewolf, I couldn't leave him stuck in that form forever. My poor boy. He'd made the best of everything and loved me even when he should have hated me. I'd love him forever for that one fact. 'Thank you, Anissa. It might be his only chance.'

'I'll give it a go. Now, I'll be back soon to give you more blood. Rest. I don't want you out of that bed. If you have to pee, you call me. Got it?'

'Yes. Thanks.'

Anissa walked out and I turned to Connor. 'There's more. Dad paid Octavius to get me turned, then Octavius made sure my parents wouldn't help me leave London.'

Connor grimaced. 'I think I know why.'

'Why?'

'That book I told you I went for? It was old and it had some details about vampires that have been forbidden for a few centuries.'

'Why are they forbidden?' I asked curiously.

'Jealousy, I think. These vampires don't need blood to survive; they don't have to battle with bloodlust. And,' he paused, 'they all have magic.'

I swallowed hard. I didn't have bloodlust and I had magic. 'What am I?' I asked Connor.

'I think you're a hybrid.'

Perfect: I was some sort of forbidden vampire. 'You think Octavius knew I'd be a hybrid?'

'Without a shadow of a doubt,' he said grimly. 'A hybrid is created when a magic user is turned, and you come from a long line of fire witches. He *had* to have known.'

'I thought that turning a witch wasn't possible.'

'That's what people believe. Even I thought it was true until I found this book.'

'I don't understand why hybrids are forbidden.' I frowned. 'Just because they don't need blood in the same way? And if I don't need blood in the same way, why am I in hospital being fed blood?'

'Blood will still help you, but you *can* get sustenance other ways.'

'Through food?' I said hopefully.

He shook his head. 'Through auras. You can feed off other people's energy.'

'Like some sort of succubus?'

'Kind of, but without the need for sex. You can feed off anyone's energy.'

'How?'

He shrugged. 'The book wasn't clear on that.'

'So again – tell me why I'm in hospital getting filled with blood?'

'Because we can't afford for anyone to realise that you're a hybrid.'

'Why? Why are they so dangerous?'

'According to the book I found, the magic and the vampirism combine. You remember I said that older vampires get extra powers?'

'Yes, like you can compel.'

'Right. Well hybrids get their extra powers when they're much younger. And you stop being vulnerable to the sun, too.'

'What?' I asked, eyes wide.

'In a year or two you may not need that charm around your neck. That's why hybrids are forbidden – no vulnerability to the sun, no bloodlust, extra powers when they are much younger... You're a threat to the status quo and the older vampires who are in power have plenty of reasons to keep things the way they are. A new breed of super-vampire could threaten to take over. Also, the book says that there were a lot of *failed* magical turnings the last time someone tried this. Those failures made the magic users turn against us vampires – and we don't want or need another war between us. Forbidding hybrids being made is self-preservation.'

'What happens if the vampire council finds out I'm a hybrid?'

He looked at me sombrely. 'They'll have you killed.'

Chapter 38

Anissa allowed me to leave two hours later. I'd had so much blood I was sloshing, but it had done its job. Whatever made a hybrid vampire tick was ticking away inside me and clearing the remnants of the curse from my system.

Connor stayed with me the whole time and I filled him in on everything that had happened, including the crazy-ass prophecy that might not be totally crazy. He wasn't thrilled at the idea that one day I'd be squaring off with the beast beyond the barrier, but then neither was I.

Once I was released from hospital, he drove me back to the office so I could find out how the search for Mum was going. The folding tables and new computer equipment had been set up and we had our own work stations again.

Fluffy bounded over to me and checked me out. I rubbed his head. 'I'm fine, buddy. Newly uncursed and ready to go.' He barked. Shadow lifted his head from Sidnee's lap, looked at me with golden eyes then snuggled back down. Typical.

'What's the news?' I asked Sidnee.

'We've cleared a quarter of our search grid, but nothing yet. We have three more suspects to interview in the next hour.'

'Did you call in the new gem witches?'

She nodded. 'Yes, they came in. No red flags.'

I suppressed the urge to point out that we hadn't had any red flags on Elsa Wintersteen until after she'd gone super-villain on us. 'What about the old gem witches?' Kostas, Vitus and Adelheid were still rumbling around Portlock.

'I talked to them all,' Sidnee assured me. 'Nothing stood out.'

'And the black market? Has anyone been there?'

She shook her head. 'It's gone.'

'What do you mean gone?'

'The market left Portlock and is on its way to the next supernatural town.'

'How can that be? It was only here for a week?'

'They only ever stay a week. It helps prevent them from being shut down.'

Fuck: that had been my back-up plan. I was sure someone at the market knew something about the curser; now I didn't even know what town it was heading to.

Laura had called Gunnar when Jeff was cursed so maybe my boss still had her number in his phone. I called him and he answered on the second ring. 'Bunny, how are you?'

'I'm fine,' I said briskly. 'Do you have Laura's phone number?'

'Laura?'

'The lady from the black market.'

'Oh, yeah. Hold on. Let me check my call log.' A pause. I could almost see him in my mind's eye thumbing through his phone looking for the number. 'Got it.'

'Send it to me, please.'

'You got it.'

A few seconds later, a text pinged with the number; now to find out if she'd speak to me. I thought for a few seconds then sent a text: *Laura, this is Bunny Barrington from Portlock. We helped with Jeff when he was cursed at the black market. I really need to speak to you – do you have a time I can call?*

I stared at the screen as though that would make her text back faster. I got lucky for once, though, and she answered quickly. *Sure, I'll call you later if that's okay. I don't know when I'll be free*. I thanked her – but now I had nothing constructive to do.

When Mum and I had searched the black market, Laura hadn't been there – or we hadn't seen her – but she seemed to be in charge. If anyone knew who was demanding protection money, surely it was she. I couldn't believe I hadn't thought of it before.

There had been too many distractions: Mum, the cursings, my dog, the barrier. It was a miracle I remembered to eat and sleep – had I remembered? Other than the blood that Anissa had made me drink I couldn't remember when I'd last had food. Huh:

maybe I was living off auras without even knowing it. That was a creepy thought.

I must have stopped moving again because Connor was suddenly at my side. 'You should go home and rest,' he murmured as he pulled me into his arms.

'I can't. Mum has limited time – I have to find her and I can't rest until I do.' If I didn't find her, the only remaining option was to hand over the gems in some sort of sting operation that would undoubtedly put the whole of Portlock in danger. Could I risk three thousand lives for my mother's?

I suddenly had an idea. 'Did anyone check the building the black market was in? Maybe we'll find some sort of clue to the curser there.'

Sidnee's head popped up. 'Um, no – because they'd left town and you never told us where it was. You said it was a warehouse by AML, but not which one.'

I hadn't? I shook my head. I was losing it. I searched my memory: nope, I wasn't because I could remember the location clearly. 'Connor, Fluffy and I will go check. Are you all right here?' I asked her.

'Yeah, go. I've got to keep this search going.' She went back to clicking on her new computer.

I turned to Connor. 'You up for trying one more place?'

'Wherever you need to go, I'm your man.'

I pulled him in for a fast kiss. He *was* my man, thank God. I grabbed my trusty black bag, and Fluffy's vest and lead. 'Put your vest on, too,' Connor reminded me firmly.

I didn't have time to argue. I went to the bathroom, strapped it on and pulled my shirt over it, then we headed out. I was battling despair, fully aware that we were clutching at straws. I had to pray that I could be Rumpelstiltskin and turn them into gold.

Chapter 39

We pulled into the empty car park at the warehouse and I took Connor to the side door where Mum and I had gone in. I stopped him from grasping the door handle. 'There was a ward here before,' I said when he raised a quizzical eyebrow.

I tentatively stretched out my hand but there was no buzz in my back teeth so I was pretty confident it was gone. As I touched the handle, nothing stopped me or zapped me. Total win.

The door wasn't locked. Inside was dark, so we turned on our phone torches until we found the lights. I flicked them on and saw that the cavernous space was completely empty. There wasn't even any rubbish. 'Do you think there's anywhere else on the property to search?' I asked.

Connor looked around then pointed. 'Up there.'

I'd missed it: there was a set of metal steps in the darkest corner that went up to a row of internal windows behind us above the door. We hurried to the stairs; although they weren't in the best shape, they held our weight. At the top were three small rooms, probably offices for whatever business had been housed here. They were dark and their lights didn't come on when we flicked the switches; either they didn't have power or the bulbs were broken.

We searched each room for a space that could hide a body but there was nothing: it was a dead end. My floppy heart seized; coming here had been my last idea. I had nothing else.

We were going back down the stairs when my phone rang. I almost ignored it then I remembered I was waiting for a call. I swiped it open. 'Hello?'

'Officer, it's Laura from the market.'

I gripped the phone tighter. 'Thanks for calling back.'

'I don't know what kind of help I can give you. I can't – *won't* – reveal our current location.'

'That's fine. Let me tell you what's going on. We've had a kidnapping. There's a good chance that the kidnapper might be the person that cursed Jeff or be involved with that person.'

'I don't know who it is,' she interrupted me.

'I realise that, but you might know *something*. Some vendors at the market told me that Jeff could have been cursed because he didn't pay protection money. Have you heard anything about a protection racket?'

'That bitch,' Laura swore loudly.

'Who?' I demanded.

'Not you. This happened the last time we came to Portlock as well. This person has been hitting up the vendors for protection money. I've told them not to pay and to come to me. I told them that they were protected by the wards and the local sponsor, but I found out that last time most of them paid and didn't tell me. The amount wasn't a lot, and most of them thought paying was easier than causing a fuss.'

'Do you know who it is?' My heart started to beat hard: this could be our break.

'Let me think. It was something to do with flowers – it started with a V.'

'First or last name?'

'Both.'

Shit, I only knew one person who had two Vs in their name: the earth gem witch. 'Was it Vitus Vogler?' I asked.

'Not V for victory, P for pants.' She pronounced the letters carefully.

'Oh.' Dammit. 'Was it a man or a woman?'

'A woman was approaching everyone, a magic user of some kind.'

I'd been pretty certain that our curser was a magic user, though there was the possibility that they'd bought the curse, like Mum had bought Fluffy's curse. Having it confirmed it was a magic user ... Liv would have my head with liver and Chianti.

'I've got it!' Laura cried. 'Posie Payne!'

I had no idea who that was, but we had a name. That was a start. 'Thank you so much, Laura! You might have saved a life.'

'Well, thanks for trying to find whoever cursed Jeff. We might be a travelling black market, but I try to take care of my people.'

'I appreciate you. If you ever come back to Portlock, let me know and I'll buy you a coffee.'

She laughed. 'You wouldn't recognise me anyway.'

I blinked. 'Why not? Are you a master of disguise?'

'I'm a Yee Naaldlooshii,' she admitted it in a tone that said she expected me to run away screaming. Luckily for her, I had no idea what one of those was.

'Does that mean you won't meet me for coffee?' I pressed.

'During which you'll try and wrangle the location of the market out of me?'

'Not for the first five minutes,' I promised.

Laughing, she hung up. I turned to Connor. 'Do you know someone named Posie Payne?' He shook his head. 'Well, she might be our kidnapper-slash-curser.'

As we headed back to the car, I called Gunnar. 'I need an address for a magic user named Posie Payne. Do you know her?'

'The name sounds familiar,' he said. 'Let me check the database.'

I heard him banging at the keyboard and my foot tapped in time with his typing. I was in a hurry. He came back to me. 'Huh. I knew the name rang a bell. I've got a J. Payne who's been given a warning for threatening behaviour.'

'That's good enough for me. Do we have a current address?'

'I'll text it to you. Do you have cuffs with you?'

I had the black bag. 'Absolutely.'

'Go get 'em tiger.'

'Thanks, Gunnar.' My phone vibrated with the incoming text before I hung up. 'I have the address,' I said to Connor. 'Let's go get her.'

Chapter 40

I'd thought that since Posie was threatening people and taking protection money she must be hard up, but I was wrong. Apparently her protection racket made a pretty penny because her house was near Connor's on another gated estate.

He frowned when I read the address. 'Give me her name again,' he said.

'Posie Payne.'

'I don't know it. I wonder if she's related to Josephine Payne?'

'Gunnar said the person he'd arrested was J. Payne, so I bet they're one and the same,' I suggested. 'Josie Payne, Posie Payne – it's not much of a stretch. You're not friendly with Josephine, are you? This could be awkward if you are.'

'No. She's been a right pain in my bahoochie.'

I grinned. I'd heard that particular bit of Scottish slang when I was at university. Though Connor may be of Scottish descent, he was as American as they came. 'What has she done?' I asked.

'Oh, the usual. Tried to stop me from building, then tried to stop me from putting the fence around my place.' He sighed. 'I had to put up the fence because she'd sent her two large dogs to crap on my lawn to punish me.'

'Punish you for what?'

'Building my house on my property. She said I obstructed her view.'

'But you're at the top of the hill.'

'I was obstructing her view of the hill.'

'That sounds ridiculous,' I scoffed. 'I didn't even see another house near you.'

'She's not that close. I'm almost in the centre of my ten acres, and she has five. We're plenty far apart.'

I shook my head. We drove up to Connor's road but where you'd turn right to go to his estate, we turned left. 'When did you build your house?' When I'd gone there the first time, I'd thought it looked fairly new.

'Three years ago.'

'Where did you live before?' I asked nosily.

He smiled. 'The cabin by Kamluck.' Connor had taken me there to keep me safe after I was shot by the crazy murderess, Virginia Tide. It was a one-room place with a twin bed, a chair, a table and a fireplace. I didn't think it even had running water.

'How long did you live there?' I figured he'd stayed in the cabin while he built his fancy mansion. How long would that take? Six months? A year? I couldn't imagine living there for a year.

'I lived there for about thirty-seven years. Give or take.'

My jaw dropped. 'Thirty-seven years? Where did you go to the loo and shower?'

He laughed. 'There's an outhouse, and I showered at the bunkhouse.'

'I can't believe you lived there that long. It's so small!'

He shrugged. 'I grew up a long time ago, Bunny. People lived in confined spaces like that for millennia. It was perfectly adequate.'

I shuddered. 'I prefer your new place.'

He laughed. 'I do, too. I guess I got tired of living like that, and I was always worried that my father would call me back. I finally stopped worrying and decided to start living.'

I'd have to unpack all of that later because we were pulling up to Josephine's gate. I hadn't thought this through. If she didn't let us in, what could I do? Get a warrant, I supposed, then I could break in legally.

There was a speaker box next to the gate. Connor rolled down his window and pressed the button. We waited; it was a few minutes before there was a response. 'What do you want?' a woman's voice demanded.

'It's Connor Mackenzie and Bunny Barrington. We wish to speak to you. Will you let us in?'

'I'm not letting any vampires in,' she sneered. 'Go away.'

'Ms Payne, this is Officer Barrington. I need to ask you a few questions. Would you please let me come up to the house?'

'No.'

'Then you leave me no choice but to come back with a warrant. If I do that, I'll arrest you and take you to the Nomo's office.'

'You can try.' She laughed. 'Now kindly fuck off.'

We had no choice. Connor was with me but I needed another council member to sign off on an arrest warrant, so we'd have to go back to town and come back. I looked at Connor but I didn't need to say anything. He turned the truck around and we headed back to town. As we drove, Connor called someone and ordered a vampire to get to Payne's residence, stat. Relief swept through me that we'd at least have some eyes on the building. She wouldn't be able to do a runner.

I called Gunnar on the way to the office, chafing at the delay. I'd been too eager. If Josephine knew Posie Payne, or *was* Posie Payne, I'd tipped our hand and put Mum in even greater danger, all because I'd been too impatient. I'd fucked up, and she might suffer for it.

'Gunnar, she refused us entry. I'm going to need a warrant. Can you get that ready for me? I have

Connor with me. I'll call and see if I can find another council member to sign off.'

'Sure thing. Thomas said he was going to swing by to see our Sidnee – I'll tell him to wait. Sidnee!' he bellowed in my ear. To be fair, he probably pulled the phone away from his mouth, but it was so loud he almost deafened me.

I heard Sidnee's voice. 'You bellowed, boss?'

'Yeah, type up a warrant for Posie...'

'Josephine,' I yelled into the phone.

'No need to be so loud, I can hear you,' Gunnar said and I rolled my eyes. Then he said to Sidnee, 'For Josephine Payne aka Posie Payne.'

'Got it boss.'

'And if Thomas shows up, tell him I need him to sign off on it. Connor's on his way to sign as well.'

'Got it.'

'Done, Bunny. See you soon. Everything is going to be okay.'

'Yeah,' I grunted. I was grateful that he didn't ream me out for my mistake, but at the same time I wasn't ready for reassurance. 'En route,' I said briskly and hung up.

'What's a yee naaldlooshii?' I asked Connor, as we jostled down the road to town, hitting pothole after pothole.

Connor raised an eyebrow. 'A skinwalker.'

'And one of those is...?'

A smile turned up his lips. 'I forget sometimes how little you still know.'

'Yeah, yeah, rub it in.'

'Sorry, I don't mean to. I like sharing my world with you. A yee naaldlooshii or skinwalker is a type of shapeshifter, but their change comes from a native form of witchcraft. They can turn into many shapes and forms, not just one.'

'She said I wouldn't recognise her next time I saw her.'

Connor tapped his fingers on the steering wheel. 'Interesting. I've heard it said that skinwalkers can change their human appearance but I haven't ever seen one to know if it's true. They are ... distrusted amongst the paranormal community.'

'Because they can make themselves look like anyone?'

He looked away. So maybe not just the ability to look like anyone.

'They deny that ability, but that comment from Laura says otherwise. It may be why she wasn't worried about dealing with you and Gunnar when the vendor was cursed.'

'She knew we wouldn't find her again?'

He nodded. 'I'd say so.'

We arrived at the office in a skid of wheels. Thomas's truck was already parked up, thank goodness. Hopefully we could grab the damn warrant and arrest Payne before she did too much damage. If she harmed my mum in the meantime, it didn't bear thinking about.

Mum may have betrayed me in the worst possible way, but she was still my mother. If Payne harmed a hair on her head, she was going to be very, very sorry.

And then she'd be very, very dead.

Chapter 41

Thomas was talking to Sidnee when we arrived. She was curling her hair around her finger and looking distinctly shy – shy but interested. Thomas was going to need to move slower than a glacier after all she'd been through with Chris.

He gave us both a nod but it seemed his smiles were reserved for Sidnee. Looking a little flustered, she handed him the completed paperwork.

'Let's go,' I said impatiently. We needed the seal from the council chambers for it to be valid. Thomas gave Sidnee an intense look as he turned to leave then the three of us and Fluffy walked briskly to the council chambers at the mayor's office.

Once there, the men filled out what they needed to, signed and sealed them. Thomas said he'd stay to file it in the records while Connor, Fluffy and I headed back to Josephine's house. I had the five-mile drive to work out how to get inside her gate. If it was too strong for two vampires to break in, we could go over the top of it or I could try to melt it to slag with my fire magic. I was up for anything at that point. My anxiety was riding high.

We pulled up to the gate and Connor pressed the button.

'I told you to go away,' the disembodied voice said.

'This is Officer Barrington, Ms Payne. I have a warrant for your arrest. I suggest you open the gate and come quietly.'

There was a manic laugh, then it cut off sharply as she turned off the intercom. 'The hard way it is, then,' Connor said calmly.

We hopped out of the truck as Fluffy watched through the windshield. Connor examined the gate, determining which way it opened: his gate slid back, but hers looked like it swung up, which seemed fancy and more breakable, but who was I to judge? I lived in council housing.

'I think if we both lift, we might be able to override the mechanism,' Connor said. 'It depends on how tough it is.'

'I'm willing to try. Our last resort is me torching it and that seems more destructive and time consuming.'

He nodded. We placed our hands under the gate and got a secure hold. 'On three.' We counted out loud, 'One, two, three,' and heaved.

At first nothing moved other than a tiny bit of give, then there was a grinding sound and the gate lifted upwards. We didn't raise it far enough to drive under, but we could bend over and walk through. I grabbed Fluffy, the warrant and the black bag, and we headed up to the house.

'Damn,' I said. 'I should have asked Gunnar if there were any notes on what kind of magic user she is. I don't want to get another fireball to the face.'

'She's threatened to turn me into an ice cube, so my money is on a water witch.'

'Wonderful.'

'Can you throw a fireball on demand?' Connor asked.

'If I'm angry, but I don't have a lot of experience and I haven't practised much. I'm full of anger right now, though, so here's hoping.'

'Hopefully she's a weak witch,' he said.

Her house was as big as Connor's but it was older, with a dark, gothic feel. 'It certainly looks like a witch's house,' I said. 'I wouldn't be surprised if she has some children locked up eating candy.'

Connor agreed. 'It has creepy vibes.'

The doorknocker was a cat set against a cauldron base. I pushed the doorbell then knocked three times, mostly because I wanted to. She didn't answer. I did it again before I tried the knob. Locked. Dammit, I needed Gunnar. 'Can you pick the lock?' I asked Connor. He had some expertise with lock picks but I wasn't sure if he had them with him.

'I can,' he said blandly, 'but I don't need to. I have a key.' He reared back and kicked the door right above the latch with his steel-toed boot. It exploded inward with an ear-splitting crack then banged into the wall.

'Nice key.' I grinned.

'It's a universal one,' he quipped.

I heard a gasp; Payne was ten feet away from the door. 'You broke my door! I'm calling the cops.'

'Honey, I am the cops.' I said flatly. Connor gave her a lazy smile; he was having fun.

'I'm going to put an official complaint into the council,' she harrumphed. 'You can't go kicking in people's doors – that's police brutality.'

'Fine, go ahead.' I held up the warrant. 'Josephine Payne, you are under arrest for the kidnapping of Victoria Barrington and for using an illegal curse against a member of the community.'

She backed away from me and turned to run. Big mistake: I caught her in three strides. I grasped her arm and twisted it back to cuff her, but her skin became icy and slick and my hand slipped off.

She turned and threw a spell at me. It was bitter cold and I started to shiver, but her action triggered my rage. Fluffy growled. When she tried to throw ice at me, he jumped up and knocked her back. She fell hard on her butt.

'Good boy,' I praised my dog. Werewolf. Whatever.

Connor tried to move around me to help but fire was rising in my core. I grabbed Josephine again and this time my hands lit up with flames. I didn't even know I could do that. Cool.

Josephine yelped and I let my flames die. 'Try the ice thing again and you'll feel the heat,' I threatened.

'Please,' she snorted, 'you're a warm-up act. I'm the main event.' She chucked more ice at me. 'I'm going to freeze you in your tracks.'

I dodged her ice easily. Her smack talk needed work. 'The only thing that's freezing are your assets,' I snarled as I threw a fireball at her. Okay, maybe *my* smack talk needed work too. 'You're under arrest!' I threw three more fireballs in rapid succession, and whilst she jumped and dived out of the way I got up close and grabbed her. I had the magical cancelling cuffs on her before she could say 'Ice Queen'.

The fight dropped from her as rapidly as her magic. 'Secure her in your truck,' I instructed Connor. 'Fluffy and I will search the house.'

Connor nodded, but first he held Payne's gaze and said, 'Tell no one that Officer Barrington can control fire.'

Payne's eyes glazed as she nodded.

He'd compelled her, not something he did often, but given that he'd said the vampire council would kill me if they found out I was a hybrid, it seemed a sensible step to take. I should have thought of that before, but all I'd been focused on had been finding Mum. I needed to do better, but I'd worry about that later. Now, I had to find Mum. I prayed she was here.

The property was irritatingly large and it took entirely too long to search every nook and cranny. Frustration raged through me. There was no sign of Mum but what I did find was a lovely textbook of curses with a couple of them tabbed: the one from the dock, and the one we'd found on Jeff. We had our curser all right, but where was my mum?

'Any sign of her?' I asked Fluffy. 'Any scent?' He looked at me then very distinctly shook his head.

If there was no sign of her here, she was being held somewhere else. I logged the book as evidence, bagged it and took it back to Connor's truck where he and Josephine were sitting in stony silence. Her jaw clenched when she saw her book in an evidence bag, but she didn't say anything.

I needed answers. Connor looked at me enquiringly but I shook my head. He started the truck and took us back to the Nomo's office, where I hustled Josephine into the interview room. After reading her the Miranda rights, I started questioning while Fluffy kept an eye on her. 'Where's Victoria Barrington?'

She looked at me blankly. 'Who?'

'I know that you demanded protection money from the black-market stallholders. I know you cursed the people on the docks, and I know you cursed Jeff. You're in a sticky position right now and the only thing that will help you is if you co-operate. So let's do this again. Where did you take Victoria Barrington?'

She shook her head. 'You're a shit cop, aren't you? I didn't kidnap that bitch! I have no idea where whoever the fuck you're talking about is.'

I stared at her for a long minute; she might be despicable and a terrible neighbour, but I had the distinct feeling she was telling the truth.

Chapter 42

I had to make sure and I didn't have time to play by the rules so I turned off the camera. She looked a little nervous. I went into the back room, came out with the truth-spelled cuffs and slapped them on her. She'd called Mum a bitch; yes, Mum was a bitch, but I was the only one who could say it.

'Where's the kidnap victim, Victoria Barrington?' I demanded.

'I told you I have no idea. Asking again isn't going to change my answer.'

She really didn't know anything about the kidnapping. 'Are you working with anyone else?'

She shut her mouth. The truth cuff worked as long as you answered, but if you didn't...

'Have you ever cursed anyone?' I asked.

A garbled noise came from her but no answer. Then she said clearly, 'I want my lawyer.'

I had my answer: she might be the curser but she wasn't the kidnapper. The interview was over. I removed the truth cuffs, let her make a call then stuck her in a magic dampening cell. I couldn't question her further until her lawyer showed up, and if she didn't use the local one that would take a while.

I checked the time on my phone: I only had five hours before the kidnappers' deadline. Actually, I only had three because I'd need two hours to collect the gems if I was going to comply with their demands.

Connor was waiting in my chair. 'Any luck?' he asked.

I shook my head. My breath felt like it was catching somewhere before it filled my lungs. He sat me in the chair and pushed my head between my knees. 'Breathe, Bunny.'

I gulped air, but it still didn't feel like it was going where it should have done. It took a few minutes before I could breathe normally again. Finally I looked up at him. 'I've got no idea where to find her. I might need those gems after all.'

'Then let's plan for that. Call Liv, get the witches together.'

I shook my head. 'If we take the gems, the barrier will fail.'

'It will have to be powered another way for a while,' he said calmly, as if that were simple.

'Can I destroy the whole town for one person?'

'The witches have contingency plans in place,' Connor reassured me. 'And didn't you say that the witches had to take the gems offline to fix them?'

I nodded. 'Yes, but that would be for a short time. If I give them to the kidnapper, they'll take them forever. They'll be gone.'

'So we plan ahead, get a team to stop them.'

I nodded, but I was full of despair. It wouldn't work and I'd be responsible for destroying everything. I couldn't do that, even for my mum. I needed to put this before the council. It couldn't – mustn't – be my decision because I was emotionally compromised and not thinking straight. 'Let's talk to the council. Can we get everyone together in an hour?'

He whipped out his phone. 'I'll get the mayor, Liv and Calliope. You call Stan and Thomas, and speak to Gunnar.'

I nodded and started dialling. I had the easiest three because I knew they'd show up. Stan was still in the hospital but he said he'd come for an hour; he was as antsy as Sigrid to get out of the hospital. Gunnar would support me, and Thomas seemed to like me; his interest in Sidnee might sway him to my side.

Connor's conversations were longer and I could tell that it was taking some persuasion to get his people to show, but finally they agreed to meet at the council chambers in thirty minutes. I was starting to think we could do it – maybe.

'Bunny, you need to eat. I'm running you home,' Connor said.

I let him take me and my pets home so we could prepare. Once home, I fed the animals, including Arabella. I'd forgotten about her and had to clean up the mess. I felt bad because I wasn't that kind of pet owner.

She was much calmer and seemed to look to me for comfort, which she never had before. I held her for a few minutes then went to get washed. I ran a brush through my hair and hurriedly put it up in a ponytail then changed my grubby clothes. Connor had microwaved some blood for us and we ate a couple of pieces of toast.

It was time to go. I let Fluffy out and put Arabella back in Mum's room, promising I'd bring my mother home soon and that I wouldn't forget her again. I put the TV on for Fluffy and Shadow, then Connor and I returned to the council chambers.

We appeared to be the last to arrive, which was interesting. I figured everyone would drag their feet, so we must have sounded desperate. Since it was the council members, Sidnee, Connor and I, we sat in a circle while I explained.

I started with the curser and ended with the kidnapping and my choices. 'So, that's where I am. I have to collect the gems and give them to the kidnapper. Connor has an idea to trap them so we can retrieve the gems, and we need to set up whatever Liv had planned to take the gems offline for an hour or so.'

Liv spoke next. 'Yes, I have a plan. I need to gather up my key magic users and the three other witches I brought in. I need at least an hour, maybe two.' She looked me in the eye. 'Listen carefully. The gems have to be back in an hour because it will take the four witches – your mother included – to get the barrier back up. If we wait much longer, it will be a two-day process to get it back and we'll be at the mercy of the beast for that whole time.'

That made me sweat. I couldn't guarantee anything; I wasn't even sure if my mother was alive.

Liv cleared her throat. 'We can't give in to threats, but we can make it look as if we are. We need to *pretend* to comply, but the reality is that we won't let the barrier fall. Not even for your mum.'

The other council members were silent. Finally, Stan, who was still looking ill, said, 'Let's vote.'

'Those in favour say aye,' the mayor intoned. 'We'll go around the table.'

Stan, Thomas and Gunnar voted aye; Calliope and the mayor voted nay and I couldn't blame them. That left Liv and Connor to decide it. Connor voted aye but I was sure Liv would say no. However, she must have been a gambler at heart because she said, 'Aye.'

I wasn't sure whether to be grateful or terrified. We were gathering the gems and putting the whole of Portlock at risk.

Chapter 43

Now that I had the council's assent and a vague plan, it was down to timing. We had to collect the stones and meet the kidnapper whilst Liv's magic users held up the barrier, then I had to get Mum back in time for her and the other witches to reset the gems and return them to their places. And we needed enough time for the magic users to get the barrier back online. Simple.

While I was cooling my heels, Connor and I popped home to get Fluffy; I hoped he'd be an asset in tracking Mum down. With my dog in tow, we headed back to the office to wait for word from Liv.

Once Liv had her people in place, it was go time. My floppy heart was thumping with the stress of it all. Was

I mad to do all this for a woman who had shoved me under a bus? Probably.

I'd contacted the new barrier witches so they'd be ready to hand over the cursed stones. We'd learned from before that the barrier would weaken after two gems were removed, but it would still stand so I had to time this right. The longer the barrier stood on its own, the better. I could collect two gems, then snatch the others at the last possible moment.

First I had to contact the kidnapper – but how? I still had the threatening note; I reread it, hoping my memory was wrong and there was a contact number listed. There was nothing.

I checked my phone: we had only three hours left and I'd promised Liv two hours to get everyone in place. I couldn't do anything until then.

I paced and planned. When I couldn't stand it anymore, I uploaded the coordinates to look at the meeting place, something I should have done immediately because it might hint at Mum's location. I almost slapped my forehead at my stupidity.

Once the numbers were loaded, I zoomed in on the location. It was the funeral home, the location of the first black market and the first serious curse. Mum could be there now, in the dark depths of the basement. I sat up straight, startling Connor and Fluffy.

'What is it?' Connor asked.

'The funeral home. Mum might be there. We should check it out before we take the gems.'

'Going to the area early could rile the kidnapper,' he pointed out.

'I know, but I can't risk Portlock by removing the gems when we might be able to rescue Mum without the gemstones.'

We drove there in Connor's brand-new truck; his last one had been torched by Aoife's father. And that gave me an idea... As we parked, I summoned the banshee. 'Aoife Sullivan!' I called. 'I need you!' Desperation leaked into my voice.

The teenager appeared in an instant, an apparition all in white. 'My mum's been kidnapped,' I said. 'I think she might be in the funeral home, but we don't want to risk pissing off the kidnapper for nothing. Can you go in there and look for me?'

Aoife considered me, before giving me a thumbs up and winking out of sight.

I looked around as we waited. The car park was deserted and the building was dark. A few moments later, Aoife reappeared and nodded. 'Is she okay?' I asked anxiously. Aoife gave me another thumbs up and I sagged with relief. 'Okay, we need to get inside. Can you show us where she is?' Aoife nodded again.

'You want to use your universal key?' I asked Connor lightly.

'Discretion is required for this one.' He pulled out a lock-pick kit and I raised an eyebrow.

He shrugged. 'What? The universal key isn't always appropriate.'

'Why didn't you do that at Payne's?'

He grinned. 'Because she's been a pain in my ass for a couple of years and kicking down her door was very satisfying.' I couldn't argue with that.

Connor patiently raked the lock and had the door open in a couple of minutes. Aoife floated ahead of us as we ran down to the space where the black market had been. Luckily, the doors down there weren't locked. Fluffy raced ahead with Aoife, his nose down: he had a scent. My heart gave two quick beats; after all Mum had done to him, he was still willing to help me find her.

Connor flipped on the lights and we hurried after Aoife and Fluffy. We didn't have to go far: Mum was tied up and gagged in the far corner behind stacks of tables and chairs. She looked at us wild eyed and shook her head.

I stopped, called Fluffy back then held out an arm to stop Connor. I'd run into booby traps before at Skylark's kidnapping, but there were no strings, no rigged shotguns, nothing that I could see.

I looked at Mum and she raised her eyes. I followed her gaze: above her was an elaborate design. Now that I'd paused to pay attention, I could feel that subtle hum in my teeth and smell blood, past its prime and rotting. To top it off, there was a weird tugging at my guts; I'd thought it was panic but it wasn't. It was dark magic.

I pointed up. 'Do you recognize that?' I asked Connor.

'I'm not a witch,' he said, 'but it looks sort of familiar.' He took a picture with his phone and texted it to someone.

'Who did you send it too?' I asked.

'An old friend who studies the paranormal, especially signs, symbols and things like that.'

'The last time I saw a curse like that, I had to disrupt the lines and it failed.'

'That works for 99% of curses,' Connor agreed, 'but I've seen few where doing that triggers a kill curse buried within it.'

'Shit. So what do we do?'

'We'll wait until my friend texts back – I told him it was urgent. Let's give him a minute to look at the design.'

Mum coughed behind her gag. She looked small and ill – she'd probably been there with no food or water for almost a full day. But her pallor was also tinged with grey, and I wondered if sitting under that thing on the ceiling was sapping her energy in some way.

A few slow minutes passed. I was about to barge in and drag her out when Connor's phone buzzed. 'It's him.' He started to read. 'It's a necromantic curse, a nasty one. It steals life force to power itself. Anyone that passes by, over or under it will have their energy taken.'

'That sounds like what happened to Jeff. He was hit with a nightmare curse but it stole his life force, too. And something like that took down Sigrid and Stan – it's why they lost so much muscle mass. I'm guessing Mum's curse is missing the nightmare element since she seems to be wholly present.' She made a noise of agreement through her gag.

Connor was still reading. Suddenly he looked relieved. 'It's easy to break. You need to disrupt the pattern of the ritualistic symbol.'

I spotted a long broom in the corner of the room, grabbed it and started frantically scrubbing at the ceiling. The old blood smeared and Mum took a quick breath. She blinked and some of her colour returned.

I threw the broom aside, untied her and removed the gag. She moved her jaw, shook out her hands and worked her mouth to produce some saliva, then she looked at us. 'It's Liv,' she said.

I felt like I'd been slugged.

Chapter 44

I frowned. 'That doesn't make sense. Liv is trying to *heal* the barrier, that's why you're in Portlock. Why would she try to bring it down?'

Connor looked as shocked as I felt. Liv was the only reason we *had* a barrier; if she'd gone to the dark side, we were all screwed. And I didn't get why she needed this elaborate game. The gems were hers; she could take them, so why kidnap Mum? It made no sense.

Was someone else involved? Was Liv being coerced? A sudden thought made me go cold. Before she'd handed the gems to the new elemental witches, she had looked after them. Was she under their influence like Wintersteen had been? Did the cursed gems want the barrier down so that they could be released?

'The gems,' I said to Connor. 'I think they might have influenced her. When we interviewed

Wintersteen's kids, they said that sometimes their mother was totally normal and other times she wasn't. They said it was like a switch had been thrown.'

'You think that's happened to Liv?'

'I don't know. Posie Payne had no reason to curse Stan or Sigrid,' I said slowly as I made a few more connections. 'But Liv was mad at Stan for his dereliction of duty when his gem stone was taken and he wasn't there.'

Connor nodded. 'She screamed at him.'

'Right. When she visited him at the hospital I thought she was burying the hatchet, but maybe she lifted the stasis so he went all rampaging bear.' My jaw clenched. 'And Sig...' I closed my eyes in despair. 'Liv has always had a thing for Gunnar. Getting Sig out of the way... She was removing her competition for Gunnar's love.'

'It's like she's giving into her darkest impulses,' Connor said grimly. 'Maybe she saw Payne's work at the docks and at the market and she couldn't resist doing her own curse work.'

'I'm not sure it's truly *her*, any more than it was the real Elsa Wintersteen. It's those cursed gems. We *have* to do something about them.' I looked appealingly at Aoife. 'We have to get the banshees out of the stones. Can you help us? *Will* you help us?'

She looked at me for a moment and winked out of existence. 'Aoife?' I called. No response. Was that a no?

My hands were shaking and I tried to make them stop; we had no time for nerves. We helped Mum out of the basement and into Connor's truck. Even Fluffy seemed concerned about her, and she wasn't his favourite person. 'We should go to the hospital,' I said.

'No,' Mum objected. 'Liv has contacts there and she'll find out I'm gone. Take me to your house. I need something to eat and drink and I'll be fine.'

I looked at her in the rearview mirror; she needed more than food and drink, but I suspected she was right about Liv. 'Okay,' I agreed reluctantly.

'How is my Arabella?' Mum looked scared. 'Did Liv hurt her?' The concern was real: Liv routinely killed goats and chickens in her line of work, so a dog wasn't a stretch.

'She's fine,' I assured her. 'Liv shoved her in your bag.'

Mum frowned. 'I think that's Good Liv trying to curb the actions of the Bad Liv. She could have easily added a kill curse above me, too – she's talented enough. But she didn't.'

It was hard to argue with that, and if it were true maybe all wasn't lost. Maybe *our* Liv was salvageable. 'It was Liv that called asking for you that made me realise you'd been kidnapped,' I said slowly.

'And Liv has been pushing Gunnar and you to put other plans in place in case the barrier falls,' Connor said suddenly. 'It's like she's trying to undermine all the gems' actions as much as she can.'

'I think you're right.'

Once home, I made sure Mum ate and drank, then she went to the bathroom to shower off the experience. 'What do we do now?' I asked Connor.

'We do what we planned to do – we wait for Liv to call then go to her. We need to lull her into believing that we're complying with her plan, only we won't let her touch those damned gems. I'll speak to the other council members and warn them about our suspicions. You take care of your mum and be ready.'

'Okay.' I felt better for having a concrete plan; for the first time in twenty-four hours, it felt like we finally had the upper hand.

He hugged me and gave me a blazing kiss before he left. I took a minute to pull myself together. I was suddenly starving so I warmed some blood and popped a microwave meal in to heat. I might be able to feed on auras but I didn't have the first clue how to do it and now wasn't the time to experiment.

As I ate, I savoured the warmth of the food in my belly and waited for Mum to come out and fill me in on everything she knew about Liv. She was in the bathroom for a long while, but I didn't blame her. She emerged right about the time that the hot water must have run out.

I switched on the kettle the moment I heard her and had a brew ready when she came out. She didn't look like her usual self: she was dressed in my leggings and a baggy top, she had no makeup on and her damp hair hung limply around her face. Looking like that, I saw myself in her for the first time; her outer veneer was gone, and she looked younger and more vulnerable. I couldn't recall seeing her without a full face of makeup, not even as a child.

'Are you feeling all right, Mum?' I asked quietly. She nodded but slumped onto the sofa, exhausted. I brought her a cup of tea and she sipped it gratefully. 'I know this is tough,' I said gently, 'but I need to know what happened. Are you up to talking?'

She sighed. 'Yes, it's important.' But she sat a while longer, staring into her cup.

'Liv came to the door and said we were meeting with the other witches. I didn't think anything of it and I left with her.' She sipped again. 'But when I got in her car, she locked the doors and took Arabella. It was like she changed – one moment she was her usual brusque self, then suddenly she was her evil twin.' Mum shuddered.

Definitely the gems, I thought grimly. 'Did Liv seem to know what her evil half was doing?' I asked.

'I really don't know. She took me to the funeral home and tied me up. She said she'd kill me if you didn't bring her the gems. That confused me, because she already has access to them. That's when I realised she was being controlled by something. She must be fighting it, or her personality has split and one side doesn't know about the other.' She looked spooked and I felt the same.

'So there's a good chance she doesn't know what she's doing when her switch is flipped, or that whatever is possessing her can't control her for long?'

'I don't know for sure, Elizabeth – Bunny. But she's very strong. I've never seen a necromancer as strong as her. She subdued me with almost no effort, and I'm one of the strongest witches in the world. I'm not dead, so she shouldn't be able to control me like she did.'

'It's because the gems are controlling her,' I mused. 'Maybe she used the fire gem to control you.'

Mum looked unnerved. 'How can the gems be that strong? Liv said they were possessed by banshee spirits but banshees, even the strongest like your little friend, haven't got a fraction of my strength.'

'The banshees in the stones are the strongest ones of all time, and the gems themselves weren't normal to start with. They had huge power *before* the banshees were forced into them. Apparently they were wielded by the archangels themselves.' No one was supposed to know that, but she was my mum, and we had to fix this somehow; she needed to know the full force of what we were facing. 'I think one of those stones might have given Liv immortality,' I admitted.

Her jaw dropped. 'Good Lord, Elizabeth. She might be unstoppable.'

'Nobody's unstoppable,' I said. 'Everyone has a weakness. Even Superman had kryptonite.'

'Superman was fictional, darling,' she pointed out condescendingly.

'Yes, I know that.' I suppressed my eye roll. 'I mean that Evil Liv must have a weakness, and I think it is probably Good Liv. The gems want to be together and they made her kidnap you as a bargaining chip, but they didn't understand that Liv has had access to the gems all along. She's kept that from them. We can't allow the gems to come together – somehow we need to block their control of Liv. Any ideas?'

'What are the gemstones in now?'

'Foot-square iron boxes.'

'Iron?'

'Yeah.'

'Let me think.' She took out her phone and began to scroll. I hoped it was a powerful ancient grimoire that had been digitised and was ready to be used. That gave me an idea. 'Mum, that grimoire you bought, do you think it has anything helpful in it?'

Her eyes lit up. 'I totally forgot about that. Oh my goodness, it might have.'

I ran into her room and retrieved the dusty tome from her dressing table. It was open – she'd clearly been reading it in her spare time. I gave it to her: she'd understand it better than me. I had passed Latin in school but I wasn't as proficient as she was, plus she understood witchy stuff.

'Elizabeth, I'm going to skim through this – I was halfway through it already. In the meantime, we're going to need new boxes for the gems. What kind of fragrant wood grows here?'

I thought it all smelled nice so I texted Connor. No one would know wood like a lumberjack, right? He texted back quickly: *Yellow cedar would work best. Have warned the others. On my way back.*

'He said we have yellow cedar.'

Relief washed over her. 'Perfect. That's in the cypress family and cypresses are guardians of boundaries. Have your lumberjack prince get to work on four boxes. They need to be the same size as the current ones, and we'll need to enchant them before we add the gems.'

'Okay, on it.' I was about to text Connor again when I heard his truck outside.

I ran out of the door and caught him before he got out. 'You've got to go to Kamluck. Mum needs four yellow cedar boxes, same size as the current gem boxes. We have to get the gems into those after they've been enchanted. Mum is still searching for a way to protect Liv from the influence of the gems – she thinks Liv is splitting into two personalities. Subconsciously she's fighting the possession, but she'll be too strong for any of us if her dark side wins.'

'I'm on it. Four boxes coming up.' He roared off.

Chapter 45

Thirty minutes later, Liv texted: *Nearly ready. Collect the gems and meet us at the GPS location.*

Shit. Was this Evil Liv or Normal Liv? If she got to the funeral home before us, she'd realise the jig was up as soon as she saw that Mum was gone. I needed to keep her far away until the boxes and the enchantment were ready. *OK,* I texted back. *When? It'll take an hour to get them all.*

I could feel the exasperation in her text, probably because I knew how she operated. *In an hour. I need an hour to get everything finalised. That's why I texted now.* I could hear her unspoken 'duh'.

At least that meant she wouldn't be checking on Mum anytime soon. I rang Connor. 'Hey, we only have an hour. Can you have the boxes done?'

'I've got four guys on it; they'll be finished in twenty minutes. The boxes won't be pretty but they'll be functional. I'll meet you at yours in half an hour.'

'See you soon.' I hung up and turned to my mother. 'Any luck? You only have twenty minutes to be ready to enchant the boxes.'

She looked up from the passage she was reading and tapped the book. 'This is the answer! But I need a few ingredients I don't have with me.'

I gave her a piece of paper and a pen. 'Write them down and I'll get them.' Somehow.

When she'd jotted them down, I looked at the list. 'Holy water? Really? We aren't religious!'

'You said the gems were wielded by angels so that will work best.'

I could get the other items, but I'd have to run around town: I could get holy water from the nearest church but she also needed silver dust. I Googled whether there was an assayer in town, someone who checked quality of metals. Being a mining town, I found not one but three – surely one of them would have silver dust? Sage would be at the witchy store on main street, or maybe even at the greengrocer's. I grabbed the list and my purse and ran out the door, using my vampiric speed to get me into the centre of town.

I went to the church first. 'Hello?' I called into the white building. 'I need some holy water. It's an emergency.'

A man wearing black with a white clerical collar came towards me. Silver hair dusted his head and he had laughter lines around his eyes. He was a little on the round side and looked friendly. 'Hello, I'm Father Brennan.' He spoke with an Irish lilt and graced me with a warm smile.

'I'm Officer Barrington, I work for the Nomo's office. We have an emergency,' I repeated. 'We need holy water.'

'Is it enough that I bless some water, or do you need water from a holy site?'

Panic rose in me. 'I have no idea!'

He gave me a comforting smile. 'Well then, let's give you water from a holy site and I'll bless it, too. Better safe than sorry.'

'Thank you!'

'Come on in whilst I get it for you.'

'Um, I'm a vampire. *Can* I come in?'

He grinned. 'You can. That's fake news, as they say these days.' I followed him and he rattled around by the altar. He retrieved a small bottle. 'It's from the Jordan River,' he explained as he blessed it. 'Here you go, it should suffice.'

'Thanks.' As I took the bottle, I thought of Liv. 'Can you do an exorcism of a curse?'

'Normally exorcisms are for demons, but I've a few rituals I could try if you have a need. What is possessing whom?'

'We think a banshee spirit from the cursed gem stones powering the barrier might be possessing Liv.'

He blinked. 'That's not good.'

'No, it's not great. Can you help?'

'I can do my best. Now?'

'Now.'

'Let me get a book and robe.' He bustled off. Mum's plan might be enough to rescue Liv but it was always good to have backup.

While I waited for Father Brennan, I called the assayers. Thankfully, the second one I spoke to thought he had some silver dust.

The priest returned, dressed in a robe and carrying a heavy book. He had some beads and a cross around his neck. 'I'm ready,' he announced.

'Great. We have a couple more stops first.' On the way to the assayer, we bought some sage.

I banged on the assayer's door and hurried in. 'Silver powder,' I panted to the lady behind the desk.

'He's checking the back now,' she assured me. 'We mine chromium here and we get a little gold and silver, but it's not our main focus.'

I nodded and waited on tenterhooks. 'Please,' I begged the universe.

The assayer came out two minutes later. 'Found some, but it's not much and it's not very pure.'

'I'll take it!'

He handed it over and I paid, yelling thanks as I ran out. I was sure I'd seemed very rude, but me being rude was better than the entire town being dead.

Father Brennan and I headed back to my house where I gave everything to Mum. She blinked at the addition of a priest. 'Not a bad idea,' she mumbled. One of her bags was open and she was measuring and adding ingredients to a boiling pot as she chanted. I knew something was working because I was itching uncontrollably and my teeth were humming.

The silver was last thing she added. 'The assayer said it's not very pure,' I warned her.

Mum hesitated then shook her head. 'It'll have to work. Let's hope there's enough.' She dumped in the entire bag. 'It's the one ingredient where more is better.' She chanted a few more words, stirred, then removed the mixture from the heat. 'Done,' she said with satisfaction. 'It looks perfect. Where are those boxes?'

Her timing was good – or Connor's was great – because I heard the roar of his truck engine and the squeal of brakes as he pulled up in front of my house. He and Lee Margrave hauled in the boxes. They were better than I'd expected: unfinished and without paint or stain but sanded, smooth and attractively made with hinged lids.

Mum nodded at them. Opening each one and using a cotton swab, she marked all the surfaces inside and out with a rune made from the concoction she'd brewed. Once she'd done, she checked the grimoire and chanted in Latin over each box. The runes flared as she completed them, and with each one I itched even more so I knew the magic was working. Soon the boxes looked like plain wood again – but now they were ready to bear the gems.

'It's done,' my mother said. She looked exhausted; she'd done all that after being kidnapped and cursed. As Sidnee would say, Mum had some moxie.

Connor and Lee took the boxes to the truck and I left Shadow and Fluffy to take care of Mum and Arabella. We loaded up and headed out to place the gems in their new boxes. I had the names and addresses of the new gem witches in my phone.

The closest was the water witch. Dakota Caples was a youthful-looking woman with pale skin and long ash-blonde hair like mine, but where my eyes were emerald green, hers were light blue.

She looked puzzled. 'I thought the witches were taking the stones to be recalibrated?'

'They are, but we need to change the boxes because the iron is no longer working. These new ones should block the gems' ability to control people and strengthen the barrier.'

'Okay,' she said timidly. 'I should call Liv to check.' She hesitated. 'But I guess it's okay since you brought a council member.'

'Don't worry, Liv sent us.' I wasn't lying: Liv had sent us, she just didn't know about the new boxes. It was important that we kept it that way.

'Come in.' She stepped back and we followed her into her home. Like the first water witch I'd met, Dakota had a decent vault for the gem. It wasn't quite as good as six-inch-thick steel, but it was substantial and new, and having a secure spot for the stone made it easier to ward.

She dropped the wards and I looked at Connor. 'It could try to possess me. Be ready,' I murmured.

He nodded. I took a deep breath and opened the box. Rather than touch the stone, I picked up the padded interior and transferred it into the wooden box. I could feel the gem in my head, telling me how strong we'd be together, what we could do, but it was water, the opposite to the element that burned inside me and it was easy to ignore.

Once it was in the wooden box, I slammed down the lid and the pressure disappeared in an instant. We thanked Dakota and ran back to the truck. Connor tossed the now-useless iron box into the back and we set off again to follow the same procedure for the earth and wind gems. I was leaving the fire gem until last.

Fire was my element and I knew full well that it called to me. Last time I'd touched the fire gem, it had made me light up like a torch and try to rule the world before Connor had saved me. I'd burned him, though, and maybe that would save me this time; I couldn't hurt him again.

We replaced the other two gem boxes and headed toward the last. As we pulled up to the new fire witch's house, I instantly felt the pull of the magical gem.

Fuck.

Chapter 46

Wrangell Baranof looked more like a bear than a witch; he could have given Mads Arctos a run for his money. He was hulking, with long, thick hair and a big bushy beard. He lived in a house that didn't seem big enough for his presence: the house was Goldilocks, and he was all three bears.

'Mr Baranof, I'm Bunny Barrington, and this is...'

'I know who you are,' he said brusquely. Most people knew Connor, and they were coming to know me too since I worked for the Nomo.

I gave my spiel. 'We're here to switch containers for the gems to prepare for the new barrier to be erected.'

'Yup? So what do you want me to do about it?'

Get a better attitude? 'Um, let us in, drop the wards and we'll be out of your hair.'

He squinted at us. 'You're lying about something,' he said.

'Some elements of this are need-to-know only. *You* don't need to know,' I said firmly. I held up the box. 'Here's the new box.'

He was still squinting at us, but after a moment or two he gestured for us to come in. He took us to a back room where a makeshift closet housed the gem. It reminded me of the closet at the first fire witch's, but it was sturdier, built of cinder block with a steel exterior door.

'Is it warded?' I asked before I approached it.

'Sure is.'

'Can you drop the wards so we can swap the boxes?' I asked.

Baranof studied us for a long minute. Connor's irritation was visibly growing and so was mine. We were on a tight schedule and his delaying tactics were slowing us down. Finally he nodded, reluctantly muttered some words, waved his hands and announced it was done.

The second the wards fell, the pressure from the fire gem nearly drove me to my knees. A sibilant hiss filled my ears. *Bunny, I've been waiting for you. We will take this world by fire and might.*

I shook my head and tried to push the thoughts from my mind. 'Connor!' I managed. The sound of his name spoken in such distress was all the clue that he needed. He opened the box and reached for the gem.

A phone rang, but I was too far gone to register whether it was mine or not. I was motionless, fighting the voice in my head. All my thoughts were turned inward as I struggled to ignore the urge to do the stone's bidding.

A sound – a grunt – made me lift my eyes: Wrangell Baranof was grappling with Connor. Apparently the fire witch had changed his mind about letting us have the gem. Was he being influenced, the same as me? These damned gems were so fucking dangerous; how they'd powered the barrier for so long was beyond me. I guessed they had some sort of half-life and had reached a point of toxic decay.

Baranof and Connor were fighting, but Connor was stronger and he forced the fire witch to the ground. Trapped, Baranof lit up with fire magic. Connor scrambled back as the fire flew towards him.

My mate! Instinctively my own fire magic burned in my chest and I tore the flames away from Connor and sent them back to the witch. He absorbed them effortlessly. I had power but no training, and this was a trained fire witch.

The gem's crooning echoed in my mind. *Let me out and together we'll leave nothing but ashes behind.*

'Nope. No can do,' I chanted silently over and over again, trying to block it from taking control of me.

Connor's shirtsleeves were burned away and some of his flesh had blackened; I could tell from his grimace that he was in severe pain. He'd heal with some blood – but we hadn't brought any.

The witch's hands were a nimbus of flame. 'Liv called. She said you're thieves,' he snarled. 'She's on her way.'

That meant his actions weren't the result of *him* being possessed, so I had a chance of getting through to him. 'Liv is being possessed by the stones. If I can get this last one in the box, it will save her. Help us,' I begged.

I could see from his face that he didn't believe us. Dammit! I ran towards him, hoping that my fire would be stronger than his. He flung fireball after fireball at me, but I let my body absorb them like he had done until the magic in my blood felt full and satisfied. Then I grabbed his wrist and pulled his magic into me. I gasped when he slumped. *What was I doing*? My magic was acting like a vampire – was I siphoning off his energy from his aura? I released him and he fell to his knees.

Before he collapsed, he threw one last weak fireball not at me or Connor but at the wooden box. I shouted to stop him but it was too late and the box blazed hot and fast. Connor and I stared in horror as it quickly disintegrated into ash and Wrangell passed out at my feet.

I sat on the floor, utterly defeated. 'Got another box somewhere?' I asked desperately.

Connor shook his head. 'No. Got any more potion?'

'Yeah, I think there was some left. How fast can your guys make us another cedar box?'

He shook his head. 'I don't know. There weren't any other boards prepared, and it'll take a long time if they have to mill a tree. If there's enough scrap lumber left, not long at all.'

'Call them. I'll call Mum and see if there's enough potion left to prepare another box. Until then, we take the fire gem and run before Liv shows up and unleashes hell.'

We both got on our phones. Mum said we had enough potion and she'd keep it warm.

Connor hung up. 'They're going to try and make a box out of scraps, but it might be smaller than the others.'

'I don't know if a foot square is important in magic, but I figure that we're good as long as it's big enough for the gem to fit inside.' Hopefully.

'I'll carry it,' Connor barked, grabbing the metal box that the jewel still resided in and shoving it under his uninjured arm. He slammed the lid shut, but even so I could hear the gem purring, promising me endless riches and servants to do whatever I desired. I clenched my teeth and tried to ignore it as we ran for the truck.

Our best bet was to grab the potion and some blood for Connor, then send Mum and Father Brennan to Kamluck to prepare the new box. We'd take the gem so it could go in the box right way, but it was a race against the clock. We had to stop Liv before she stopped us.

Permanently.

Chapter 47

We screeched to a stop outside my house. Mum came out with her grimoire, a plastic container, a bag of blood and a handful of cotton swabs; Father Brennan followed carrying his own book. They climbed in the truck and Connor drove, gritting his teeth against the pain.

Mum gasped at the extent of his injuries and shoved the bag of blood at him. His fangs shot down to pierce it and he drained it dry in a minute, then we were off to Kamluck. Hopefully the box would be finished by the time we arrived.

That ten-mile drive felt like a thousand miles even though Connor was going as fast as he could on the winding road. We shot into the warehouse car park and he was out, racing towards the door.

The fire gem was sitting on the seat in its metal box, and my head was pounding from fighting it off. Unfortunately, I'd forgotten about Mum's affinity for fire as well.

Panic laced through me as I saw the faraway look in her eyes. She absent mindedly put the pot of potion on the floor and reached into the back of the truck for the gem. 'No! Mum! You have to fight it,' I yelled. She hesitated and looked at me but then she turned back to the box. She was too far gone.

'Fuck!' I pushed her away from the truck, reached inside and grabbed another set of cuffs from the black bag I'd thrown in there. When I turned around, she was smiling at me but her hands were covered with fire. 'Mum, it's me, Elizabeth! You have to stop. Lower your flames.'

'We will not stop. This world is ours.' Her voice was echoing like Elsa Wintersteen's had done when she was under the control of the gems. I blinked and my stomach sank. Whatever the problems between us, I didn't want to hurt her and I didn't want to take her power like I had taken Wrangell's. If I did that,

I'd take everything from her including her position as High Priestix, and I couldn't risk that. I needed to put the magic-cancelling cuffs on her and hopefully they would clear her mind enough so she could apply the potion and ward the box.

'Mum, stop! I don't want to hurt you,' I pleaded one more time.

'You cannot hurt us, together we are unstoppable,' the gem said through mum's mouth. The stupid thing was arrogant, that was for sure.

As I took a step towards her, she launched a fireball at my face. I let it hit me, let the magic sink in and add to my own like I'd seen Baranof do. She kept launching and I kept absorbing until I was close enough to her.

I thought of all I could do and decided only one thing might work. I lifted my hand and slapped her—hard. Her head snapped back and she gasped in outrage. Her now fire-free hand rose and touched her cheek. I had built up a lot of hurt and resentment towards her and, if I'm honest, slapping her was a tiny bit satisfying.

She blinked and her eyes cleared. Her hand fell away from her face – which bore a bright red handprint. I cringed: that was probably going to swell. I'd controlled my strength, but it had still been a mighty slap.

She looked around. 'Oh my God! I'm so sorry, Eli– Bunny,' she said.

'I'll try and keep it contained,' Father Brennan said. He had his book open and he started to chant in Latin.

Connor chose that moment to come running towards us with a wooden box in his hands. 'Mum, you have to fight the stone,' I pleaded. 'I know it's hard – it's calling to me, too. Use the potion. The sooner we get that bloody thing in the box, the sooner we can both relax.'

She nodded and picked up the potion container. Connor put the box on the bonnet of his truck and Mum started painting the runes and chanting the words. She stopped and started a number of times, panting, clearly trying to fight the gem as she worked. It was the longest three minutes of my existence but finally she stepped back. 'Hurry, Bunny. I don't know how much longer I can resist it.'

'Me neither,' I admitted. I wanted to put my hands over my ears and sing loudly like a child, but that wouldn't help when the voices were in my head. But Father Brennan's chanting was doing something because it seemed easier to resist and my head wasn't splitting with the effort.

As I pulled the iron box out of the truck and set it on the ground, I heard an engine straining up the road. I glanced over my shoulder: it was Liv's sedan. Shit. 'Hurry!' Connor yelled.

My hands were shaking. I flipped open the lid and almost keeled over at the gem's strength. It was screaming in triumph at me, and I could feel it trying to pull my power forward as it had done once before. I had to lock it down or it would destroy the wooden box.

Sweat was pouring down my back and into my eyes. I grasped the velvet lining to avoid touching the gem then I lifted it and laid it inside the wooden box.

Liv's door slammed shut. She started screaming words in a language I didn't know – some kind of spell – and the decaying stench of her magic filled the air. Hot winds swirled around me, so hot that they took my breath away. I felt something tugging at my middle and I knew that she was trying to control me. 'Lift the gem out of the box,' she commanded.

'Bunny! No!' Connor shouted, barrelling towards me.

'Stop!' she ordered him and he froze where he was, his eyes furious as her necromantic magic held him still. 'Lift the gem out of the box!' she yelled at me.

The tug came again, but it was easy to push aside and she seemed confused that I wasn't complying with her orders. But I was a hybrid vampire, neither undead nor truly alive, and she couldn't control me. I slammed the box lid shut.

Liv let out a guttural scream and fell to the floor.

Silence reigned. The gem was quiet and the pressure in my head was gone.

I looked around to see what Liv's first spell had done. Thankfully, she'd missed us; maybe that had been Good Liv's influence. Connor, Mum and I were fine, but the new truck was disintegrating before our eyes. The ear-splitting sound of breaking metal had us all covering our ears as it twisted in on itself and fell, flake by flake, into nothing but rusty dust. Her spell must have been concentrated death and decay.

Liv's face was twisted in horror as she sat on the ground, shaking her head. She reached up to touch her face. 'Bunny?' she said faintly.

'Yeah, I'm here.'

'I tried to fight it,' she mumbled. 'I tried so hard.' She looked at me bleakly. 'That's why I insisted that Gunnar put another barrier plan in place. I was scared I'd somehow sabotage the magic users' plan. I'm sorry.' She shuddered.

'You should apologise to Connor. That's his second truck destroyed in a couple of weeks.'

She struggled upright. I'd never noticed how small she was; her forceful presence made her seem seven feet tall. But Liv was from an ancient time and she was petite, only a couple of inches over five feet tall. Her usually perfect hair was wild and unkempt. She clutched her head. 'What did I do? I know I cursed someone.'

'What do you remember?'

'Bits and pieces. Who did I curse?'

'A couple of people,' I admitted evasively.

'Did anyone *die*?' She looked concerned; maybe she did have a conscience somewhere.

I shook my head. 'No, we stopped you in time.'

'What did you do? How did you stop me?'

I pointed to the two boxes sitting next to the heap of rust. 'We put the gems in new boxes that blocked their control. I don't know how long they'll hold, but we're good for now.'

She nodded. 'I thought about doing something similar but I think I was already under the influence before I could act on it.' She stared at me suddenly. 'I cursed you. A note, on your door.' She frowned, 'They wanted to kill you but I managed to make it a weakening curse instead.' She shook her head as if trying to clear it. Her hands shot to her mouth. 'Fuck! I cursed the black market mug,' she blurted, eyes wide in panic.

'Stan and Sigrid are okay,' I relented enough to say.

Liv's eyes slid closed. 'No thanks to me, I visited them in hospital and removed the stasis spell from Stan. I – *they* – deliberately let him loose to cause havoc. The gems were going to do the same to Sigrid but she'd already been uncursed and there were too many doctors and nurses around.'

'How did you manage to curse just those two? Anyone could have touched the mug.'

She shook her head. 'No,' she admitted. 'I broke into Gunnar's house when it was empty. The dog went nuts, so I cursed him to sleep for an hour or two whilst I placed the curse on the mug. The nightmare curse was targeted at Stan and Sigrid specifically. I used their blood to make it.'

'And how did you get their blood?' I asked, trying to keep my voice level, remembering poor Loki's exhausted behaviour before dinner.

She opened her mouth and then slammed it shut abruptly. 'I think I've incriminated myself enough, haven't I?' She looked suddenly weary, and I felt a pang of sympathy for her. She'd been through hell.

Yes, she'd done bad things, but were they really her fault if she'd been acting under possession?

'Let me check you over, my child,' Father Brennan said to her.

She huffed at him. 'We both know I'm no child, Brennan.'

He smiled at her and chanted softly in Latin. 'She's clear,' he said finally. 'I sense nothing foreign in her.'

'Lucky me,' she groused. 'Come on. We'll drop Father Brennan back at the church, then we need to collect the other three elemental witches and get this shit over and done with for good. I need you to call your banshee friend.'

I stared at her. Did I really trust her? What if she was trying to trap Aoife, the way Elsa Wintersteen had wanted to? Was Liv really back to herself – and if she was, did that make her trustworthy?

Connor's hand warmed my back. 'We'll watch and see,' he murmured; as always, we were on the same wavelength.

I nodded. We picked up the two boxes and packed into Liv's car like sardines. Either we were going to fix the town or we were going to orchestrate everyone's doom.

Chapter 48

Liv drove us to her funeral home. She held up a finger after she parked. 'Wait here, please.'

We looked at each other uneasily, but waited while she went inside. A few minutes later she emerged with a small box that she handed to me. Inside it was a large gem. My blood ran cold. 'What is this, Liv?' I asked, my voice was full of suspicion.

'A large, very expensive gemstone,' she said bluntly.

I got that. The gem was blue, so I assumed it was another sapphire like the Water Gem. 'What's it for?' I demanded. If she was planning on trapping Aoife, I would stop her no matter what.

'I know you have no reason to trust me right now, but after falling under the control of the gems I think the only recourse we have is to pull the banshee spirits out of them. They are too strong and too unpredictable in their current states.'

She took a deep breath. 'As you said, we don't know how long the new containment boxes will work, and I'm sure that they won't control the barrier like the iron boxes did. We have limited time and we need the gems to power the barrier, preferably without powerful evil spirits. We have to break the curses and free the inhabitants. I need this gemstone, the four elemental witches and your banshee friend to do it.'

I couldn't make that decision alone and we had no time to ask the council. I had Connor to represent them, my mum to represent magic users and my own judgement. Did we trust Liv?

I looked at Connor. 'Yes,' he said simply. Mum nodded as well. So it was up to me.

I weighed the choices. Liv knew the gems and their issues intimately, and we needed her whether or not she was trustworthy. She'd protected the town for years at her own personal cost, and I had to trust her to continue to do so. The cursed gems in their current state were under control but they would eventually make their presence felt again. We needed the barrier to protect the town, so we had no choice.

I nodded firmly. 'Do it.'

Liv pulled out her phone and sent a text. 'We need to gather the gems and the elemental witches. In fifteen minutes, the barrier will fall to the magic users I have in position and we'll have one hour to cleanse the stones, replace and reactivate them. Bunny, where do you think your banshee friend will be most comfortable appearing to you?'

'She's appeared in a bunch of places, but probably she'd be most comfortable near her house.'

'Okay, let's go there. I'll drop you off, then gather the other elemental witches.'

'I'll come with you.' Connor's tone brooked no argument.

'Fine,' she snapped. 'We're going to need your friend to call the banshees from the gemstones. This new gem is a focus stone that is unique to her kind, similar to the original gems in configuration. It should increase her power.'

'It won't trap her?' I asked anxiously.

'It won't as long as she doesn't touch it. Give her this incantation.' Liv handed me a slip of paper. 'She needs to chant this while connecting with the gem through her power.'

Could Aoife do that? I wouldn't know until she appeared, and I could ask her.

I directed Liv to Aoife's home. Mum and I climbed out of the car and watched as Liv and Connor drove off to get the others. 'Ever call a banshee?' I asked Mum curiously.

'Can't say that I have,' she answered.

I lifted my voice. 'Aoife Sullivan, we need your help.'

'That's all you do? No spell?' Mum sounded incredulous.

'I haven't one to use.' I looked around. No banshee. 'Aoife,' I called again. 'It's life or death. Please appear.' A cold prickling enveloped me and a pale form raced to me from the woods. Aoife was floating a foot above the ground, staring at me.

'We must save the town. I need you to call the banshees from the cursed gemstones. There's an incantation.' I held out the paper and was surprised when she managed to take it. She studied it silently.

'You need to push your power out and connect with this gem,' I explained, offering it to her. She shrugged; even though she was now a fully-fledged banshee, she was a teenager and new to the job. She wasn't sure she could do it.

'Please try,' I pleaded. 'But be careful. Once you say the incantation, you mustn't touch the gem otherwise it could trap you.' She looked scared but nodded.

The entire town, the trapped banshees and the fate of the cursed stones were dependent on one frightened, dead teenager.

Chapter 49

I felt the change in the barrier fifteen minutes later, as Liv had predicted; I hadn't realised there was always a faint vibration in the back of my teeth until it was gone. The vibration was replaced with a slight itching sensation: witch magic.

A few minutes later, Liv screeched to a stop near us and Lee Margrave followed with a car full of vampires. Connor had ordered some additional security; he didn't fully trust Liv – fool him once and all that.

He and Liv climbed out of her car. The other elemental witches were carrying the wooden boxes and Liv had her giant bag in which she carried her supplies. My mum nodded at the other elementals and they greeted her solemnly in turn. Everyone was braced for the difficult task ahead.

Mum murmured their names to me as they approached. 'Flora Sanchez, earth witch from the United States.' Flora was tall, Hispanic, wearing jeans and a long-sleeved T-shirt. Her dark hair was short and her face fiercely intense.

'Enyo Kiyomizu, water witch from Japan.' He was a stately looking man dressed in business casual.

'Kaia Rangihau, wind witch from New Zealand.' The dark-haired woman appeared to be Māori. Her long hair drifted in the slight breeze. She looked calm, determined and focused.

They gathered around Mum, each holding the wooden box that contained their element stone. Their job was to wait until Aoife pulled the banshees free from the cursed gems.

Liv put down her bag and told Aoife it was time.

Aoife looked at me wild-eyed and I nodded. *You can do it,* I mouthed. She blinked a few times and wrung her hands, then she read the spell aloud, her voice a mix of a shriek and a wail. It was visceral and terrifying and the hairs on my arms and head rose. The air seemed thicker and I felt as though it were tugging me apart. The sound of her cry ripped through us all like a storm.

We sagged with relief when she fell silent, but as Liv opened each of the gem boxes a new level of anxiety enveloped me. Any one of us, particularly Liv and the elemental witches, could fall under the stones' control if Aoife failed. She couldn't fail: she mustn't.

Aoife reached her hand towards the huge, clean gemstone but was careful not to touch it. Her eyes closed and her voice changed to a full banshee wail as she intoned the final three words: 'Come to me!'

We covered our ears, hands grasped tightly to our heads, even though we knew full well we couldn't escape the sound.

The gemstones glowed white, red, blue and green, then pulsed brighter and brighter as Aoife's scream lengthened past words into the banshee howl. The light intensified until I had to look away.

Abruptly it went dark. I swung round to check on Aoife; her wail had stopped but she was still standing there. And she was not alone. Next to her stood four ghostly figures.

Her face was solemn as the other banshees surrounded her. For a moment I feared they would attack her, but their faces were radiant with joy, glowing with a soft light. They smiled at Aoife and spoke words to her, but they were not for human ears and we heard nothing at all.

Aoife smiled and nodded, chest swelling with pride. She made a gesture and the gem banshees winked out of existence – but had they gone forever or just for now? Aoife gave me a smile, raised her thumb and then she also faded from view.

The sapphire that had been the focus of Aoife's power had turned black and, as we watched, it crumbled into ash and dust. I hope Liv hadn't been expecting her hugely expensive stone back.

I jumped when she broke the moment with a barked order. 'Don't stand there, we have work to do. Take the gem that represents your element,' she commanded the witches.

Each one took a coloured stone – Mum grabbed the giant ruby, the fire gem. I realised that it was still powerful, but it felt clean like a new flame. It was no longer trying to control me; now it was an instrument infinite in depth and incredibly pure.

Liv positioned the witches with a compass: earth to the north; wind to the east; water to the west, and fire to the south. She picked up her bag and stood in the middle. I had never seen her reset the barrier. Her magic required death and I shuddered to think what she would pull from her bag.

First she took out some papers and gave one to each of the witches. They seemed prepared and started mouthing the words on the page, practising. Next she pulled out a cord like a regular piece of thin rope. She said something – probably an enchantment of some kind – and strung the cord around the four witches. I figured that must represent the barrier.

She took a jar of something thick and dark red from her bag: it had to be blood. My nose confirmed it when she opened it: it was old, dead-human blood, and I almost gagged. I wasn't going to ask where it had come from but my mind flashed to the funeral home. Please God, let it be from there.

Lastly, she motioned to Connor who went to her car, opened the trunk and led over a pure white goat on a rope to the centre of the circle. The sacrifice. I shuddered.

Liv poured the blood over the cord, making sure that every drop was gone, then went to the centre with her goat and nodded to the witches. Each witch raised their stone with both hands and held it above their heads. Starting with north and going clockwise, they spoke their incantations and poured forth their power. As each one completed their words, the itch under my skin got worse. The gems started to glow, increasing in intensity until the last witch had done their part. A beam from each gem joined in the air above the circle. Mum's was thin, thready.

Liv raised her hands and chanted something in a strange language. She smiled at the goat and it gazed back at her with adoration, its eyes glowing with light. It knelt before her and without hesitating she slit its throat. She held its loving gaze until the light faded from its eyes.

'Hold steady,' she called to the witches. 'A few moments more.'

Mum started to sway. She'd been afflicted by an energy-draining curse and she'd been a full day without food and drink, then she'd made potions. She was spent. She swayed again. 'Hold!' Liv barked at her.

I growled. She could bark orders at my mum all she wanted, but Mum had nothing more to give. I strode towards her. 'No! Stay back!' Liv shouted.

I ignored her. Mum needed me, and even though she'd failed me in a multitude of ways, I didn't intend to fail her. I held her in my arms so that no one could see what I was doing then I gently summoned my magic, my heat and fire and strength, and sent them into her.

Eyes wide and shocked, Mum absorbed my magic; she didn't need to see a fireball coming from me to know what I was doing. She hadn't seen my fire magic yet but now she knew I had it. Her and my father's machinations had borne fruit; for good or ill, I was a fire witch, too.

Ever the consummate professional – it wouldn't do to be seen to be *incompetent* – Mum refocused on the job at hand. She poured the addition of my magic upwards and her magical thread strengthened and glowed.

Finally the spell was complete – and the result was explosive. Light burst out so strongly that we all went flying. I literally tumbled ass over teakettle. I landed with a whump and stared up at the sky. I was winded for a moment but then I scrambled up to check on the others. The light had gone and I hoped the barrier was properly in place.

The witches were pulling themselves up to sitting positions, as was Liv. I helped Mum up and looked around for Connor, who gave me a relieved smile. No one seemed to be injured; we might be bruises and sore but we were all moving. 'Did it work?' I asked out loud.

Liv brushed herself off. 'Yes. The barrier is healed. It is strong again,' she said triumphantly. 'Thank you all for your contribution.' She gave the elemental witches a bow.

They each handed her their stones, which she dropped unceremoniously into her spell bag. I gaped. 'Close your mouth, Bunny, you'll catch flies,' she sassed.

'Should you do that?' I asked. 'Dump them together in there?'

She gave a satisfied smile. 'It doesn't matter now because the gems are cleansed. They can be together – they don't even need to be returned to their holding places. Without the spirits in them, all is good.'

Well that was a relief – but she was wrong about one thing. 'Not *all*, Liv. I hate to do this, but now that you've fixed the barrier you're under arrest.'

Chapter 50

She gawped at me incredulously. 'Under arrest? Are you fucking kidding me? You dare arrest *me*? I'm a council member! Without me, you'd all be dead!'

'Even so, you kidnapped a woman, cursed several members of the community almost to death, sponsored the black market and tried to steal the gems that were protecting the town.'

'They were my gems in the first place!' It was notable that she said nothing about the other accusations. 'The evil spirits didn't even realise I already had them through *my* sheer strength of will. The kidnapping wouldn't have been necessary if they'd realised I had them in my possession all along. And I took your mom on purpose, to point you in the right direction! I held your mom in my own damned funeral parlour, I even gave you the co-ordinates! I did everything but write *Liv has her* in big letters. It's not my fault you couldn't put it all together! With my actions, I saved this town!'

I winced internally. That was a direct hit. Why hadn't I checked the co-ordinates sooner? I guess I'd just been running down the roads of panic, not thinking straight. It turns out you don't do your best critical thinking when a family member is kidnapped.

Regardless of all of that, I had a job to do, even if it was unpleasant. 'My job is to arrest you and let the council decide your fate. Don't make this harder than it needs to be,' I said firmly.

She was visibly furious but she allowed me to put the magic-cancelling cuffs on her wrists. 'I won't forget this, Barrington,' she hissed.

I winced a little; she probably wouldn't but that couldn't influence my actions.

We'd come in Liv's car, which was awkward because I had to drive her back to the Nomo's office. I didn't think the council would allow her to remain incarcerated for very long; she was integral to the whole town so they'd probably cut her some slack.

Connor followed with Lee and the others after they had buried the goat and taken the elemental witches back to the hotel.

Gunnar and Sidnee, who had been busy keeping the rest of Portlock safe as we dealt with the gems and the barrier, were open-mouthed as I took Liv in and locked her up in the magic-cancelling cell. Posie Payne was in the next cell and she couldn't stop staring. She must have been as shocked as I was that I'd arrested Liv.

Gunnar shook his head. 'Liv's gonna make you pay for that one.'

'She cursed Sigrid and Stan. Do you want me to release her?' I asked sharply.

His head whipped round to stare at me and his voice dropped low. 'Liv was the curser?'

'Yes,' I confirmed.

His face flushed and fury boiled in his eyes. 'I'll kill her,' he snarled.

I placed a hand on his arm. 'She was under the influence of the cursed gems,' I pointed out. I didn't add that Liv had only cursed people she had a genuine beef with; the gems' influence had made her carry out the actions but I suspected the intent was already there. On some level she'd wanted to hurt Stan and Sigrid: Stan for his disrespect, and Sigrid because she stood in the way of Liv getting with Gunnar.

My boss ground his teeth; his fury wasn't going to die down easily. He stormed out of the door and I figured he needed to walk it off. Meanwhile I told Sidnee everything that had happened and we filled out so much paperwork that I could hardly see. Luckily Connor came back to save me a couple of hours later.

The barrier was up, Mum had been saved and Liv and the gems were de-cursed. It had been a monumentally long day – and even now it wasn't done. Mum and I had things to discuss.

Connor drove me home. 'Do you want me to come in with you?'

'I do, desperately, but I need to talk with my mum first.' I looked into his eyes and placed a hand on his warm cheek. 'You don't deserve to be thrust into my family drama.'

He chuckled. 'You'll have to face mine some day, so it's only fair.' The thought warmed and scared me in equal measure; I loved that he envisaged introducing me to his family – but his father was the vampire king of the US.

He kissed me gently. 'Call me later.'

'I will.'

I climbed out and waved him off then took a deep breath and walked into my house. Poor Fluffy and Shadow had been ignored for most of the night and I felt bad. Hopefully we'd have time to spend together now that the curses and the barrier had been dealt with.

I brushed my hand over Shadow and gave Fluffy a full body cuddle. 'I'm super happy to see you both.'

Mum was sitting on the sofa; it looked as though she'd had a shower and was ready for bed, but she was clearly waiting up for me. 'We need to talk,' she said softly.

'Yeah,' I agreed.

Neither of us was quite sure where to begin. Finally she spoke. 'Bunny, I'm so sorry for everything. I really am.'

I nodded. 'I think I believe you. But regardless of how sorry you are, what you and Dad did to me will take me a long time to deal with.'

'Of course. I understand.' She searched my face. 'But you do have magic?'

'I do. And it's dangerous because it makes me a rare vampire – a hybrid. My very existence is forbidden.'

'You took a great risk giving me the magical boost when Connor and his vampires were nearby.'

'Connor knows what I am. I have nothing to fear from him. We're fated mates.'

'Oh!' Tears filled her eyes. 'I'm so happy for you.' She moved as if to hug me but stopped and let her arms drop. 'Well, that's lovely news.'

'I don't want you telling Dad,' I said firmly. 'I don't trust him.'

She blanched but nodded. 'If he could come here and explain himself, maybe you could start to repair things.' She paused. 'I'd love to come back, if you'd let me.'

She sounded so hopeful that I couldn't quite bear to quash her. 'Maybe. Give me a bit of time to get over all of this.'

'Of course.' She gave a tremulous smile. 'Oh!' She patted her pocket then drew out a piece of paper. 'I called some people when I got back here. This is the spell to uncurse the werewolf.'

I put it into my own pocket; I'd give it to Anissa tomorrow. I was running on empty and I had nothing left to give for today.

'Is there anything else I can do to make it up to you?' Mum asked quietly.

I shook my head. I honestly didn't know. This would take *time*. She'd hurt me as a child and I understood why; in her mind she'd thought she was justified. But the truth was that I had deep psychological scars.

'You can't.' I said simply. 'I have to deal with your choices – *you* have to deal with your choices. Right now, I'm still deciding if having you and my father in my life is a choice I want to make.'

Mum looked like I'd punched her. She stifled a sob. 'I wanted you to have everything.'

'I know, Mum, and that's why we're talking now. I understand that.'

'Elizabeth...'

I put up a finger to stop her. 'You can start by calling me by my name.'

'I've been trying but it's hard to remember. Bunny, I do love you. It's taken me a lot of therapy to realise how damaging it must have been that I hardly ever told you that, let alone showed it.'

'I love you too, Mum. That's never been in question.' I had always loved her, despite her many and varied flaws.

'Forgive me,' she begged.

I took a deep breath. 'I don't know if I can. Like I keep saying, I need time.'

She slumped and looked away. 'I never knew why Nana called you Bunny. It hurt to know you two had secrets – you had a far closer relationship than we did and I was jealous. It was petty and I'm sorry, but it's the truth.'

I looked at her in surprise. She'd never asked me or her own mother, and s*he* was hurt?

'It's simple, really. Nana read *Peter Rabbit* to me when I was very small and she said that Peter was like me, unrepentantly curious. She started calling me her little Bunny Rabbit, which morphed to Bunny.' It was a lot simpler than all the elaborate stories I gave everyone else, a pet name between a grandmother and her granddaughter, a name filled with love and laughter in a home with none of those things. The name that reminded me that I was loved.

Mum's eyes filled with tears again. 'I should have been there, darling. That should have been me reading to you, concocting pet names. I'm so sorry.'

I could tell that she was. It was a first step, a baby step, but still... 'I'm sorry too, Mum. I've got to go to bed. I'm exhausted. Talk to you tomorrow, okay?'

She nodded regretfully. 'Goodnight, darling. Sleep well.' She took Arabella and went to her room.

I fed my animals and let Fluffy out. After that I showered and climbed into bed with my pets snuggled close. I tugged out the book on fire elementals and started to read the introductory chapter, but it was an old grimoire and it was heavy going, not really bedtime reading. I was struggling to keep my eyes open.

I was relieved when my phone rang and I had an excuse to put down the book. *Connor calling.* That was exactly what I needed. 'Hi!' I answered happily.

'Hi, doe.'

'I'm tired,' I warned him.

'That's okay. I'm tired, too, but I needed to hear your voice.'

I melted. 'Tell me about your day.' Then I drifted to sleep with the sound of his warm baritone voice in my ear.

Chapter 51

The first thing I did when I woke up was call Anissa.

'Hello?' she answered after a beat.

'Hi, Anissa, it's Bunny. I have the spell to uncurse my dog.'

Her voice grew warmer. 'That's great news. Are there other instructions – potions or anything?'

I hadn't looked at it, just shoved it in my pocket. 'Hold on, I'll look.' I dug the folded piece of paper out of my pants and opened it. 'No, it's an incantation as far as I can tell.' Mum's handwriting was neat and precise.

'Oh.' Anissa sounded disappointed and my heart sank. That didn't bode well. 'No matter. I'm not familiar with witch magic but I'm sure it'll be fine,' she said, once again upbeat. 'Can you text it to me?

I'll talk to the elders and prepare, then call you back with more details when I'm prepped.'

'Thanks so much, Anissa. I'll text you a pic of it now. Talk to you soon.' We hung up. I made sure to take a good clear photo of the spell and texted it to her. 'Fluffy, we're one step closer. I sent her the spell and now we wait. We'll have you de-cursed soon!' He wagged his tail so hard the entire bed shook.

I got up, slipped on my clothes and shoes and went out of my bedroom. The house felt odd, somehow empty. I looked in the kitchen diner, then in the lounge. Nothing out of place. I frowned and knocked on Mum's door but Arabella didn't bark. I opened the door and blinked in surprise: Mum's bags were gone, all seventy million of them, and she was gone too. So was Arabella who, I would now concede, wasn't as evil as I'd originally thought.

Mum had stripped and remade the bed. On the pillow there was a note; I gave a small smile at the *Bunny* written on the front.

My dearest Bunny,

I know I have apologised a lot for my past actions and I think I will be apologising forever for them. I am so sorry that I let you down so much. I've taken enough of your time and you deserve your space. I'll return to London post haste.

I'll guard your secrets forever.

Mum X

It was hard to say what I felt, but my primary emotion was relief that she'd gone home. She'd been a constant strain on my emotions and I was looking forward to having some space again. I felt bad that her month-long trip had been cut drastically short, especially given how I knew she felt about flying, but I also wondered if her retreat wasn't a little cowardly. Was she nervous about the werewolf that Fluffy would become?

I fed my animals and made myself some breakfast. When I felt ready, I took the animals and marched to work. We entered the Nomo's office in time to hear raised voices. Sidnee was sitting at her table, leaning towards the sound – the shouting was coming from

Gunnar's office. I sat down and whispered, 'What's going on?'

'Mafu, Thomas and Calliope are in there with Gunnar. They're arguing about Liv.'

'Where's her lawyer?'

Sidnee shook her head. 'She refused one, said she wants an immediate ruling by the council. We're supposed to take her over to the council building in an hour.'

Even if Gunnar would like to see her locked up for a millennium, it almost certainly wouldn't happen because Liv had made herself indispensable to the town. 'What do we need to do?' I asked.

She pointed to my chair. 'Sit and help me get the paperwork ready, I'm only halfway done. Oh, and Payne's lawyer will be here Monday.'

I nodded. Posie's charges would have to be changed as well; I needed to drop the kidnapping, but we still had plenty on her. I'd need to get a few statements from the black-market vendors about the racketeering, but I was confident Laura could facilitate them if it meant that Posie would be locked up. Still, it all involved paperwork.

I blinked when I saw new animal beds lying next to my desk. 'What this?' I said to Sidnee.

She grinned. 'Connor dropped them by. He's so thoughtful.'

I sighed happily and settled Fluffy and Shadow down in their brand-new beds. April had left a few notes, but there was nothing too pressing. I turned on my new computer and loaded up the program I needed.

Calliope and the mayor strolled out of Gunnar's office ten minutes later. The mayor left looking steamed but Calliope stopped by my desk. 'Hi, Calliope,' I said.

'Bunny.'

I studied the powerful woman. 'Any chance you'll tell me the next time the black market is in town?'

She smiled. 'Maybe.' She sashayed out of the office without a backward glance.

Thomas came out, nodded at me and gave Sidnee a smile, which she instantly returned. 'How's the paperwork going?' he asked casually.

'Slowly,' she admitted.

'You reckon it'll be done in an hour?'

'It will be now Bunny's helping.'

'Great. Well then, maybe after all this is over we could grab a coffee.'

Sidnee smiled again. 'I'd like that.'

His eyes lit up. 'Great. I'll see you later.'

I waited until he'd gone then looked at Sidnee. 'You going there?' I asked, waggling my eyebrows. 'He seems smitten.'

Sidnee blushed. 'I think I'd like to,' she admitted. 'I'm feeling a bit smitten myself.'

I was pleased; I liked Thomas and he'd be good for her. And only the thickest of mermaids would dare to mess with Sidnee if she was dating Thomas. He might be human but he was a council member and we all knew that he was deadly as hell.

We fell silent as we typed away at the mountain of forms.

'Bunny, Sidnee, get back here,' Gunnar hollered.

We both jumped but scrambled to our feet. 'You bellowed, boss?' Sidnee said cheekily.

I smiled at how quickly these little things had become part of my new norm: Gunnar's loud bark, which was surely worse than his bite, and Sidnee's inevitable response. I really did love everything about my job.

'Bunny, go get the prisoner. Sidnee, have you done that paperwork?'

'Yes, sir.' We both snapped out sloppy salutes then laughed.

Gunnar rolled his eyes. 'Well, get to it.' He shooed us away.

I wasn't looking forward to seeing Liv; I'd be lucky if she didn't try to turn me into her personal vampire slave after I'd arrested her. I'd thought she was growing to like me until this –but she still scared the shit out of me. I grabbed the green cuffs and went in the back.

Someone must have brought Liv a change of clothes and her toiletries because she was made up, her hair was tied into tight bun and she was wearing an ivory dress with golden jewellery at her throat, neck and ears. I didn't even know we allowed those things in jail. I guessed she was getting special treatment.

She held out her hands and I cuffed her. 'I thought we understood each other, Bunny,' she said, her tone heavy with disappointment.

'I think we still do,' I shot back.

She smirked. 'You may be right.'

The four of us walked to the council chambers at the mayor's office. Sidnee, Liv and I sat on the front row facing the paranormal council and Gunnar took his place with them. Everyone else was there – Connor, the mayor, Calliope, Stan and Thomas.

Once we were settled, the mayor stood up. 'This informal hearing has been called by council member, Liv Fox. We are here to decide if this matter will be brought to trial. The charges are that Liv cursed two members of the community, including one of our council members, Stan Ahmaogak. It is suggested that both of the cursed would have died without the intervention of the Nomo's office and the medical team at the hospital. It is further alleged that Liv Fox knowingly sponsored the black market. Finally, it is alleged that she attempted to subvert the gems that are powering the barrier in such a way that the barrier would fail.'

He looked at everyone to make sure they understood the gravity of the charges then at Liv, who looked down. 'Each council member will have ten minutes to state their piece. We'll start with Gunnar.'

Visibly upset, Gunnar got to his feet. For once Liv didn't look at him salaciously but stared down at her hands. I could almost believe that she felt remorse for her actions, but this was Liv we were talking about…

Gunnar's jaw was clenched and when he spoke it was a rumbling growl. 'I vote that Liv Fox be tried for her crimes against this town and her fellow Portlockians.' He didn't elaborate: we all knew his wife was one of the cursed. Liv had also attacked Stan, Gunnar's *de facto* son. He would like to see her booted out of town at the very least.

Stan was next. I was surprised that he was allowed to vote given the clear conflict of interest. Liv looked resigned.

'Although, I nearly died as a result of Liv's actions, I think this town needs her. Necromancers of her skill and moral fibre are rare. At the time of her actions she was under the influence of some powerful, malicious magic. I understand that she has been freed from the influence of that magic and is no longer a threat to this town. I vote to drop the charges.'

I was stunned – and so was Liv. He'd called her *moral*. Stan was far more mature than I'd given him credit for; a lot of people would have struggled to see past being cursed.

The mayor called Calliope to speak. Since she and Liv were often on opposite sides of an issue, I expected her to vote in the negative. 'I agree with my learned colleague Mr Ahmaogak. Miss Fox's actions, though egregious, were under the influence of potent deadly magic. I vote to drop the charges.'

The mayor, Mafu, stood up as Calliope sat down. 'I think that council members should be held to the highest standard. I vote that Liv be tried for her crimes, at which juncture she may be exonerated –

but the town deserves a full trial.' He looked over at Thomas. 'Patkotak?'

Thomas looked at Liv; he was a wild card and I had no idea how he'd vote. He took his place at the podium. 'I don't think council members should be above the law.' He held Liv's gaze until she looked away. 'But I've never seen anything as strong and perverse as those gems. It's a miracle Liv remained free of their influence for as long as she did. It is noteworthy that she was resisting them and still trying to help us even when she was under their influence. I don't think her actions under the gems' influence are indicative of her natural responses. I vote that the charges be dropped.' He sat down again.

It was three to two. Whatever Connor said at this point would either free Liv or tie the vote and automatically send her to trial.

Liv looked worried. Vampires disliked necromancers because they were the walking undead. She was an extremely powerful necromancer; she could play with vampires like they were puppets and she'd had no compunction in letting Connor and the other vampires know it. She enjoyed messing with him; it amused her to let us know she could control us with little effort. If anyone actively disliked her as well as Gunnar, it was Connor.

He was quiet for several beats. 'God knows, Liv and I are tolerant of each other at best and I could easily condemn her for her actions. I'm of the opinion that the black market is a necessary evil and I believe it is better if it's under the control of the council; however, it should have been brought to the *entire* council.' He looked at Liv sternly, then let his gaze linger on Calliope. He knew that she was also involved somehow.

He continued, 'But I was there when we broke the gems' hold over Liv, and again when we broke the curses and freed the possessed souls inside the gems. Although I believe that we councillors are beholden to the law, in this instance I cannot condemn her for actions beyond her control. I vote to drop the charges.'

Four to two: the council was going to free her with no charges. I wasn't sure how I felt about that.

Mafu stood up. 'The council has spoken. Formal charges will be dropped. However, you will undertake community service at a date and period to be determined, and you will pay for the damage caused to the Nomo's office.'

Gunnar leapt to his feet, outrage on his face. When he spoke to Liv, his voice was low and dangerous. 'You may be a free woman but if you ever come near my wife again, I'll kill you myself.'

Everyone froze. The air was charged with static and he was glowing slightly as his magic amped up. The hairs not confined to my braid were standing up, as were Sidnee's. Thomas reached out and touched Gunnar's shoulder lightly. Gunnar shrugged him off but the static died down.

'Don't look at me,' he snapped at Liv. 'Don't come on to me. Don't call me if it isn't council business. If it *is* council business, call someone else. You and I? We're *done*.'

Liv was trying for a poker face but her eyes showed how miserable she felt. As Gunnar stalked off, she slumped into her chair as if she'd been punched in the gut. Maybe she'd learned one thing from all this: Gunnar may be nice, but he had a hard line and she'd crossed it.

Since she was now free, I carefully removed the cuffs from her wrists. She gathered what dignity she had left and stood with her head high. 'Thank you for fixing the barrier,' I said. 'I'm sorry I had to arrest you, but that's how *I* protect the town.'

She gave me a curt nod. 'Given Gunnar's comments, I'll be dealing more with you in the future, Bunny. I'll do my best to move past the arrest.'

I smiled tightly. 'And I'll do my best to move past you cursing my friends.'

She flinched but gave me another nod, then swept out. The dynamics had undoubtedly changed between us; the question was, for better or worse?

Chapter 52

Anissa called two days later; she was ready to try and free Fluffy. I was scared, nervous and happy all at once. I'd miss my dog, but hopefully the werewolf that he really was could also be my friend. And it would be nice because he could actually talk back to me. God, I hoped he wasn't an opinionated asshole.

Anissa wanted us to meet at the building known as the Alutiiq Centre, a large place where the various native groups could meet and run their own interests. The largest native group in Portlock was Sugpiak or as most Alaskans referred to them, Alutiiq. There were several other tribes represented as well. As a foreigner, I'd never been invited.

When I arrived, I was directed to a large open room where Anissa and her elders were waiting. The seven elders sat in a circle on plastic chairs; they were all dressed in traditional garb, and each wore a mask and had a drum resting on their laps. The white plastic chairs seemed incongruous when everything else was steeped in tradition.

Anissa waved us in and took Fluffy to the centre of the circle. She gestured for Connor and me to sit out of the way at the side of the room. I was relieved that we could stay and witness the magic; I wanted to be sure that Fluffy was okay.

She appeared to be the focus for the curse-breaking spell, but she looked calm and confident and her manner reassured me. She had the spell, she'd done her research: she could do this.

At some unseen signal, the elders started to drum and chant rhythmically, the men chanting one thing, the women another. The multi-choral sound swept around us as Anissa danced around Fluffy, manipulating the mask in her hands, raising it, moving it about, looking at it, all the while chanting the spell between words in her own language.

I could feel the magic starting to build. It wasn't witch magic, so there was no itching, but the pressure bowed my shoulders and pushed me back in my chair. The air became tense, full of *something*.

I kept my eyes focused on Fluffy; he didn't seem distressed even though the magic must be buffeting him more than it was me. The spell built and the chanting and drumming grew almost painfully loud. A misty cloud surrounded my dog, swirling around him until I couldn't see him.

As one, the drums stopped. The elders and Anissa broke their masks and the mist surrounding Fluffy parted instantly. Only it was no longer *my* Fluffy.

Standing in the centre of the circle was a man, broad shouldered and tall. He was young – no more than eighteen or nineteen – and dressed all in black: black leather boots, black jeans, and a black leather jacket covered with colourful patches. His clothes must have been retained in the change because he'd been cursed into dog form, rather than him willingly shifting. His shoulder-length dark hair was shaggy and he had a strong, square jaw, but his bare chin seemed to emphasise his youth.

He swayed and I ran over to him. 'Fluffy?' I said, not meaning for it to sound like a question.

He looked around and seemed to find his balance, then he grinned. 'Hey, Bunny. My real name is Reginald Watson – Reggie – at your service.' He sketched me an off-balance bow. I grabbed his arm when he wavered. 'I ain't stood on two legs for a bit,' he joked in a Cockney accent.

Tears pricked behind my eyelids as I threw my arms around him. 'I'm so pleased to see you Fluffy – I mean Reggie. I am so sorry my mum cursed you.'

He hugged me back tightly. 'Wasn't your fault, mate. It's actually been pretty cool. I'd never been outta London before and now I'm in America!' His smile faded. 'You won't send me back, right? I've kinda grown to love Portlock.'

'Of course you can stay!' I said. I turned to Connor, 'He *can* stay, right?'

Connor nodded. 'We'll do some paperwork.'

'Actually...' Reggie started. 'It's probably best if we don't leave too much of a paper trail, guv. I was part of a werewolf biker gang, joined it when I got bit at sixteen. But they're not too good at letting people go, if you know what I mean.'

'We can fudge it,' Connor assured him. 'Reginald Watson might have to die, but Reggie Fluffsen can be reborn.'

Reggie grinned. 'I can roll with that.'

Anissa came over looking worn. 'Well, I've got some bad news. We didn't break the curse exactly.'

I got a chill. 'What do you mean?'

'The shamanic magic transformed the curse but didn't break it.' She looked at Reggie, 'The good news is you can now shift into your dog form at will. The bad news is we're not sure if you can change into your werewolf form.'

'Ever?' Fluffy – Reggie – looked disappointed.

'Honestly? We're not sure. Time might wear down the curse until it dissipates, but then you might lose your dog form. I'll keep looking into it – but you can be dog or human now.'

He nodded gratefully. 'I have options. Ta, Anissa.'

'You're welcome. We need to clear up here,' she added, in a not-so-subtle attempt to make us leave.

'Sure thing,' Reggie said instantly. 'We'll get out from under your feet.'

I still had my arm around him and I gave him a squeeze. 'Come on, let's go home.'

He grinned. 'Shadow is going to lose his little head when he sees me on two.'

Chapter 53

Connor ordered a tonne of steaks and chicken drumsticks and had Lee bring over a brand-new barbecue that he placed in my back garden. I invited Gunnar, Sigrid, Sidnee, Thomas and Stan to come on over and meet Reggie. I'd invited John, but he'd politely declined. He said that he needed time to process his loss, and he didn't want to bring the party down. I told him it was a standing invite, and whenever he was ready, he'd be welcome.

Happy to be able to use his hands again, Reggie cooked some potatoes and veggies whilst Connor grilled. It felt like a party – and we all needed one. I introduced Reggie properly to everyone and saw tears in his eyes as Sigrid enveloped him in a hug. I got it.

'You want to still work at the Nomo's?' Gunnar asked, in between chewing some greens. 'If you can still shift into a dog, your nose would come in handy.'

'I don't have anywhere else to go,' Reggie admitted. 'I'd love to stay if you'll have me. I know you have April now, though, so I'd understand if...'

'Pshhh.' Gunnar waved a chicken leg around. 'We're always run flat out. It'd be great if we could train you up a little, show you the ropes. Though I guess you probably know a lot of it already from hanging with Bunny here.'

'Yeah,' he agreed. 'But seeing and doing are different.'

'Right you are, kid. We'll get you on the right track in no time.' Gunnar was in a gregarious mood, delighted that Sigrid had been released from the hospital although she was under strict instructions to take things easy and had a few more days of potions to take. Her recovery had been markedly slower than Stan's, even though he'd been worse off; as a shifter, his body was primed to heal at warp speed but her witchy one wasn't.

Somehow Shadow seemed to know exactly who Reggie was. He was miffed at all the attention his friend was getting, so he upped his antics to steal back the attention. He jumped up on the table, knocked things over, took off with Sig's scarf. Reggie finally picked him up and cuddled him, and Shadow settled down to sleep in his arms.

After an evening of laughing and joking – and longing glances between Sidnee and Thomas – everyone finally left me with a messy home and a happy heart.

Connor helped me tidy up and clean whilst Reggie had a shower. Once we'd restored my home to an acceptable level, I walked into my living room and stopped abruptly – because there was Fluffy curled up on the sofa, next to Shadow.

I walked over to him and his tail thumped happily. 'Hey,' I greeted him, stroking his head. 'Everything okay?' He licked my face, making me grin. 'You can take the spare bed, you know. Now that Mum's gone that can be your room for as long as you want it.'

His tail tapped happily again but he laid his head back down. For now he was happy as a dog on the sofa. I guessed it would take him a long while before he felt normal in his human form.

I locked up, checked the shutters and turned out the lights, leaving Fluffy and Shadow to sleep. Connor and I went to my bedroom. I had so much in my headspace. I was a forbidden vampire – a hybrid – and I'd barely scratched the surface of what that meant, or what my powers would be. My father was responsible for turning me into said hybrid vampire, he and the vampire king of London who undoubtedly had his own agenda – and I wasn't sure if Octavius was done with me yet. He'd sent John here to fuck with me, so my gut said no.

I'd be going to the police academy soon and I hoped they'd give me the skills to track down Chris Jubatus and his black-ops buddies. It didn't sit right that they were free, wreaking havoc on the world with their horrifying drugs, and I no longer wanted to let Calliope take point on that.

Then there was a prophecy about me and the beast beyond the barrier. It had mentioned my cursed wolf, Fluffy – Fluffy who was Reggie, and Reggie who was Fluffy. I didn't know Reggie yet, but I loved Fluffy and I was sure that Reggie and I would bond properly once we got to know each other as humans.

'He's in dog form again,' I said to Connor.

'It's going to take time for him to adjust.'

'Yeah. He'll be okay though, right?'

'I'm sure he'll be fine. After all, he has a very understanding roomie.'

'And you're okay with that?' I said lightly, searching his eyes. 'Reggie staying here with me?'

He raised an eyebrow. 'Why wouldn't I be? Fluffy has looked after you since the day you arrived in town. He's been by your side through thick and thin, he crossed the barrier with you and faced the beast. It turns out he's a brave young man still trying to find his way into adulthood.'

'Yeah. He's young and he's already been through a lot.' I paused. 'He didn't mention family or parents.'

'I noticed,' he said softly. 'We need to give him time to tell us his story. Like you, he was pedestrian most of his life – he was only bitten at sixteen. The paranormal world must still be daunting.'

I snorted. 'It's not daunting, it's amazing! Coming to Portlock is the best thing that's ever happened to me!' I grimaced. 'Though it turns out I accidentally abducted a man from London to come with me.'

'Did he seem upset when you left England?' Connor asked me.

I replayed the whole crazy series of events in my mind. Fluffy had been protective, but he hadn't resisted once when I was trying to escape. He'd happily gone into a pet carrier and come to the airport with me. 'I don't think so,' I said finally.

Connor pressed a kiss to my forehead. 'There you go, then. You didn't kidnap anyone. If you want a life in crime, you'll have to start somewhere else.'

I grinned suddenly and pushed him back onto the bed. 'Maybe I should start with soliciting.'

His eyes darkened. 'I could get on board with that.'

I climbed onto his lap and he rolled us over so that he was pinning me down. When he leaned down and seized my lips, the zing between us made me gasp. 'Hold on,' I said abruptly. 'Can you make the zing happen? Because it always seems to come at the most opportune time.'

'It comes when one of us is riding high on desire.' His voice was gravelly. 'Are you feeling a rush of desire, doe?'

I groaned and rocked against him. 'You bet I am.' I seized my courage. 'Is that all there is between us Connor? Desire?'

'You know it's more than that.' He looked into my eyes. 'I love you, Bunny Barrington, with all of my tattered heart.'

Thank God. He loved me, not that I'd doubted it, not really, but it was something else to hear those words fall from his lips. I felt like my heart would burst from love. I'd never felt this way about anyone before. Connor made me feel safe and grounded, loved and cherished. Everything he did, his every action, had *our* best interests at heart. I'd never been the centre of anyone's world before and it was a heady feeling.

'I love you too, Connor MacKenzie.' I wrapped my arms around his neck and pulled him down to me.

'Thank God for that,' he murmured, lowering his lips to mine again. I swear his kisses were divine; they should have been listed as one of the wonders of the world. The way he touched me, was like he always knew exactly what I wanted. But then he'd had a lifetime to get really good in bed, several lifetimes probably.

'Since we're confessing things,' I whispered against his lips, 'do you want to tell me how old you are?'

'Nice try.' He grinned. 'You're going to have to work harder for it than that.'

'Harder than declaring my undying love for you?' I protested.

He ground his hips against my centre, making me gasp. 'Much harder.'

'My head is too full,' I admitted. 'Distract me?'

'With pleasure,' he purred as he peeled off my clothes.

I reached up to undo his black and red flannel shirt, revealing a muscular torso the gods would be jealous of. 'I love it when you wear flannel,' I blurted out.

A slow smile tugged his lips. 'I've noticed.'

'You did?'

'I did.' He kissed my collarbone. 'Since we're confessing things...'

'Yes?'

'I only owned one flannel shirt but I lent it to you that time after you were shot and all I could think of was you wearing it. So I bought fifteen more.'

I burst out laughing. 'Really? Fifteen?'

'Fifteen. For you.'

I was still giggling. 'I'll wear your shirt for you later,' I vowed. 'But first you promised me some distraction.'

'I'm on it,' he said mildly, snaking down my body. 'Get ready to see stars,' he purred.

Oh boy.

The End... For now!

You have begged and Jill and I have listened. There will be more tales from Bunny and the magical town of Portlock, coming 2025! Don't forget to pre-order your copy of The Vampire and the Case of the Hellacious Hag!

In the meantime, here to tide you over, is a bonus scene – this time from Fluffy's point of view! Grab it here: https://dl.bookfunnel.com/524rlc6h4n

Other Works by Heather

The *Portlock Paranormal Detective* Series with Jilleen Dolbeare

The Vampire and the Case of her Dastardly Death - Book 0.5 (a prequel story),

The Vampire and the Case of the Wayward Werewolf – Book 1,

The Vampire and the Case of the Secretive Siren – Book 2,

The Vampire and the Case of the Baleful Banshee – Book 3.

The Vampire and the Case of the Cursed Canine – Book 4

The Vampire and the Case of the Hellacious Hag – Book 5

The *Other Realm* series

Glimmer of Dragons- Book 0.5 (a prequel story),
Glimmer of The Other- Book 1,
Glimmer of Hope- Book 2,
Glimmer of Christmas – Book 2.5 (a Christmas tale),
Glimmer of Death – Book 3,
Glimmer of Deception – Book 4,

It is recommended that you read *The Other Wolf books 1 to 3* before continuing with:

Challenge of the Court– Book 5,
Betrayal of the Court– Book 6; and
Revival of the Court– Book 7.

The *Other Wolf* Series

Defender of The Pack– Book 0.5 (a prequel story),
Protection of the Pack– Book 1,
Guardians of the Pack– Book 2; and
Saviour of The Pack– Book 3.
Awakening of the Pack – Book 4
Resurgence of the Pack – Book 5
Ascension of the Pack – Book 6

The *Other Witch* Series

Rune of the Witch – Book 0.5 (a prequel story),
Hex of the Witch– Book 1,
Coven of the Witch;– Book 2,
Familiar of the Witch– Book 3, and
Destiny of the Witch – Book 4.

About Heather

Heather is an urban fantasy writer and mum. She was born and raised near Windsor, which gave her the misguided impression that she was close to royalty in some way. She is not, though she once got a letter from Queen Elizabeth II's lady-in-waiting.

Heather went to university in Liverpool, where she took up skydiving and met her future husband. When she's not running around after her children, she's plotting her next book and daydreaming about vampires, dragons and kick-ass heroines.

Heather is a book lover who grew up reading Brian Jacques and Anne McCaffrey. She loves to travel and once spent a month in Thailand. She vows to return.

Want to learn more about Heather? Subscribe to her newsletter for behind-the-scenes scoops, free bonus material and a cheeky peek into her world. Her subscribers will always get the heads up about the best deals on her books.

Subscribe to her Newsletter at her website www.heathergharris.com/subscribe.

Too impatient to wait for Heather's next book? Join her (ever growing!) army of supportive patrons at Patreon.

Heather's Patreon

Heather has started her very own Patreon page. What is Patreon? It's a subscription service that allows you to support Heather AND read her books way before anyone else! For a small monthly fee you could be reading Heather's next book, on a weekly chapter-by-chapter basis (in its roughest draft form!) in the next week or two. If you hit "Join the community" you can follow Heather along for FREE, though you won't get access to all the good stuff, like early release books, polls, live Q&A's, character art and more! You can even have a video call with Heather or have a character named after you! Heather's current patrons are getting to read a novella called House

Bound which isn't available anywhere else, not even to her newsletter subscribers!

If you're too impatient to wait until Heather's next release, then Patreon is made for you! Join Heather's patrons here.

Heather's Shop and YouTube Channel

Heather now has her very own online shop! There you can buy oodles of glorious merchandise and audiobooks directly from her. Heather's audiobooks will still be on sale elsewhere, of course, but Heather pays her audiobook narrator *and* her cover designer - she makes the entire product - and then Audible pays her 25%. OUCH. Where possible, Heather would love it if you would buy her audiobooks directly from her, and then she can keep an amazing 90% of the money instead. Which she can reinvest in more books, in every form! But Audiobooks aren't all there is in the shop. You can get hoodies, t-shirts, mugs and more! Go and check her store out at: https://shop.heathergharris.com/

And if you don't have spare money to pay for audiobooks, Heather would still love you to experience Alyse Gibb's expert rendition of the books. You can listen to Heather's audiobooks for free on her YouTube Channel: https://www.youtube.com/@HeatherGHarrisAuthor

Stay in Touch

Heather has been working hard on a bunch of cool things, including a new and shiny website which you'll love. Check it out at www.heathergharris.com.

If you want to hear about all Heather's latest releases – subscribe to her newsletter for news, fun and freebies. Subscribe at Heather's website www.heathergharris.com/subscribe.

Contact Info: www.heathergharris.com
Email: HeatherGHarrisAuthor@gmail.com

Social Media

Heather can also be found on a host of social medias:

Facebook Page

Facebook Reader Group

Goodreads

Bookbub

Instagram

If you get a chance, please do follow Heather on Amazon!

Reviews

Reviews feed Heather's soul. She'd really appreciate it if you could take a few moments to review her books on Amazon,

Bookbub, or Goodreads and say hello.

Other Works by Jilleen

The *Paranormal Portlock Detective* Series with Heather G Harris

The Vampire and the Case of Her Dastardly Death: Book 0.5 (a prequel story), and

The Vampire and the Case of the Wayward Werewolf: Book 1,

The Vampire and the Case of the Secretive Siren: Book 2,

The Vampire and the Case of the Baleful Banshee: Book 3,

The Vampire and the Case of the Cursed Canine: Book 4, and

The Vampire and the Case of the Hellacious Hag – Book 5

The *Splintered Magic* Series:

Splintercat: Book 0.5 (a prequel story),
Splintered Magic: Book 1,
Splintered Veil: Book 2,
Splintered Fate: Book 3,
Splintered Haven: Book 4,
Splintered Secret: Book 5, and
Splintered Destiny: Book 6.

Splintered Realms Series:

Borrowed Magic: Book 0.5 (a prequel story)

The *Shadow Winged* Chronicles:

Shadow Lair: Book 0.5 (a prequel story),
Shadow Winged: Book 1,
Shadow Wolf: Book 1.5,
Shadow Strife: Book 2 ,

Shadow Witch: Book 2.5, and
Shadow War: Book 3.

About the Author - Jilleen

About Jilleen

Jilleen Dolbeare writes urban fantasy and paranormal women's fiction. She loves stories with strong women, adventure, and humor, with a side helping of myth and folklore.

While living in the Arctic, she learned to keep her stakes sharp for the 67 days of night. She talks to the ravens that follow her when she takes long walks with her cats in their stroller, and she's learned how to keep the wolves at bay.

Jilleen lives with her husband and two hungry cats in Alaska where she also discovered her love and admiration of the Alaska Native peoples and their folklore.

Stay in Touch

Jill can be reached through her website https://jilleendolbeareauthor.com/

Jill has also just joined Patreon! What is Patreon? It's a subscription service that allows you to support Jilleen AND read her books way before anyone else! For a small monthly fee you could be reading Jill's next book, on a weekly chapter-by-chapter basis (in its roughest draft form!) in the next week or two.

If you're too impatient to wait until Jilleen's next release, then Patreon is made for you!

Social Media

Jill can be found on a host of social media sites.

Review Request!

Wow! You finished the book. Go you!

Thanks for reading it. We appreciate it! Please, please, please consider leaving an honest review. Love it or hate it, authors can only sell books if they get reviews. If we don't sell books, Jill can't afford cat food. If Jill can't buy cat food, the little bastards will scavenge her sad, broken body. Then there will be no more books. Jill's kitties have sunken cheeks and swollen tummies and can't wait to eat Jill. Please help by leaving that review! (Heather has a dog, so she probably won't be eaten, but she'd really like Jill to live, so... please review).

If you're a reviewer, you have our eternal gratitude.